Enjoy
The Trip!

Marshall

SANTA FE COCKTAIL

A NOVEL BY

JERRY L. MINSHALL

Cold Tree Press

Cover Illustration by J.D. Parker
© 2005 J.D. Parker

Edited by Lee Cirillo

Published by Cold Tree Press
Nashville, Tennessee
www.coldtreepress.com

© 2005 Jerry L. Minshall. All rights reserved.
Cover Design © 2005 Cold Tree Press
This book may not be reproduced in any form without express written permission.
Printed in the United States of America
ISBN 1-58385-031-7

To Jan...

and to dinner with Jan.

JLM
Nashville, Tennessee
2005 A.D.

PROLOGUE

...*even silence has its sounds: the slow steady creak of the rocking chair on the back porch; the intermittent whissshh of a slight gust of wind on a rare, almost windless night; a low metallic screech as each new gust moved the old tin weathervane atop the house.*

Silence also has its smells. The aroma of pipe tobacco seeped into the kitchen from the porch despite the closed door. It was something she hated. Not the tobacco; she hated the smell because it was the same as his. And she hated him.

She stared through the darkened window into a darker night. She could've turned on a light but didn't. That would've made him more visible—and she'd seen quite enough of him in her life.

Crack! This time she was certain it was the snap of a twig, and he heard it too. She saw a shadow; a blur, for a fraction of a second. Then she heard the sickening thunk! as the blade found its mark, followed by a tormented scream of pain. A slight sliver of moon peeked from behind a cloud as her husband staggered from his chair.

How many times had he heard cries of torment from his own victims? She had often been his victim; but seldom did she dare give voice to the pain. Perhaps that was the reason she survived.

The woman sat frozen in her chair too afraid to move. How long she sat there she didn't know. But it was long enough to know she could be of no help to her husband, had she even wanted to help him.

Finally she picked up the telephone. "Sheriff's office, please."

A sense of relief and exhilaration swept over her frame with sensations she'd thought never to feel again; a calm that came from knowing ("God forgive me," she breathed), she was rid of her husband.

SANTA FE COCKTAIL

A NOVEL BY
JERRY L. MINSHALL

CHAPTER 1

Monday, November 1, 1948—

It was an unseasonably warm day in Raton—sixty-seven degrees, the radio said. A gold-orange sun blazed overhead and one puffy white cloud, a small one, was visible on the southwestern horizon. Otherwise the sky was like a vivid blue bowl, unblemished, turned upside down over all the earth.

And it was quite windy; not that high winds were unusual in Raton. That was frankly the norm. This was after all, New Mexico.

The Santa Fe's eastbound *Chief* pulled into the station on the dot, one fifty-five p.m., Mountain Time. The FT engines, with their vivid war bonnet colors of red, yellow, and silver gleamed in the sunlight. In fact the entire train looked as though a steam-machine washing had occurred only moments before. To gaze at the string of silver stainless steel coaches for any length of time, sunglasses of decent quality were a must.

Jed Easton noticed her twenty yards away waiting to board—eye-catching, astounding good looks. She wore a full-skirted silky dress draped at the shoulders by a striking fox stole. Topping off her ensemble was a fashionable wide-brimmed hat, straight from New York's celebrated Fifth Avenue. The hat was the same brilliant green as the dress. Long red hair tumbled from under the hat and fanned out over the stole. The sunlight glistened from contrasting strands of gold and auburn in curl after curl.

She chatted amiably with her husband; or was it a boyfriend, a cousin, or a boss? No matter; since she had an obvious male companion Jed got no closer.

Then, just as *The Chief* pulled in, the lady's escort looked at his pocket watch, reacted as though he was late as hell, kissed the gorgeous redhead on the lips, and sprinted to a new maroon coupe in the parking lot. The Buick roared away from the train depot.

The conductor stepped off the train before it came to a dead stop. He dropped a metal and rubber step stool from his hand. It bounced and clanged on the cement platform.

"*All aboooARD!*" came the call. Raton was a very short stop for *The Chief.*

Jed headed to the streamliner, but paused as any gentleman would to allow the redhead to go first. Then came one of those moments; a moment of which all men dream. If they are honest men they will even admit to the dream.

As the redhead reached the train; just as she put a tiny stiletto-heeled foot on the stool, but before the conductor could take her luggage, a gust of wind that would have made hurricane devotees envious came barreling down the Sangre de Cristo Mountains. The full skirt of the young lady's silky green dress was everywhere *except*—where it was supposed to be; everywhere *except* covering her exquisite derriere and mile-long legs. A slender silk-stockinged gam perched atop the step stool, green fabric rippling high in the wind; it was a classic pin-up pose in real life and real time. The scene could not have been more riveting, even if staged by a tinsel-town publicity agent. The three-dimensional display would be etched forever on Jed's mind.

And that this woman would wear a garter belt and short silk tap panty that *matched*—matched everything else! *Wow!*

A week earlier Jed would not have known a tap panty from a dust cloth. But as it happened, he'd been Christmas shopping for his mother in the Montgomery Ward catalog; (not that he'd buy underwear for his mother, heaven forbid)! However, as he turned the pages he lingered a little at one point. The particular attraction was a lovely young model holding a towel over her upper body—and the garment around her hips was identified as a "top-fashion rayon tap panty, a dollar thirty-nine, in white, blue, pink, or green." Thank you very much!

At this moment Jed could easily believe the "Monkey Ward" gal had found her way to the Raton depot. The entire outfit of the wind-swept redhead was the same color—the hat, the dress, the high heels *and*...the undies. Jed had never seen such a creature aside from the silver screen.

"I'm sorry, ma'm," the conductor mumbled, "let me help you." The trainman could not bring himself to look the woman in the eye, nor could he prevent the restrained smile that crossed his face.

On the other hand, when the woman turned to look at Jed (as he knew she would), he made intentional and pronounced eye contact. For a brief second he thought he was getting the *"Drop dead!"* look anticipated. Then it changed to a shy smile across the gorgeous lady's still crimson face. Jed was close enough that the delicate fragrance of her perfume surrounded him. Simply put, he was smitten.

The redhead, her skirt now firmly in hand, climbed the steps and handed her ticket to the trainman.

"Bedroom 3C, second car to your left, ma'm." As an afterthought the conductor called after her, "I'll have your luggage sent down in a second."

Jed set down his suitcase and fumbled for his ticket. "Bedroom 5B," said the conductor as he glanced at the tiny square piece of perforated paper, "this car right here to your right."

"Damn!" The mild profanity was mainly a sigh of resignation by Jed, and the conductor chuckled. It was easy to understand the disappointment of being unable to follow the redhead.

"I got it, suh," said a porter as he picked up the suitcase and led Jed down the narrow aisle.

Jed handed the man fifty cents (he was feeling magnanimous) and entered the small convenient bedroom, the bed of course now hidden. The configuration was currently club car style: two seats facing each other. He put his briefcase on one seat, removed his jacket, and hung it in the open closet. He opened the briefcase and took out the morning edition of the *Albuquerque Journal.* Before he sat down to read he reached for his suitcase to stash it in the corner. It felt light, lighter than he remembered. He frowned and took a closer look. The nametag—*(Nametag? My luggage has no nametag.)* The tag said 'Erica E. H. Swanson—Colorado Springs, Colorado.'

Jed Easton smiled. Heaven's fortune was shining down.

"Thank you, God," he mumbled aloud. Jed hadn't noticed before, but Miss Green Garters had a suitcase just like his—and the porter obviously delivered the wrong one to each compartment.

He immediately picked up the case to take it to her—then hesitated. His smile broadened as a devilish little plan invaded his mind.

Jed set the case back down, removed his jacket, and tossed his Boss o' the Plains Stetson on the closet's top shelf. He relaxed in the seat facing forward, stretching his long limbs straight out in front of him. His size twelve Tony Lamas wound up on the empty chair opposite.

Jed had discovered that the tools for persuading a jury worked pretty well in romantic pursuits also. His next meeting with Miss Green Garters deserved a little precise planning; just like a presentation in court. So he loosened his necktie and got to the contemplation with due diligence—and exuberant expectation.

CHAPTER 2

Four days ago Jed had no idea he'd be speeding eastward to Kansas City. On Thursday his boss had walked into the office with the announcement.

"Jed, got a mighty good lead on that Stickett murder, mighty good lead." Thomas James Johnson (everyone called him TJ) was the elected District Attorney in Colfax County.

"What lead, Boss?" Jed knew little about the case. There was no reason he should because the sheriff had yet to make an arrest in the stabbing death of Claude Stickett. "And TJ—don't you believe what everybody in town is sayin'? His wife killed him, Boss. Wouldn't you kill that ol' codger if you had to live with him?"

When Jed's mother heard the news she had merely mumbled, "The meanest ol' man I ever knew."

Claude had been found dead on his own back porch. A long-bladed hunting knife with an artistic and meticulously carved bone-handle was buried in his chest.

Now, the D.A. smiled. "Could've been the wife, my boy—could've been. We just gotta check everything out."

"Besides, what are we doin' messin' in this now?" Jed's smooth tanned face wore a perplexed frown. "I thought this office was supposed to wait for the sheriff to arrest somebody." Jed believed in strict observance of territorial boundaries in the legal profession.

"Aw, Jed, come on, you know better than that." Johnson's face screwed up in a cynical smile and he leaned back in his archaic wooden swivel chair. It creaked as though it would break into a million pieces at any moment. "If we didn't give a little assistance on the sly to Sheriff Emwiler—whhewww!" It was just an exaggerated sigh but coming from TJ it sounded like excess steam escaping from a locomotive at the end of its run. "And good lawd, Jed, you know that deputy he's got. I don't think that Robertson kid even finished the sixth grade. Besides, what's Emwiler, 'bout a hundred-and-two?"

"Well, it's your show, TJ. Whadya want me to do?"

"Get yer desk cleaned up of anything ehhhm-minent." TJ loved the word imminent but he always pronounced the first syllable like the bawl of a young calf. "If you need to reschedule something with the court for next docket, do it. You're leavin' for Kansas City, Monday."

Jed shot up from his chair, his posture straight as though someone had punched him between the shoulder blades. "What's Kansas City got to do with ol' Claude Stickett?"

"That's what we got to find out." The D.A. hauled his massive frame from the ever-creaking chair. His laborious movement suggested a block-and-tackle might make the effort easier. He slapped on his Arizona-style cowboy hat, with a brim worn ragged to the point of embarrassment, and headed for the door. "I'll fill ya in later. Right now I'm goin' to Jody's Café for some ham 'n' eggs."

"It's two o'clock in the afternoon, TJ!"

"Damn straight, my boy. That's when I eat breakfast. You know that." His voice wafted up the staircase even though he was halfway to the ground floor. "Can't stand to look an egg in the eye till the bourbon wears off. Don't ever eat eggs when you're hung over! Didn't yer mama teach you nothin', son?"

Jed sank back in his own chair across from TJ's desk. *Hmm. I wonder where the hell my old brown suitcase is.* And for the first time, really, Jed began to wonder what actually happened that brutal night. Could that quiet old lady—sad Mrs. Stickett—

could she have actually done ol' Claude in? *Maybe she hired someone to kill him!* The thought made Jed smile and shiver at the same time.

*Two weeks earlier—
October 14, 1948—*
Fall evenings in Raton are seldom warm—not after the sun goes down. If you intend to be outdoors you need a sweater, at least a heavy shirt.

On this particular evening Claude Stickett stepped onto the back porch and noticed a deeper chill in the air than usual. It unnerved him and there wasn't much that unnerved Claude Stickett. He returned to the kitchen for his jacket. It hung where it always did, in the corner by the Frigidaire. He had personally mounted the row of five brass hooks when he moved in. He put up five, because there was room for five; there was no practical reason. Stickett had never owned more than two coats at any one time in his life. And the woman kept her wraps in the bedroom closet. (Claude really thought of his wife as he did all women: a "whore-bitch").

If there was anything at all exemplary about Claude Stickett it was that he actually had bought a home; not that he was always there, far from it.

Then!—he noticed the shotgun still in the corner under the hooks. I'm slippin', he thought, gettin' old. Claude never went out at night anywhere, not even to his own back porch without his double-barreled twelve-gauge or some other firearm.

He put on the sheepskin jacket but didn't button it and picked up the twelve-gauge. Returning to the porch he settled his long bony frame into the old wooden rocker. The chair's groan seemed to elicit a yelp from a coyote a hundred yards away up Goat Mountain.

Smoking his Doctor Grabow pipe was the only harmless pleasure Claude Stickett enjoyed. He took the tin of Three Nuns tobacco from his right shirt pocket, his pipe from his left. Miser that he was he tried very hard not to spill a single shred of the tobacco as he shook it into the pipe's bowl. He had no idea that Three Nuns was a fine English tobacco of renown, but a few years back had snatched a tin left behind by a soldier; an officer just returned from duty overseas. The soldier had left a Lubbock, Texas bar in much too big a hurry; understandable, when one saw the lovely young brunette on the officer's arm. That's why he forgot his tobacco.

Stickett tried Three Nuns, liked it, and had smoked it ever since—when he could find it, which was often difficult. He would take a long time to tamp the tobacco down firm. It made for a longer-lasting smoke and gave him time to think. His thoughts tonight were just as usual: of past moments in his life—some from long ago, some much more recent. They would have been disturbing memories to most—not necessarily to Claude.

How many men had he killed—seven? eight? He wasn't sure. Stickett was especially adept at shadowing cowboys with their payday stash, cowboys who drank too much, too quickly. If the cowpoke woke up at all, he awoke in some alley or stable with a huge bump on his head, his pockets empty, wondering how the hell he got there—and where exactly <u>there</u> was. The now penniless cowhand never knew how lucky he really was; never knew how close he came to pushing up daisies like the rest.

But Stickett did not like to kill a woman. He could think of no particular reason to do so. They provided more gratification when alive; and for Claude Stickett his personal gratification was all a woman was good for.

But there was that one time—two years ago in Gallup, New Mexico. Things had gotten out of hand. Stickett was, as usual, running from the law.

He had been in a poker game in Prescott, Arizona. One man caught him cheating. Claude pulled a two-shot derringer from the tiny holster on the calf of his leg, and shot the man dead; a perfect shot right between the eyes. Claude always carried the small weapon on the road. He had stolen it years ago from under the seat of a horse-drawn hearse, while a funeral service was in progress at a tiny white-washed church.

He bolted from the card game and two blocks away hot-wired a '39 Plymouth parked on the street. He headed east; but the car broke down five miles outside Gallup.

Stickett's rage was at the breaking point; and at such times he always wanted to hurt something—or someone. Sadly, he usually took those feelings out on a woman.

"What's your name, honey?" Claude Stickett could be charming if he tried.

"Morning Star," she smiled.

"Are you Navajo?"

"Yes, sir, I am." The sun had just gone down and the girl became nervous. She looked around to see if anyone was in sight. The street was deserted.

The <u>Gallup Independent</u> reported that the seventeen-year-old beauty had moved off the reservation, diploma in hand from the mission school, just weeks earlier. Morning Star wanted to live in the modern world. She got a job at a dry cleaning establishment. It was her dream—somehow—to save enough money eventually to enroll at the University of New Mexico, in Albuquerque.

The police found her face down in a culvert under a seldom-traveled alley. The ugly black and purple bruises on each side of her windpipe immediately told investigators the cause of death. She was only a block-and-a-half from the dry cleaners.

An hour later on the other side of Gallup, Claude Stickett was finishing off a half-pint of rye. He reached for his tin of Three Nuns tobacco. It was <u>gone</u>! And it had gnawed at him ever since.

So now, on this chilly fall night in 1948, he sat on his own back porch—and there was a noise so slight. Was it a boot kicking a stone—or did a twig snap? Whatever it was, it snapped Claude Stickett from his reverie. He squinted—nothing <u>there</u>...or <u>there</u>. He sat completely still—then resumed rocking and sucking his pipe.

Damn coyote, he thought. *<u>Worthless</u> creature.*

Moments later, and for only a second, Stickett saw the shadowy figure. It was ten yards away, slowly raising its left arm as though participating in a ceremony, a ritual.

It was rare for Claude Stickett to be afraid, but he suddenly knew fear. He'd never been more afraid in his life. He staggered up from the rocking chair grabbing wildly for the twelve-gauge; but it was too late!

The eight-inch blade of cold blue steel, sharpened with precision and care, sliced into Stickett's chest, dead on its mark. His heart was pierced completely from front side to back. Claude screamed in pain, an awful roar. He reached for the carved bone handle to pull the knife from his chest but there was no feeling in his hands. He sank to his knees, a muffled gurgle emerging from his throat. Blood now soaked his shirt and the sheepskin of his open jacket. A small river of bright red trickled from the left corner of Stickett's mouth. With one final anguished gasp he flopped back on the porch, a grotesque scene, his eyes staring blankly at the ceiling.

Claude Stickett's final memory this side the veil was of a brown-skinned face. The hair was covered by a blue and white bandana. The figure bent over him, but there was little emotion in the face; no sadness, no joy; just satisfaction—for a job well done.

CHAPTER 3

Back on the Santa Fe Chief—
November 1, 1948—

Jedidiah D Easton had just concluded one of life's most pleasant tasks: a leisurely perusal of the *Albuquerque Journal's* sports section. He always read the sports page first. Of course the joy of the exercise was enhanced considerably by doing it aboard *The Chief.*

The New Mexico landscape was breathtaking as the streamliner's diesel engines labored up Raton Pass. The afternoon sun filtered through the mountain pine to bounce off the grays, purples, and reds of the rocky slopes, before shining on the dry scrub of sagebrush and sand. The golden rays made the ground seem warmer and less desolate than it could possibly be. Even as he flipped through the paper's other sections, Jed glanced again and again out the window, awestruck by the cascade of semi-desert colors in this vast majestic place.

"Shhhit!" he suddenly exclaimed aloud. The flash of irritation wasn't brought on by the gorgeous view; it was really more exasperation than anger anyway. He'd been busy as hell the last couple of days and had neglected something very important. That which prompted the sudden profanity was a bold headline across the *Journal's* page one. Tomorrow would be Election Day and in the frenzy of last minute preparations for the trip, the fact completely slipped his mind. No matter, it would have been too late to request an absentee ballot anyway; but it pained him. This would've been his first presidential election. As a 22-year-old in 1944 he'd been eligible to vote but the military ballot never reached him with Patton's Third Army in Lorraine.

His time in combat was quite short. Uncle Sam had sent him to Fort Polk, Louisiana where he excelled at basic training; but then he just waited—waited for orders. No one ever gave him a reason for the delay, although the military term "SNAFU" came often to Jed's mind.

He finally landed in Brest, France on October 31, 1944. He joined up with "Ol' Blood 'n' Guts" a week later and on November tenth, just outside Metz, Jed took a Nazi bullet in his left leg. His thighbone was shattered.

Jed's memory of the next few months was mostly a haze. He remembered army hospitals—three or four of them. And he had distinct memories of two extremely pretty nurses; but for the life of him he could not put names with their faces. He'd always hated that part especially—and chocked it up to the morphine (or whatever), they were injecting into his body.

He remembered the doctors as being kind and proficient, but always in a hurry. And they weren't optimistic for full recovery. Thankfully they were wrong. On the rare day that Raton was truly damp, Jed limped a little. That was all. He finally arrived back in his hometown, grateful; but a little ashamed. He knew it wasn't his fault; but he still felt he hadn't quite done his duty.

If you believed the common "wisdom" about the '48 election Jed's vote would make no difference anyway. From all accounts Tom Dewey and Earl Warren would win big. However, the prognostication made no difference to Jed. He would've cast a ballot for Ol' Harry just because he liked the guy. Harry laid it on the line. He didn't mince words. The President's blunt speaking style reminded Jed of his dad.

And there was another reason; a silly reason. But it was not unusual for Americans to cast ballots, based on something of little or no seminal importance. This was Jed's silly reason: Mister Truman was the only other man Jed knew of, who put no period after his middle initial. That was proper when the initial stood for no particular name. Jed, therefore, felt a personal connection.

"Why is my name so different?" An eight-year-old Jed had been a little tired of the teasing he took at school over his out-of-the-ordinary moniker.

"It's a wonderful name, Jedidiah, it's a Bible name," and Mrs. Easton was happy for the excuse to encourage a little righteous study time for her son. "That would be a great devotional for you today."

"But I won't know all those big words." Jed, like most kids, wasn't naturally inclined to read the Bible, but since he'd be learning about his own name his curiosity was slightly piqued.

"Let me help," Mrs. Easton said. "Book of Second Samuel, chapter twelve. I'll show you how to use the index."

Jed learned that his namesake was the second son of King David and Bathsheba. They named him Solomon—but God called him Jedidiah.

"Jedidiah D! Does the 'D' stand for David?"

"Well, yes and no," his mother replied. "Obviously that's the inspiration, but your father and I thought both names together a little long, a little clumsy. So we just made it the letter 'D'—that's why there's no period."

Jed remembered the conversation with his mother, when Truman became President. He read that ol' Harry's parents couldn't decide which ancestor to honor with their son's middle name, Shippe or Solomon; so they called him Harry S—at least that was the story as told.

"That's why you shouldn't use a period after the 'S,'" Truman instructed the press, "it doesn't stand for anything."

It was much later that Jed learned the untoward circumstances of David and Bathsheba's getting together in the first place; her bathing on the roof as King David "peeked," and all that. (At least that's the way a neighbor boy, a Baptist, had mischievously retold his Sunday school lesson to Jed as they played catch one Lord's Day afternoon). The biblical account also said that King Solomon, or Jedidiah, was the wisest man who ever lived. If the Bible said it Jed wasn't prone to argue. But he did wonder how the wisest man who ever lived wound up with a thousand wives.

    Twenty-five minutes had passed since the *The Chief* pulled out of Raton. Jed was surprised that the lovely lady in green hadn't already sent the porter knocking on his door. He chuckled. Just *maybe* she was still blushing from her wind-blown expose`.

    He again checked his father's gold pocket watch. It would always be his father's pocket watch, even though his father gave it to *him* two years ago, the day Jed left for law school at Washburn University in Topeka, Kansas. It was a proud and smiling Dad who waved goodbye from the depot platform. His son was doing what the father had always wanted for himself; but was unable to afford.

    Jed put the watch back in its small pocket and thought of his dad at the train station. It was the last time he saw him. His father's death had been sudden, a heart attack just three months later.

    Jed decided to give Miss Green Garters a little more time to discover the porter's mistake with the luggage. In a couple of hours or so, *The Chief* would be highballing across open prairie at ninety miles-per-hour near the Colorado-Kansas border. There was no experience in all the world so likely to take you from your own "universe," and drop you in one completely new, than that of riding the long silver snake: the modern-day streamliner. It allowed people who'd never met before—total strangers, to momentarily feel they were intimates. And the fact they'd never meet again brought an even more relaxed attitude to the social setting. On a train, men and women share thoughts, ideas, stories, and life experiences (some true, some not so true), more readily than anywhere else in the world. He hoped the switched suitcase would, at the least, allow him to buy that gorgeous creature in the green dress a drink in the club car—maybe even dinner in the diner.

CHAPTER 4

Jed Easton never found his old brown suitcase. That's why he bought a brand new one for the trip; one just like Miss Green Garters'.

The Chief was now highballing across the southeastern Colorado prairie and in eager anticipation Jed walked two cars ahead, steadying himself with his free hand on the walls of the narrow aisle. He was now in the proper car. *Let's see, 'E', 'D'— 'C', here it is.* Jed distinctly remembered the conductor telling the redhead it was Bedroom 3C.

He lifted his hand to knock—just as the lady opened the door from the inside—and just as the Pullman car gave a sudden lurch. A sunken roadbed or a heat-curved rail, Jed would never know. But it was enough to land him full on the floor atop the beautiful gal in the silky green dress.

Now it was Jed's turn to blush. "I am so sorry, ma'm." He grabbed both her hands to help her up but she quickly pulled one hand free to adjust her skirt. For the second time today, in a too short space of time, she was showing much more to a gentleman than was socially acceptable.

"Is it your job to embarrass ladies, or do you just show up at such moments by pure dumb luck?" Her tone was brittle and derisive sparks shot from her eyes.

Jed couldn't blame her. "I—I'm t-truly sorry," he stammered. "Are you hurt—uh—Erica? It is Erica, isn't it?" Jed realized his full-weight fall against her, with a solid floor beneath, might well have caused injury.

"No, I'm fine," she said sternly—"I think." She moved her

hands lightly over her hips and ribs. "And yes, it is Erica. But how do you know my name?" She was wary; very suspicious.

Jed pointed to the bag he'd just brought. "The nametag; we have bags just alike. The porter switched them."

"Ohmigosh! Or, do tell," she added suddenly as though the instinctive use of slang was beneath her dignity. "I hadn't even noticed. I've just been looking out the window," and she warmed a little. "I love to ride the train, don't you?"

Jed was relieved to see a slight smile from the lady. Maybe she didn't hate him completely after all.

"I'm headed to Kansas City to visit my sister," Erica continued, "she's lived back there for ten years; married a guy from there."

Jed picked up his suitcase. "Well, sorry again, hope I didn't hurt you." As he'd already planned he turned as though to leave—then turned back. "Uh, you seem to be headed out; maybe to the club car? Could I buy you a drink to make up for my clumsiness?"

"Wellll"—she hesitated and Jed held his breath—"sure, why not?" she concluded. And this time the gorgeous smile came comfortably and lit up her face. "Goodness though, let me powder my nose."

She turned to the small washbasin by the bed and looked at her reflection in the tiny medicine cabinet mirror. "Just a moment, please."

"Shall I step out?" Jed certainly did not want to appear more oafish than he already had.

"No, no, I'll just be a minute." She removed a pearl pin from the stylish hat, placing the pin back in the hat before setting it on the seat. "Do you mind if I take off the hat? I love to wear them but they make me a little weary after awhile." She brushed her long red hair as she talked, glancing at Jed in the mirror, then at herself.

"Don't mind a'tall, ma'm. In fact, if it'll make ya feel better

I promise to take off my Stetson when we get to the club car."

Jed could *not* take his eyes off her. He loved watching a woman brush her hair. It was such a feminine thing; just one of those little attractions God threw into the mix to ensure the continuation of the species; the population of the planet. Then, as she put the brush aside and raised both hands for a final three pats to her hair, Jed saw what he'd hoped not to see. It was on the fourth finger of her left hand. It caught the light and twinkled at Jed as though mocking him. 'Twas an elegant gold band.

CHAPTER 5

The *Chief's* observation club car, the *Coconino*, was packed and noisy, but it suddenly fell silent as they entered. The men (and there were only men at the tiny counter bar) followed Erica with their eyes. Jed took her hand and she didn't seem to mind. He led her down the narrow aisle, past the men, past the bar—and spotted what he was looking for. Near the huge wraparound windows at the very end of the train was an empty couch with a small coffee table. As they sat down the hum of conversation resumed.

The November sun, as though taking its cue from the sage and the evening haze, was turning a purplish orange as it sank near the horizon. Through the rear windows Jed again took note of the spacious beauty of his native southwest. "Look at that!" The sky and landscape was a tableau on canvas, an ever-receding canvas. Yet it never ended. There seemed always to be more.

"Oh, yes! I never get tired of *just looking* at this country," Erica smiled.

They settled on the couch and a moment later the train pulled into La Junta, Colorado.

"Why didn't you get on the train here, or Trinidad?" Jed asked. "Wouldn't either be closer to Colorado Springs?"

She looked at him, the cool look again, and he hated himself for asking.

"I'm sorry," he mumbled, "that's none of my business. I'm really not that nosey. I'm just making nervous conversation, can't you tell?" He hoped self-deprecation would break the ice.

"Oh, I don't mind—" she stopped in mid-sentence as

though debating whether to continue, then repeated the phrase with a warm smile. "I don't mind, really."

Jed almost believed her.

"A friend," Erica continued, "came up to The Springs last Wednesday." She'd apparently decided no harm would come from satisfying a portion of Jed's curiosity. "Oh, excuse me—'The Springs'—that's what we natives call Colorado Springs."

"Right, I know."

"Anyway, my friend; he wanted me to see an old ranch, a small ranch, he just bought near Maxwell, New Mexico. That's just south of Raton so I had Santa Fe re-do the ticket."

Jed was very curious about this rancher but bit his lip, determined not to pry all over again. Fortunately at just that moment the bar steward arrived to take their order.

"What'll you have?" Jed was relieved to be back in the role of gallant gentleman.

"Oh my, what time is it?" Erica asked as she glanced at her petite gold wristwatch then answered herself. "Almost five—a little early for me but what the heck! Scotch and soda."

"Beefeater on the rocks," Jed told the steward.

The man moved back toward the bar with a quiet, "Yessuh, right away, suh."

Conversation fell silent for a moment and Jed had a silly urge to tell Erica he thought of her as Miss Green Garters. He stifled a smile and held his tongue. The drinks arrived. Erica took a lady-like sip; Jed swallowed half a glass in one swig. This wasn't like him to be jittery around women, even one as beautiful as Erica. He prided himself in being "Mister Suave" in such situations. *Take control, buddy, get this thing back on track!*

"You say you love the train; do you travel a lot?" Good, he thought. He didn't even sound nervous.

"Every chance I get," she smiled. Her voice was controlled, well modulated, and her poise gave credence to the sophistication she was about to reveal. "I teach history and geography at

Colorado College in The Springs, so I consider travel my continuing education." She took a longer sip of her scotch and soda.

"American history?" Jed asked, his eyes lighting up. It was his favorite subject since sixth grade.

"Yes," she responded, "world geography but American history." As she spoke she crossed her legs demurely but the silky skirt slid upward anyway. Jed again caught a glimpse of green garter.

"I can't wait until the summer of 1950," she continued. "A benefactor of the school has set up a fund for one professor a year to do a sabbatical in their field. Fortunately, I get the grant that year. I'll do three weeks in Washington working with the Senate parliamentarian before the Congress takes its summer break; then it's off to Italy and France for five weeks."

Jed couldn't help but think that this benefactor, if he were male, would undoubtedly love to accompany Miss Green Garters on sabbatical. Jed knew *he* sure the hell would.

"I *really* can't wait!" Erica concluded triumphantly and her face beamed like an exuberant college freshman instead of a professor.

"Geez, I'll bet. That sounds wonderful!" Jed couldn't imagine TJ ever sending him to Europe. He noticed her glass was empty. "Another drink?" he asked and drained his own.

"Oooh, I shouldn't, but yes!" she chirped. "But only if we then get some—uh, s-something; something to eat I mean." Erica was embarrassed by her stumbling and unintended suggestive remark. She brushed imaginary lint from her skirt.

"I understand." Jed pretended he'd noticed nothing. "Breakfast was a long time ago; comes early on a ranch."

Jed caught the steward's eye and held up his glass and two fingers. The steward nodded and moved to the bar. In a moment, Jed thought Erica relaxed enough for him to plunge ahead. So he took a deep breath—and plunged.

"So, was that *Mister* Swanson with you at the station?"

"No. No it wasn't." She teased him with her smile. "That was my rancher friend." Now Erica seemed to enjoy the interrogation, taking some delight in Jed's none-too-subtle curiosity. Had she concluded that Jed was on the make? That he was trying to determine if she were capable of "stepping out?" *Women!* Jed wondered if his bewilderment showed. *What's this gal's story? Does she wanna flirt or not?*

Erica caught Jed glancing at her ring, and a somber look came to her face. After a long moment she spoke. "There is no Mister Swanson," she said. "Well—there was. I just can't bring myself to, uh"—her voice broke slightly and she cleared her throat—"I just can't stop wearing the ring."

Jed didn't know what to say so said nothing.

"The war," Erica continued, "Battle of the Bulge."

"I'm sorry, Erica." Jed hoped he wasn't too forward but it was a natural response. He reached over and touched her hand. "I'm truly sorry. I really must quit asking questions."

"No, no—it's all right," she whispered. She brushed away a tear as their second round arrived.

"For guys like me who got a quick ticket home from that little scrap, it—uh, it makes me feel a little worthless."

"No need," the redhead responded and smiled through her tears, "I'm glad you made it. I'm glad you're here"—she patted his hand and leaned close—*"despite* your propensity to see everything I've *got* every time I turn around!" Erica gave a throaty chuckle and seemed ready to switch the conversation to something that didn't make her sad.

Jed raised his glass to the lovely redhead. "To fond memories of true loves," he toasted.

"Hear, hear!" came her soft response.

It was another natural but impulsive reflex: Jed lifted her hand to his lips and kissed the gleaming gold band. Then, Jed *and* Erica downed half the refilled glasses—in one deep swig.

CHAPTER 6

6:24 p.m., Mountain Time—

The streets of Holly, Colorado were deserted. Of course if every citizen in town were out and about, there still wouldn't be much of a crowd.

A lone man—a tall brown-skinned man—walked down the main street, which was U.S. Highway 50. He walked slowly and limped slightly as though the thin moccasins no longer cushioned his feet from pebbles in the sandy soil. The orange ball of sun was almost gone but its flaming light, low in the sky, was still a backdrop for the barely visible eastern rim of The Rockies. A faint long shadow was cast in front of the man.

The sound began quietly in the distance. Within seconds it was louder, then louder still; a crescendo that seemed certain to obliterate all in its path. However it brought no fear to the lone pedestrian. The sound was part of his life.

The air horns on The *Chief's* lead FT engine blared ominously as the streamliner stormed through Holly, the railroad tracks just yards from the tall man.

He watched the silver streak as it tore to the east. If only he were on it. He could envision himself in amiable conversation with a beautiful lady over cocktails or discussing the news of the day with a gentleman peer as the train carried them away to a world free of problems. But he knew it was just a daydream. He feared he'd never escape the circumstance into which he'd placed himself. He had wanted to do the right thing. But now he wasn't sure.

The tall man was upon the building before he realized it was there. Had he any warning he'd have looked in another direction—because it wasn't what he wanted to see on this day, at this hour. The building was small, mere cinder blocks painted white. But the gold cross on top made its purpose unmistakable.

He walked on past—but walked ever more slowly. Finally he stopped, turned around, and with eyes glistening walked back to the chapel and through its simple door. The confessional booth was up front to the right. He entered and closed the curtain not knowing if a priest was available, not knowing if he really wanted to see one. But for the moment, there was a degree of solace here.

The man was a creature of two cultures and his conscience was confused. Which set of mores was he to follow? Where did his supreme loyalty lie?

Shuffling footsteps approached the confessional. The man heard the rustle of a cassock as the priest settled in on his side of the booth and slid open the screen.

"Bless me, Father, for I have sinned." The man kept his voice at a whisper. How far his confession would go he still didn't know; but he certainly did not want to be identified.

"Yes, my son. How long since your last confession?" The priest's voice was that of a young priest, a tired young priest. Perhaps he'd already heard his share of confessions this day.

"I don't remember exactly, Father. I'm sorry. It's been too long."

"And what sins have you to confess?"

It would be difficult to assess who was more surprised—the tall brown-skinned man who blurted it out or the young priest who had never heard a confession like this.

"Father, I have killed a man!"

There was silence from the priest's side of the confessional.

"He was a very bad man, Father, *very* bad."

The priest finally found his voice. "My son, I—I am

empowered to impart grace in Christ's name, but...uh—"

"You *can't* tell the police, Father! I *know* that!" In his sudden excitement the man forgot to whisper.

"And I won't, my son, but you must—you *must* examine your conscience with painful scrutiny—hold nothing back."

Panic overcame the tall man and he leaped from the confessional, ran down the short aisle, and out into the dusk. In less than a minute he was out of Holly, Colorado, running with even more speed than he had as a youngster.

The priest sat silent for a good two minutes. He was quite sure he'd never see the man again and thankfully he hadn't recognized the voice. But he didn't want to risk seeing the stranger, not even for a moment in the dim light of evening. He had no desire to know his identity.

The priest bowed his head in brief prayer and made the sign of the cross. For a second, he wondered if God would countenance his granting absolution, even though the fleeing penitent seemed far short of the act of contrition. The priest knew better than to give the proposition serious thought.

CHAPTER 7

It was a quarter past nine and they were now in the central time zone. *The Chief* had left the sun far behind and was highballing down Santa Fe's mainline just east of Dodge City. She was doing ninety-one miles-per-hour and there'd be only two stops—very brief stops at the towns of Hutchinson and Newton—before the silver streamliner arrived in Kansas City in the wee hours of Tuesday morning. Jed and Erica lingered at their table in the Fred Harvey dining car savoring the final sips of expensive wine. The candle gave off a soft glow, its flicker exposing two or three fresh wine-colored spots on the white linen; precious drops that failed to make it to the glass or their lips.

There was one other couple still dining half a car-length away. They were middle-aged, late arrivals for dinner and Jed thought that fortunate. Since the crew was still serving them he and Erica could stay.

The meal had been a gourmet's delight. A starter of raw fruit with French cheese followed by Kansas City sirloin served Steak Diane style, mashed potatoes whipped in butter, and baby limas mixed with several other vegetables, also served with a heavy pat of butter and a touch of seasoning delightfully indigenous to the Great Southwest. The meal was so satisfying neither thought of ordering dessert.

When they arrived Jed and Erica hadn't noticed him; but the nattily attired businessman, already seated, saw them the moment they stepped through the door. He appeared sophisticated, wealthy, and envious of a couple so happy in each other's company. Lonely people live vicariously; and this gentleman was lonely.

He heard their order and in a gregarious state brought on by four bourbons with branch water, surmised something far beyond his power of discernment.

"Suh, madam," the steward had bowed in his most stately manner as he presented the bottle of Chateau Lafite Rothschild. "Our finest Bordeaux, compliments of the gentleman there in the gray pinstripe. He conveys his warmest congratulations on your honeymoon."

Jed hoped the man was too drunk to notice the shock on their faces as he and Erica turned as one to look at him. The gentleman was so pleased with his own hospitality they couldn't disappoint him. They did the polite thing.

"Thank you!" They spoke almost in unison and, the wine not yet poured, lifted their water glasses in a salute.

But Jed couldn't leave it there. He couldn't resist the opportunity to over-play the incident. Being a "ham" in such situations was part of his personality. He rose from his chair, bowed to the gracious gentleman and said, "You're very kind, sir, and thank you for noticing. Thus far, it's been a fan-*tastic,* unbelieveable honeymoon!" He spoke the last words slowly, deliberately, and loudly for Erica's benefit—and flinched at the kick she delivered to his ankle under the table.

Jed sat down laughing and rubbed his ankle. The steward poured the wine almost reverently. Jed was no expert in these matters but even he knew you could probably feed the entire car for what the bottle cost.

Conversation was easy during the long meal; talk of families and background. Jed shared his southwest Catholic upbringing and his education at the all male Jesuit college in the High Sierras of California: a jam-packed, year-round, three-year program. And the Raton draft board left him alone until he finished. The whole scenario was something of a mystery to Jed for the school was beyond his parents' means. But through the years Jed developed opinions on the matter. He believed he was indebted to the family wealth of Father Benson McKinnon, the parish priest when Jed was born. Father McKinnon had died when Jed was six but the priest's memory was always revered in the Easton household, and Jed was grateful (to whomever) for the solid education he received. However, he was certain the Reverend McKinnon would be disappointed that Jed's manner of speaking, even his basic cultural tastes, were more Main Street, Raton, than Jesuit academia.

As Jed told his story he touched briefly on his post-war law school days in Topeka and his return to Raton; to the D.A.'s office, the apprenticeship that every young lawyer dreads and looks forward to all at the same time.

Erica was a little older than he, six years to be exact. Her parents were natives of Colorado Springs as his were of Raton. Her father had practiced medicine (a family doctor) and her mother—"Well, to put it simply Mother read books," Erica laughed. She said they weren't wealthy people, but comfortable and her parents were retired. They moved to Tucson for better winters and, hopefully, longevity. She loved them dearly, corresponded often, and went to see them in Arizona for Christmas and Easter. Her sister in Kansas City (Jean was her name) was her best friend ever.

Erica glossed over her own two-year marriage to Ronald Swanson who gave his life for his country. It was obviously still painful—very painful—for her to speak of him.

There was a half-inch of the Rothschild in each of their glasses. The bottle stood empty, a silent sentry. They were quiet now. Two or three minutes passed. But it was not an uncomfortable silence. The jitters of strangers were long gone. They were quite comfortable as though they'd known each other since childhood. Alcohol will do that to people, Jed thought, for better or for worse.

The clackety-clack of steel wheel against steel rail was the only sound. Jed gazed dreamily at Erica across the table. Her eyes were light brown mixed with pale green. *What do they call that, hazel?* Jed barely knew the color of his own eyes. He knew his hair was black with streaks of gray sprinkled here and there, even though he was only twenty-six.

*Clackety-clack, clackety-clack...*the sound was accompanied intermittently by the clang of a bell and the flash of red lights as *The Chief* sped through crossing after crossing. It was lullaby time. They were like babes in a cradle. *Could we make that one cradle?* Jed thought the idea attractive.

He pulled out his father's pocket watch. "Gosh, why did we pay for bedrooms? We'll be in Kansas City before we get any sleep," he chuckled.

Erica returned his dreamy gaze; then her lips formed five inaudible words.

"What did you say?" Jed laughed but was shocked at what he'd just witnessed.

"Nothing—nothing! I'm sorry, it's the wine—I mean, I didn't say that," she mumbled.

How many times now (Jed was losing count) had he seen her face turn crimson? "Say what? You didn't say *what?*" He moved his leg against hers under the table. She didn't pull away. He knew what he knew, and he knew what the five words had been.

At his mention of bedrooms she had breathed, "We could use just one."

"Really, I'm sorry," she smiled, "and a little, uh—ashamed. I'm not used to drinking this much. The wine really went to my head. I think I'd better go to my room," and she giggled at that line. "I sound like I'm my own mother. Besides," (she leaned closer and pressed her leg strongly against his) "you wouldn't take advantage of an indisposed lady, would you?" She was now flirting quite shamelessly.

"No, no, I wouldn't Erica." Jed's smile and tone were full of sarcasm and he laid his hand on her knee. "Now, I'd really *love* to. I really would. But I'd *hate* myself in the morning."

"Of *course* you would!" Erica mocked him and the sarcasm. "Take me to bed—I mean take me to my room." She was pleading now. "And take my arm. I hope everyone thinks it's the train's rocking that makes *me* wobbly."

Jed and Erica managed to negotiate the narrow aisles of the five cars between Fred Harvey's place and hers without any undue stumbles. At her door Jed lingered, hoping for an invitation in but doubted he'd get it. Erica, even slightly drunk was too classy for that. She turned the key in her lock, opened the door, and put one foot inside. Then she turned, looked up at Jed, and said nothing for a long time. But her eyes spoke volumes.

Jed, somewhat self-conscious, steadied himself by placing one hand above the door. His other hand fell straight in front of him. It was at that moment that Erica stood on her tiptoes and placed both her hands, softly, on the back of his neck. Her touch reminded Jed of a cool silk scarf and her fingers drew slow circles through his hair at the collar line.

She pulled his lips to hers. It was a warm, open-mouth kiss and their tongues touched—lightly at first, then with more intensity. Whether by accident or design Jed would never know but as Erica stretched up to kiss him she pressed against the back of his hand. He gently turned his palm toward her; and felt soft thighs meeting at that special spot. He applied no pressure but she pressed against his fingers; then pulled away.

"I'm blushing," Erica whispered. "Go, Jed. Good night." And she closed the door.

Jed now lay alone between the crisp white sheets, which had been turned down and smoothed, the soft pillow fluffed, while they were at dinner. He wondered if she were still awake. Was she seeing the same brilliant stars dotting the vast Kansas sky? Was she thinking of him? *And why the hell did I strike out?*

As the train rocked gently, the prairie a passing blur, Jed Easton arrived at that juncture where dreams and reality merge. And on the dreamland side of the crossroads Erica was with him in his streamliner bedroom; *with* him in that small bed, their naked bodies pressed together between the cool sheets. In his dream they rocked together *with* the train, then *against* the train, on and on (and on and on) until his sensual and loving release inside her. And with the release his dreamland sky had stars more brilliant than those of the Milky Way. Jed couldn't calculate their number, or even the number of their contrasting shades of color. But many were a bright, bright green—as green as Erica's garters.

The Santa Fe *Chief* roared eastward.

CHAPTER 8

A look back—
Tuesday, November 3, 1936—

She stood out, this pretty young coed; a real head-turner, tall and slender, "…a gorgeous redhead with legs up to her neck!" That's how one lusty old professor described Erica to a colleague. And everyone on the Colorado College campus knew her; not personally but they knew who she was. Erica was hard to miss.

She carried a double major, history and geography, and was in her senior year. She knew she was good-looking, but had a special grace and demeanor that gave no overt hint that she knew. Some would say she was slightly aloof but not in a snobbish way. She merely reflected a refined upbringing and seemed comfortable in her own skin. She was Erica Elaine Harlan, no apologies necessary.

Her walk was the topic of conversation in many a male bull session, on campus *and* in downtown Colorado Springs. Erica could've been the pin-up for proper posture; always standing erect, shoulders back in confidence, and when she walked it was a vision of relaxed elegance. There was a certain swing and sway of the hips that no man missed—and the ladies were all too aware their men were aware. *The walk* went along perfectly with the spark in her eyes and the easy smile. Some even called her a flirt but Erica didn't think of herself that way. She was aware upon occasion of the commotion she caused but honestly wondered what all the fuss was about.

It was a situation that somewhat amused her father, particularly since it *disturbed* her mother. In fact Mrs. Harlan had mentioned it to Erica—once.

"Erica, dear, uh, sometimes, upon occasion—well, sometimes a lady, uh"—(it was obvious that Erica's mother was having trouble putting a delicate matter, delicately. But Mrs. Harlan wasn't one to give up.) "Well, even though one feels it's a glorious day...and—er...one *feels* so wonderful—dear me, how *do* I put this?"

"Just try, Mother, *try*," Erica said with a fair degree of irritation. "Use the English language." Erica was standing at the vanity applying lipstick, her back to Mrs. Harlan. And she was weary of this conversation.

"Well, Erica,"—(Mother Heather plowed bravely on)—"sometimes a lady needs to be a little re-*served* shall we say, in—in the way she carries herself, in the way she walks. Uh—do you know what I mean, dear?"

Erica turned with a combined smile and frown. "No, I really don't, Mother. What on earth are you talking about? I walk the way I walk!"

And that was the end of that. If Erica really knew what her mother was talking about she'd never admit it anyway.

And in the quiet of the parents' bedroom on the night of the aforementioned mother-daughter talk, the amused father (who overheard the conversation) sweetly said to the mother, "What *is* the problem, Heather? You know, my dear," and he looked adoringly at his wife, a gleam in his eye, "she got that from *you!*"

"What *are* you talking about, Doctor? I'm an old lady." Heather feigned disgust at the suggestion but the glint in her eye telegraphed she knew exactly what her husband was talking about.

"You remember, dear"—the doctor would not quit—"what I *told* you on our first date; what I found so attractive about you when you walked by—the first day I saw you?"

"I *don't* know what you're talking about." But there was the glint again—it gave the lie to her response.

Mother Heather never discussed the subject with Erica again. Heather Harlan knew she was seeing more of herself in Erica than she wished to admit. But she'd never heard it put so bluntly as from Doctor Harlan that evening. (She always called her husband Doctor Harlan).

From that night on the mother tried to cease her worry over Erica. After all Erica's older sister, Jean, seemed as perfect as any child could be as a youngster; yet her life had been anything but pleasant. Jean had two failed marriages by the time she was twenty-two, an inauspicious start for a young lady in the 1920s. Divorce, of course, was almost unheard of; but Doctor Harlan was not without friends in high places. The annulments were arranged.

Heather Harlan took great comfort in one thing. In fact she marveled at it. She'd never seen two sisters so close despite the ten-year difference in age. Jean from age fifteen had assumed more and more of a mother's role and Heather didn't mind. It allowed her more time to read. Heather knew it was undoubtedly a key reason Erica matured so swiftly. To this day, on the rare occasion Jean was in town, she and Erica were inseparable.

On this November evening in 1936, Erica turned her coat collar up against the brisk breeze streaming down from Pike's Peak. It was a short six-block walk from the campus to the Harlan residence and Erica relished the exercise and the time—time to reflect on her day, time to dream of her certain and glorious future; in short, the dreams of youth.

Light snow flurries swirled in the wind and glistened in the streetlamps. A few landed on her perky nose and rosy cheeks and competed for attention momentarily with barely visible freckles.

Her spirit was especially buoyant because of the party ahead. Election Night was always exciting at the Harlan house. There would be friends of parents and friends of her own, coming and going, Republican and Democrats alike. Ribbing among the hardcore partisans was always loud and usually friendly— occasionally not so friendly. The nation was still struggling through a horrific depression, and the wives more than once during the evening might well be called on to step between (and sweet-talk) their husbands, if the rhetoric got above an acceptable degree of volume and "enthusiasm." (It was undoubtedly helpful that this particular group was a bit more insulated from the country's woes, than the majority of their fellow citizens).

The radio would be blaring with music and special network up-dates on the election returns. From time to time a bunch would cram into a large automobile and take the short trip to the El Paso County courthouse. They'd congregate with scores of other citizens to watch the latest local returns posted on a huge blackboard fastened high on the wall. Someone in the group seemed always to bring a half pint of whiskey—which was always passed around. And before long, some guy would suggest that Erica or one of the other pretty girls climb the step ladder with the chalk to post the latest tally. One of the girls would often comply but Erica, completely aware the guy was interested in seeing something besides returns, would respond with a cool dallying smile. She'd then tell the brash young gentleman to behave himself, "…or I'll tell your *mother* on you." Erica was always amused at the expression those six or seven words brought to men's faces, no matter their age; as though they'd taken a blow to the solar plexus.

On the Harlan dining room table there would be an abundant supply of ham sandwiches, cold fried chicken, home-canned pickles, deviled eggs, home-baked light bread, piping hot Mexican corn cakes, spicy beans and rice, and Mrs. Harlan's specialty: apple pie baked with twice as much crust as apples. Heather and their Mexican housekeeper, Rosetta, had been making these epicurean delights for years and before a platter was empty it was replaced with a full one.

The living room, the foyer in front of the grand staircase, even around the dining room table itself—anywhere you could hear the radio, such areas became impromptu ballrooms. Young and old alike kicked up their heels at the Harlans.

There were always two punch bowls on the table, one at each end, and each specifically marked: "YOUNG ADULTS" (this meant no booze included) and "ADULTS," which meant the bowl had been plentifully spiked.

This arrangement was at the center of an episode that became family folklore:

Election night, 1920, the Harding-Cox contest, and back then the Harlans were one of the few families in Colorado Springs with a radio. If the weather was right you could pick up three or four signals on the headset; even as far away as Pittsburgh, Pennsylvania. The newspaper said a station in that city, KDKA, would report election tallies from each state throughout the night, a first for radio. The novelty was a big hit at the Harlan party, as guest after guest took their turn with the earphones.

Erica had heard such words as prohibition, liquor, and hooch; but at age four had no idea what any of it meant. However, she knew the punch bowls were segregated and was enchanted by the forbidden. As the punch bowls emptied and the room became louder Erica surreptitiously got her own full cup from the "ADULTS" bowl. What followed were a healthy sip, a childish yelp and sputter, and a mouthful of the hooch-laden punch spewed on Jennie Thomas' beautiful new white filmy dress, shipped especially for this party from New York City. Jennie Thomas was the Mayor's wife, the First Lady of Colorado Springs.

Erica truly believed these election night soirees had piqued her interest in history and politics in the first place. She decided such topics would always be of primary interest, hence, her college majors.

But tonight, Election Night, 1936—this night would live in Erica's memories for specific reasons.

"Now, Erica," Heather told her the day before, "do not get your hopes up; but I got a letter from Jean. She says she and some friends might—*might*—drive down from Denver." Erica received the possibility with kid-like glee, jumping up and down and clapping her hands.

It would also be special because five of Erica's best college buddies would be in attendance. These included Roscoe Squire. Roscoe was a fellow senior and quite good-looking. Upon graduation he planned to apprentice with a local attorney of good reputation.

Erica was already going over in her mind the darkened hallways and secluded rooms where Roscoe could (and would) follow her. He always tried to steal a kiss in such circumstances. Erica always acted like she hated it (sort of), but she knew he knew, she loved it.

She couldn't wait to put on her new dress purchased at the ladies apparel shop in Colorado Springs' exclusive Broadmoor Hotel. It was for such occasions that Heather Harlan would dip into her own household money, ("Doctor Harlan need not know about this," she would quietly tell Erica), to supplement Erica's clothing allowance.

"It's beautiful!" Heather told Erica when the exuberant girl pulled it from the shopping bag, "but dear *girl!* The fabric is *so* thin. Do *not* forget your slip!"

"Of course not, Mother!" Erica replied with mock horror—but just to be safe decided *against* showing Heather the virtually sheer, gauzy slip she bought to wear with the dress.

The dress *was* thin, a silk crepe number in light gray-blue from Hollywood designer Edith Head. Erica had seen a picture in a Hollywood movie magazine; a starlet was wearing the exact same dress. It sported a shawl collar that draped all the way to the center of the slender waist. There were no buttons but two strategically placed snaps inside the long collar would keep the wearer modest. With such a low neckline it was stylish to show a touch of elegant underwear; hence, the gauze slip trimmed in Italian lace. The skirt of the dress was also *very today*—not quite full, not quite slim, and falling to mid-calf.

Erica smiled dreamily as she walked home thinking of Roscoe's hand on her back tonight. With such gossamer fabrics she thought his touch would make her feel *naked!* She hoped the idea would cross his mind as well.

Erica was also certain she'd be called on to salve some hurt feelings; specifically, those of her father whom she loved dearly. It was impossible for him to accept reality in politics even when he should know better. For weeks he'd been forecasting to all who would listen a very close win—the return of the Republicans to the White House.

"The American people will not continue this road to socialism," Doctor Harlan said of FDR and his New Deal. "I have too much faith in them. They've seen the light and Governor Alf Landon of Kansas, is just the man to send Franklin and Elea*nooooor* back to Hyde Park."

Erica, more analytical than ideological, thought otherwise. Professor Arthur Aldredge, her favorite American History teacher, corresponded regularly with many officials in Washington. For weeks the professor had assured his class (*warned* would be the word for those with Republican leanings), this election was all but over. Erica couldn't yet determine which side she was on, but was sure she'd make up her mind by the time she was old enough to vote. She admired her father so much and agreed with him that America was about liberty and freedom for the individual; freedom to be all one could be. To Erica, Doctor Harlan's argument made a good deal of sense: that even well meaning government assistance had the potential to curb creativity and determination, the very appetite necessary to reach for the stars.

"This is *America!*" Doctor Harlan would mutter; usually, as he read the newspaper description of the most recent New

Deal program. "Americans *do* for themselves!" The doctor made no secret of his low opinion of socialists and communards. He did not consider The President to be one of *those*—but as to some of the people around Mister Roosevelt, he wasn't so sure.

But Erica also admired The President; this, after several conversations with Professor Aldredge.

The professor was one of the prominent Colorado Democrats who encouraged the New York governor to seek the Presidency in 1932. Erica was deeply touched by his description of FDR. He could not know for certain, but was personally convinced that Mister Roosevelt could not actually walk.

Aldredge was invited to a reception, a few weeks prior to the '32 convention, at the Waldorf Astoria in New York City. Governor Roosevelt stood for the entire forty-five minutes of the receiving line. As Professor Aldredge approached he could see beads of perspiration on FDR's face. Interestingly the room was quite cool.

Aldredge took note of the two men standing with the governor. One was James, Roosevelt's son, the other a uniformed New York State policeman. Neither man *ever* left the governor's side.

As Aldredge shook hands and introduced himself to Roosevelt the future President smiled, chatted, and sucked on his cigarette holder as though nothing in the world was wrong. But the professor noticed Roosevelt's left hand, the hand that gripped James' arm. The knuckles were bright white with intensity. It was then that Aldredge assumed that FDR couldn't even stand unassisted—and his determined effort at such events must have taken every ounce of strength he could muster.

Erica was now just two and a half blocks from home. She pulled her coat collar higher, a shield against the gusty wind swirling down from Pikes Peak. It cut like a knife. Snow was falling now beyond the flurry stage. She heard a car approaching behind her. It was an old Marathon touring car with the driver's seat exposed and it inched slowly alongside. The bundled-up driver mumbled something in a loud voice. Erica—innocent, vivacious, and always helpful—assumed he was asking directions. She walked to the car and rested her arms on the passenger door.

"Excuse me, what did you say?" Erica smiled at the middle-aged but weather-beaten face.

For a long moment the man said nothing. A clammy fear enveloped Erica's body—but the instinctive warning was almost too late. Like a flash the man grabbed her arm and yanked hard. Erica screamed with pain and fright as she tried to pull away. But the man yanked again even harder.

Erica panicked. "You—you *BASTARD!*" she screamed. She was shocked she used the word. It apparently shocked him. The man let go and Erica took off down the sidewalk, running as she never ran before, stylish pumps to the contrary. Fear rushed over her in waves, each wave more traumatic than the last. She hiked her skirt to mid-thigh to run even faster, and the terror of the moment made her appear a candidate for the Olympic Games.

The grizzled man stared blankly at the fleeing figure. He'd been too brazen this time. Debauched desire had triumphed caution. The girl saw his automobile—*and* his face.

Claude Stickett made a u-turn with the old Marathon and headed out of Colorado Springs. This gal; this luscious redhead was so different from the first; but with each successive victim—even when an attempt failed—Claude Sticket was always reminded of that first time:

At age fifteen, he was already a six-foot-four-inch ruffian; wiry, tough as beef jerky, and strong as an ox. Young Claude had no

interest in professional girls, those willing to comply for a small fee. He delighted in brutal force, the weaker his victim the better.

She was a tiny Mexican waitress at a barroom and whorehouse in Roswell. He was the only customer that night downstairs, she the only employee on the lower floor. It was almost midnight and the shy girl pressed down hard on the musty dishrag, giving the massive bar a final wipe. She was not a hooker—just a young girl pouring drinks trying to make a few coins to help her mother raise five siblings.

Like a flash he grabbed her long black hair and with his other arm around her waist he dragged the petite girl across the bar and out the door to the wooden porch. The horses at the hitching rail whinnied nervously.

Around to the back and the darkness, and the sordid deed was dirty, quick, and violent. At the horrid conclusion Claude again grabbed a handful of the girl's hair and yanked her to her feet. With his other hand he clutched her tiny throat until she gagged and gasped for air. The stench of his foul breath stung her nostrils.

"You Mexican bitch!" he growled. "If you ever breathe one word of this, I promise I'll hunt you down and _kill_ you."

In the New Mexico Territory of 1889 that was enough. No Mexican girl of fourteen, with a limited English vocabulary, would dare talk of such things.

Stickett returned to the barroom often, his routine menacing and frightening. He sat in a corner, drank rye whiskey, and stared at the girl. A cold leer was on his face, as her face turned ashen and clammy, her eyes on the floor so as not to meet his gaze. The longer he sat, the more her hands trembled as she tried gamely to pour drinks without a spill.

However, Claude Stickett never touched her again. Why would he? She was yesterday's stuff. He wanted something new.

Erica arrived home winded, and in a dreadful fright. But she was absolutely determined to let nothing destroy the long-awaited party for her and her friends. She possessed that capacity so identified with exuberant youth: to believe you are indestructible; to push to the far recesses of the mind anything you want to forget; to pretend it didn't happen. Everything will turn out fine because it always has. Today is wonderful, tomorrow will be brilliant.

Despite the horrific scare, she was the designated junior hostess for the evening and she *had* to make herself outrageously beautiful. But neither project advanced before Hilary Smith and Judith Webster, two classmates from Latin who had already arrived, whispered in unison, "What's the matter?" Their eyes were wide. They'd instantly noticed Erica's ashen face and rapid breathing.

She pulled them into her room to tell the story, not wanting her mother to hear. Erica knew Heather would demand that Doctor Harlan deliver her to and from college each day and she enjoyed her independence too much for such restriction.

"Besides," she concluded to her breathless friends, "he was probably just an old drunk, a little lonely. He didn't even realize what he was doing."

"But shouldn't you tell your parents?" Hilary asked.

"Heavens, *no*! *Daddy* will just get upset and *Heather* will 'mother-hen' me to death. Besides, the old coot was undoubtedly just passing through. I mean, *I've* never seen him and *I* know *everybody* in The Springs."

And so it was that Erica went on to more "important" things, such as pulling her new dress from the closet for Hilary and Judith's approval. On the heels of their "Ooohs" and "Ahhhs" she asked if they'd please check with her mother.

"See if she needs help. Roscoe will be here any minute—I *must* get ready. I'll be out shortly."

Erica never mentioned the scary episode again. In the years to come she'd occasionally awaken from a deep sleep and bolt upright in bed, drenched in clammy sweat. For an instant she'd see the leering wrinkled face and feel his bony fingers around her wrist. But being the feisty girl she was—"Piffle!" she'd say to herself. "He was just passing through. I've *never* seen him again." Erica would turn over and go back to sleep.

She stepped into the claw-foot bathtub in the large bathroom between her room and Jean's old room. There were four such bathtubs in this house and they were about as close to big city living as anyone got in Colorado Springs. If the tub was even half full a woman of Erica's body weight could float all evening—but not tonight. She moved the soap-saturated, luxuriant washrag over her body more quickly than she liked. A long hot bath was one of her very favorite things. Next time, she promised herself. Erica stepped from the tub and toweled dry.

She stepped naked from the bathroom into her bedroom—just as Roscoe Squire opened the door from the hall.

"Roscoe, get out!" Erica gasped. But possessing more spunk than most young girls she couldn't help laughing, even as she felt her face flush. She grabbed the first thing she could find on the bed and held it in front of her nude body.

Roscoe stood there with the door (and his mouth) open. "Oh, my, I—I'm *sorry!* Hilary told me you were dressed!"

"*DRESSING* was the word, Roscoe, *dressing!*" She was embarrassed but also amused at Roscoe's state. He seemed frozen and looked as though his oxygen supply was down to its last five seconds.

"*Puh-LEEZ get out!*" she giggled.

Red-faced, Roscoe stepped back into the hallway and closed the door behind him. He rolled his eyes as he headed down the hall—and to the punch bowl.

It was only then that Erica noticed she'd "shielded" her totally naked body with the new, extremely sheer, gauzy slip.

CHAPTER 9

It was almost eight o'clock when Erica circled her lips one last time with a soft red, evening lipstick. She stepped back to survey the finished product in the full-length mirror, which tilted on its own stand in the corner. *Oh, my! But it's okay—I think.* Erica now saw what her mother had known immediately: in the 'daring' department the dress was on (if not over), the borderline. The slip barely performed its task. *Well, the lights are dim, Mother won't notice, and fashion is fashion!*

The party was well underway even though returns were scant at this early hour. Libation flowed freely, which was why the party was well underway.

The floor-model Stromberg-Carlson radio, its thickly lacquered wood reflecting flickering candles, was blasting out "Jumpin' At The Woodside" by the Count Basie Orchestra. The fabulous band was on a network feed live from Kansas City. The Sparks-Withington table model in the kitchen was tuned to the same station. The younger crowd was showing off new dance steps. A few older citizens were also on the dance floor; those accustomed to an early nip *before* the evening out. It was easy to pick out the early nippers, particularly among the older gentlemen. They kept asking the ladies to dance—mostly, ladies who were much younger.

Whenever the announcer at KVOR or a national reporter on CBS would break in with election news the room grew silent.

Roscoe, still blushing a little from their earlier encounter approached Erica timidly. He said nothing at first but over a sixty-second period inched ever closer and casually slipped his arm around her waist. The dress had the effect Erica hoped for.

"Oooh," Roscoe moaned, "that feels nice; the dress I mean." They laughed. "Wanna dance?"

"Sure," Erica replied, "I love this." She referred to the strains of "Embraceable You" now filling the room from the Stromberg-Carlson. For this tune, Basie used only a small section of his orchestra, a French-style combo: accordion, guitar, string bass and, of course, the Count's piano. The ensemble was perfect for Gershwin's romantic little ballad. Roscoe was a graceful dancer and he pulled Erica close.

"Has this place got an attic I haven't seen?"

Erica laughed at his honesty. "Roscoe, I'm running out of places. We've been to every dark corner in this house. Besides, our 'tours' occur so often, people talk."

And then Mother Heather saved the day. "Erica, dear, get another ham. Doctor Harlan put them on that high shelf in the garage to keep cool. Better take Roscoe, it's heavy; too heavy for you to get down."

They spotted the baked hams covered in brown paper wrapping but Roscoe decided the crowd could just damn wait for another sandwich. He took Erica in his arms and pulled her tight against him. The garage was more than cool, it was cold and Erica welcomed the embrace. She ran her fingers through his thick chestnut hair and put her face against his chest. He lightly touched her chin and tilted her lips up. His kiss was not so light.

"Erica," Roscoe whispered, "I want you! I mean I really *want* you. Here! Now!"

For the first time in her life, really, Erica felt restraint slip perilously away. She took his hand and touched it lightly to her lips; then guided it lower, slowly, teasing him with her eyes. Over the rise and fall of her firm breasts ("I love this dress!" Roscoe whispered), across her lean torso, and Erica moved his hand even lower. *Lower..lower—*

"Erica? Erica, dear, the ham?" Heather Harlan called from the back door of the house.

Roscoe, cursing in a hoarse whisper took a huge ham from the shelf. He and Erica returned to the party, both (particularly Roscoe) in need of a cold shower.

They entered the dining area as the front door burst open.

"Jean!" Erica screamed so loudly Roscoe almost dropped the ham. The sisters hugged each other as Mom and Dad arrived to greet their oldest daughter.

"Hey, everybody, meet my friends," Jean exclaimed brushing snowflakes off her coat. "This is Shirley Hamilton and her fiancé, Lieutenant Ronald Swanson, United States Army."

Erica thought her sister, now thirty years old, the most beautiful woman in the world, and told her so often. Jean thought the same of her kid sister but was more hesitant to say so. Deep inside Jean feared her own good looks had been the cause of much trouble. Jean attracted men wherever she went, even early on. So early in fact, she was too young to discern the good guys from the not-so-good guys.

However, two failed marriages to the contrary, she refused to be bitter and chocked it up as experience. She more often than not, went out with friends in a group. And Erica loved the friends Jean brought home. They were sophisticated, or so it seemed to young Erica.

Jean currently worked as a stenographer for the Colorado Supreme Court in Denver, as did Shirley.

"Where did Shirley meet the lieutenant?" The sisters were freshening up in the bathroom and Erica hoped she asked the question nonchalantly.

"An old family friend, I think," Jean answered. "He's ten years older than Shirley. He's thirty-five and plans to make a career of the Army."

Erica did the math in her head *(he's fifteen years older than me)* and felt slightly ashamed at being attracted to him.

When they returned to the party Lieutenant Swanson was talking politics with Doctor Harlan in the kitchen doorway and Shirley Hamilton was with Roscoe near the front door. Shirley laughed gaily at one of Roscoe's stories and it crossed Erica's mind that Shirley might be enjoying the story (and Roscoe's company) a bit too much, for a lady engaged to an Army officer; an officer in the room. *Why am I suddenly so bitchy?*

She went to the punch bowl for another drink. Her parents had allowed her to move to the "ADULTS" container at age eighteen. She glanced in the direction of her father and the lieutenant. Doctor Harlan's back was to Erica and Lieutenant Swanson was listening to him, nodding politely. But as Erica risked a second glance the lieutenant's eyes were on her. His eyes were dark and glistened with a sensuous mischievous twinkle; and were exactly the color of his wavy hair. And one short sprig of a curl persisted in falling over his forehead.

Erica smiled and he gave her a sly wink. She turned away and felt her face flush from the giddy surge that went through her body. She walked to the Stromberg-Carlson and stood by herself listening to the music and sipping the punch. The network was still broadcasting Count Basie and Erica couldn't help but move to "The One O'clock Jump." Drink in hand, she twirled in her solo dance and each time she looked in the direction of Lieutenant Swanson he was still nodding at her father's political lecture—but watching Erica. She glanced his way again. Again, their eyes met. But this time neither would look away. She was afraid someone would notice—but a 'devil may care' mood won the day.

What is he thinking? Erica danced on, her movements becoming ever so slightly suggestive, their eyes still locked in the daring gaze. *Jean will kill me if she sees me flirting so brazenly with Shirley's fiancé.*

This time it was Roscoe who saved Erica from herself.

"Wanna dance?" He was at her elbow.

"Like a *gypsy!*" she laughed, and everyone stopped talking to watch. The "One O'clock Jump" never jumped so much as it did that night for Roscoe and Erica.

11:00 p.m., Mountain Time—

The snow fell heavily now. It was apparent to all that Alf Landon would carry only Maine and Vermont—New Hampshire if he were lucky. (He wasn't lucky). But the party was still lively and loud, and no one wanted to leave. The Democrats drank more because they were happy; the Republicans drank more because they were sad.

By one o'clock in the morning the crowd, a little bleary-eyed, began to drift away. Shirley Hamilton, Lieutenant Swanson, (and Roscoe), were among the last to leave.

"You aren't staying with us?" Erica asked of the handsome couple, admitting inside she'd love to see the officer at the Harlan breakfast table.

"No, but thank you," Shirley responded. "My brother manages the Broadmoor. He called today to say they're not heavily booked and insisted Ron and I stay there. He has a huge suite for each of us."

Erica, Jean, and Mother Heather were in the vestibule to say goodbye. They each kissed Shirley lightly on the cheek and shook hands with Lieutenant Swanson. But the lieutenant, the last in line, held on to Erica's hand a bit long. Then after letting go he moved close once more, so close it hid their hands as he again gripped hers. Their fingers interlocked and his affectionate squeeze was much more than a formal goodnight.

As he reached the door Swanson turned back. "Oh, I really should give my regards to Doctor Harlan," and he headed for the good doctor sitting in his favorite chair by the fireplace.

Doctor Harlan was not at the doorway because he was one of the sad Republicans. Much more bourbon than usual had crossed his lips this night.

Erica watched as the handsome officer exchanged pleasantries with her father. Her father nodded and said something though Erica doubted he knew who or what was in front of him.

As the lieutenant approached the doorway for the second time, he again came close and clasped Erica's hand so tightly *and so long* she feared Shirley would notice.

"Goodnight." Everyone said it in unison, even Roscoe who gave Erica a mere peck on the cheek and a wan smile. With all the guests gone, Erica, Jean, and Heather went to the fireplace for a nightcap with Doctor Harlan.

Erica was giddy with infatuation and her body tingled from the handsome officer's intimate, sensual approach. She wanted to tell Jean of the officer's sly flirtation (she hoped it had been sly), but knew this wasn't the time for that conversation.

Outside, Roscoe stood on the sidewalk in the falling snow. He watched the disappearing taillights of Lieutenant Swanson's car. He had noticed a couple of those revealing glances between Erica and the officer. He even saw their final furtive hand squeeze, not as secret as they thought, in the vestibule.

"Cocky West Point-er!" For the second time tonight Roscoe cursed hoarsely under his breath. "Fresh bastard!" He knew in his soul that earlier tonight, that once-in-a-lifetime quest for the ham; that was it. He would never again get so close to having Erica.

"Damn the 'One O'clock Jump' after all!" he muttered.

CHAPTER 10

A year and a half later—
May, 1938—
Near Dalies, New Mexico—

The fast freight had begun to slow its speed ten miles back. It now was approaching a crawl. Claude Stickett slid open the door of the box car just enough to peer ahead up the track, but was careful to stay out of sight. He wanted no railroad detective discovering his favorite method of free transportation.

It was clear the freight was pulling onto a siding; most likely to let a passenger train pass, but Claude would take no risk of being discovered. He could always hop a later freight; besides, he was hungry.

He slowly stuck his head out the door and seeing no one, jumped to the ground before the train came to a complete stop.

The sky was threatening, the clouds dark with a purplish hue. The wind had a biting chill for the month of May. There was probably hail in those clouds.

To avoid any railway personnel who might question his presence, Stickett walked a quarter-mile away from the tracks before turning to walk parallel to them. He hoped he wouldn't have to go far to find a town, at least a homestead, where he could get sustenance.

He was going to need it. At that moment the rain started, a heavy downpour; and yes, there was hail. He found a small knoll with a natural overhang and was able to avoid the worst of the deluge; but with the wind whipping every which way his clothes still became soaked. As if it would help, he shook his fist at the sky and cursed God. But then, that was something he did regularly with little or no provocation.

The rain finally diminished to a light drizzle and Stickett renewed his trek along the Santa Fe tracks. He'd walked a couple of miles when dusk fell, and half a quarter due north he spotted the dim glow of a lighted window.

The house was little more than a clapboard hut; two, maybe three rooms at the most. There was a small front porch with a roof.

Claude rapped softly on the door, which was opened by a gray-haired man, likely in his sixties.

"I'm cold, wet, and hungry," Claude said in the softest voice he could muster. "Just wonderin' if I might come in and warm up; maybe get a cup of coffee."

The man gave Stickett a kind smile, and said, "I'm sure this wouldn't apply to you, but there's some mighty rough characters ridin' the rails these days. Makes me a little uncomfortable invitin' 'em into my home."

Sticket just stared at the man, saying nothing.

"But," the man continued, "I'd be mighty happy to get you a bowl of stew and a couple of blankets. Don't think it's gonna get too cold tonight. You're welcome to stay on the porch."

Stickett stared at the man for another five seconds; then pulled the derringer and shot him in the center of his forehead. The man crashed backwards against the rickety kitchen table with two chairs. One of the chairs was smashed to pieces by the weight of his fall. Coins from his pants pocket jangled across the linoleum. He was dead when he hit the floor.

Claude took the coal oil lamp from the table, and with the derringer in his other hand, crept across the kitchen to a door just slightly ajar. It was a pantry barely three feet square, but well stocked.

He tip-toed across the kitchen and through the open door on the opposite side of the room. It was a bedroom. A double bed with a simple brown enamel wrought-iron headboard, and a tiny chest of drawers, was the only furniture he saw. There were no closet doors. Stickett looked under the bed—nothing.

The mirror above the chest of drawers was so old, or of such poor quality (maybe both), it reflected merely a blurred glow of the lamp. Stickett could scarcely make out his own features. One at a time he jerked the drawers open. There were only two: one with clean pillow cases, the other held a single pair of bib overalls.

Then—he saw the trunk. It was a tall trunk—and a long one, a good six feet. It took up most of the wall behind the open door. Claude was instantly suspicious.

The metal latch on the lid was unlocked. He set the lamp on the chest, and with his pistol aimed at the trunk's center, stealthily approached—and threw open the lid.

Quilts—and clean sheets; all neatly arranged. That was it. He ran his free hand deep, rummaging through the stack of material. Just more of the same.

Stickett, with a sense of relief, put the derringer in its holster and took the lamp back to the kitchen table.

He took comfort that he'd found no clothes for a woman. He now noted there were no plates at all on the table; another good sign the man lived alone. Had there been two bowls waiting for the hot stew steaming on the stove, or the slightest hint of a feminine presence anywhere, he would have torn the place apart until he found her.

Stickett got a bowl and ladle from the pantry and dipped up a serving of stew. Then, back to the pantry for a salt-cured ham. He found a butcher knife on a shelf and sliced off a huge chunk of the meat.

He opened the tiny oven door of the wood stove and discovered a pan of biscuits, almost over-baked. For the next twenty-five minutes he sat at the table and gorged himself.

Stickett seldom glanced at the body of the murdered homesteader; but felt no emotion, and lingered not at all on any particular feeling he may have had.

He scooped up the scattered coins from the floor and stuffed them in his own pocket—but something had struck him. He took the handful of change out, and looked at one coin closely. It appeared to be gold; gold of good quality, and bore the image of a structure. Nothing in Stickett's past would have allowed him to identify the coliseum in Rome on one side; Julius Caesar on the other. But that coin he put in the derringer's holster; in the tiny side pocket with a snap.

Stickett thought of going to sleep on the double bed but felt it too risky. There was always the possibility some other wanderer would drop by. He also thought of smashing the coal oil lamp on the floor as he left, knowing the place would go up like dry wood on the desert. But he reconsidered, thinking that might draw more attention than the alternative.

In the end, he blew out the lamp, walked out the door, and again began his trek along the tracks. He was certain a freight would come by soon. He didn't care which direction it was going.

Twenty minutes had passed since Stickett left the homestead. Ever so slowly; ever so silently, the trunk in the bedroom began to move.

A woman, in the darkened house, crawled on all fours to the kitchen. She was sobbing uncontrollably.

The storm was over. A sliver of moonlight came through the window. She felt for a pulse, knowing she would find none. Blood still oozed from the wound in her husband's head. In the darkness, she found a clean dishrag. She did not bother to light the lamp—or heat water. She feared _he_ might still be out there.

She had heard the muted voices, mixed with the sound of the rain. Her husband was talking to someone, but she could see little through the crack in the door.

Then—the terrifying shot! And she leaped for the trunk.

Now, she cleaned her husband the best she could—and kissed his lips. Then, she got a clean sheet from the trunk, and covered him.

At daylight, if she saw no one through the windows, she would try to start the old model T truck and drive into Dalies to tell the authorities. She hoped she could manage all that; she'd never driven before.

She had married her husband seven years ago; he was twenty-five years her senior. The first thing he had shown her, when bringing her to his house, was the trunk. He had installed a false floor, two-thirds the way down from the top. In the hollowed out bottom, he had placed two metal handles at the front. He showed her how to slip underneath; then pull the trunk and herself, against the wall. It was a small degree of added security—but some was better than none.

She had never complained, because she loved her husband. But in her mind, she was often despondent over the lack of finery in her life. She had hoped for more.

But tonight she felt differently. She prayed, thanking God for sparing her. She realized it may well have been the very <u>sparseness</u> of her wardrobe that saved her. For on this night—she was wearing the only dress she owned.

She kissed her husband's cold lips again; this time through the sheet.

CHAPTER 11

Back on the Santa Fe Chief—
Tuesday, November 2, 1948—
8:10 a.m.—

The sudden blast from the switcher diesel's air horn would have startled Gabriel himself. It rumbled by on the next track, a matter of inches from Jed Easton's Pullman. He sat up in the bunk so quickly, and in such shock, he was short of breath. For a moment he was unsure where he was, but was aware of the prominent throbbing at the base of his skull—in the back of his head where it joined the neck. And his eyebrows throbbed. He immediately knew the cause: wine, wine, *too much* wine.

"Ooooh!" Waves of nausea swept over Jed. He glanced around his Pullman compartment realizing everything was still—motionless. There was no movement.

Then, he remembered: this was the procedure and Jed knew it. He would've remembered he knew it, had his mind been less enshrouded in the grape. *The Chief* was scheduled to arrive in Kansas City at two-forty a.m. All sleeper cars with Kansas City-bound passengers were shunted to a sidetrack where slumbering travelers could finish their night's rest. But Jed recalled nothing of the clanging and jolting which undoubtedly accompanied such an exercise. This could only mean his sleep had been truly sound—or downright drunken. The thought made him smile, but even smiling made his head hurt worse.

Jed hated hangovers. Other than that, he was glad to be awake. After falling asleep the night before, enveloped in warm fantasies of Erica, the air horn had blasted him conscious from a frighteningly horrible nightmare:

(Jed was standing in the back yard of Claude Stickett's house. That was strange enough, because Jed had never been to Stickett's house. Nevertheless, here he stood, looking at the porch—and he sensed he was invisible. But the *really* weird part: Jed seemed to witness what was going on in Claude Stickett's mind on that awful night).

Claude's unseeing eyes stared up at the brown face. But somehow he saw the face—and a blue and white bandana covering the figure's head. The face disappeared; and as Claude stared into the void, which to one alive would be a back porch ceiling, something unusual was happening behind his eyes. Was it in his brain? his spirit?

Stickett sensed his eyes bulging, his mouth open wide. His jaws seemed about to burst from their sockets. He screamed loudly! He knew he was screaming—but no sound came forth. He was in a tube, a long black tube—oily, slimy, and greasy. He fell faster and faster down the tube. Was there an end to the tube?

There was total darkness, yet he saw—but saw nothing. He was <u>HOT</u>! and getting hotter! Sulfur—the smell of sulfur! It burned his eyes, his nose and throat. His complete existence seemed singed. On and on and on—he gagged on the sulfur. He wished he were dead—then realized <u>he was</u>!

Claude Stickett's soul had arrived in Hell.

Jed jumped from the Pullman bunk and dipped his head to the compartment's tiny sink. He splashed handful after handful of cold water on his face, as though it would clear his head of the bizarre nightmare. It would be an added blessing if it cured his hangover.

Jed pulled his father's pocket watch from his trousers in the closet—8:13 it read. *Damn! Am I supposed to be somewhere this morning?*

Jed's preoccupation with Miss Green Garters had kept him from opening the big manila envelope TJ left for him at the Raton depot ticket window. He'd received a phone call from Mrs. TJ that the information would be there.

"The silly ol' fool's sick," she said. "I tell him every day I'll cook for him but *no*, he has to go to Jody's Café. He got some bad eggs," Mrs. TJ opined. "I know what happens in restaurant kitchens"—(she was wound up and wouldn't shut up)—"they leave stuff set out," she said. "They leave stuff *set out!*"

Jed found the packet and ripped it open. He was feeling better and even chuckled at remembering his conversation with Mrs. TJ—and at the pleasant memory of Erica taking over his every waking thought since boarding the Santa Fe *Chief.*

Jed scanned the single page, stunned at what he was reading but relieved he wasn't late for an appointment. TJ's first sentence suggested Jed show up at this guy's office unannounced.

TJ needed only one page to explain any subject even when quite complicated. He wrote (scribbled would be a better word) in short three-or-four-word, incomplete sentences. But the message was always clear:

> don't call first
> john deerman—kc lawyer
> firm: steadman, swift, and jones
> deerman's real name: john little deer
> grew up Navajo reserv., gallup
> sheriff out there sez rumors in town

little deer hated c stickett
thinks stickett killed little deer cousin (see clipping)

How odd, Jed thought. In his nightmare he had seen a brown face—and here he was in Kansas City to interview a Navajo attorney.

Jed unfolded the strip of yellowed newspaper in TJ's packet. It was from the *Gallup Independent*, dated August 7, 1946. There was a picture, probably a high school graduation photo of a dark-skinned beauty, long hair falling well below her shoulders. She was obviously Native American with a cautious smile and a look of calm determination.

The gruesome facts chilled Jed's blood and his upset stomach returned, doing a couple more flip-flops. The article was straightforward, small-town newspaper reporting; brutally plain, concerning the strangulation death of Morning Star. Gallup was known as a high desert town with rough edges but a ghastly deed such as this was far from common.

Was John Little Deer a real suspect in Claude Stickett's murder? *Amazing!* Would a Navajo kid who somehow managed to make his way to the practice of law, revert to the old ways of retribution? A knee-jerk reaction to avenge the horrible death of a loved one was understandable. But with so much to lose, why would anyone actually carry it out? And how in hell did Deerman, aka John Little Deer, become a lawyer? Jed looked forward to his surprise visit to Steadman, Swift, and Jones.

But now there was Erica—he must see Erica. He hurriedly dressed, wondering if she was still asleep. What if she'd already left the train? He had no address or telephone number for Miss Green Garters; Colorado College, that's all he knew of her. And at this moment he wanted to see her more than anything else in all the world.

Jed left his bedroom, luggage in hand, and headed for 3C, two cars ahead. However, direct passage from his Pullman to the next, was blocked by folding metal gates. This meant he had to exit to get to Erica's coach.

Jed stepped off the train and grabbed his Stetson to keep it on his head. The prairie wind swept through the un-walled shelters of the Kansas City railroad yard in forty mile-per-hour gusts. He started for Erica's car but a stern neatly dressed man blocked his path.

"Sir, the stairs to Union Station are here to your right." The man was pointing to a wide stairway leading up from the tracks.

"But I wanna see a friend in another car," Jed protested.

"I'm sorry, sir, you can't re-board the train once you've left. Just take the stairs, please." The man's hat brim was pulled so low Jed could scarcely see his eyes.

"May I ask why?" Jed was getting irritated. To have some hard-ass prevent his seeing Erica was too much to take.

"Sir, this is a secured area. *Please* take the stairs!" The man did not budge and two other men similarly dressed appeared around the corner of Erica's car. They stood silent, staring at Jed.

Intuition told Jed not to resist and he picked up the suitcase he'd just set down. "Yes, sir!" he said crisply and noticed two or three more of the strong silent types at the rear end of his own sleeper.

Slowly, deliberately, he walked to the staircase, not turning back till he was on the fifth step. Only then did he understand.

Beyond the three Santa Fe sleeper cars, four or five tracks away, was a long, heavyweight sleeper car. The roof was black. The rest of the car was a deep Army green, save for the highly polished handrails and trim—all brass—on the rear observation deck. *Pullman,* said the large gold letters above the coach windows. Four more of the no-nonsense guys stood around the car, looking first one direction then another. But it seemed to Jed they always wound up looking at him.

Then, a schoolboy shiver of excitement shot through Jed's body as he focused on the smaller gold letters below the windows of the green Pullman. *Ferdinand Magellan* they proclaimed, and next to the observation deck was more gold lettering: U.S. No. 1.

That long green Pullman was the private railroad car of The President of the United States! Jed had just experienced a first-hand encounter with the United States Secret Service. Ol' Harry was in town to cast his ballot in Independence. This was Election Day, 1948.

CHAPTER 12

Jed walked into the cavernous halls of Union Station wondering what his next move should be. There were questions for which he had no answers: had Erica already left or was she still in Bedroom 3C; and how could he find out?

He stopped an elderly porter walking toward the down staircase. "Excuse me, do you have a second?"

The old Negro turned, "Of course, sir, what can I do for you?" His voice was mellifluous, his elocution perfect. He was obviously a man educated far beyond the average porter.

"Uh, I've a friend who came in on *The Chief* this morning. Might she still be in a side-tracked sleeper car?" Jed asked. The porter's eloquence made Jed self-conscious of his own flat prairie twang. He suddenly felt unsophisticated, like a country boy in the big city—which he was.

The porter pulled a large gold watch from his pocket. "She certainly could be, sir. It's nine-o-seven. Santa Fe gives them until ten o'clock to clear out. That's when the cleaning crew goes in."

"Well, is there anyway I could find out? I hope I haven't missed her."

"Ordinarily, 'twould not be a problem, sir, but I hear we have a VIP car down there this morning. The powers that be aren't allowing unnecessary access. So sorry." The porter tipped his cap, bowed slightly, and moved on toward the stairs.

Jed turned to look at the huge Roman numeral clock hanging from the high ceiling in Union Station. There were actually four clocks, one on each side of a square suspended pedestal. The time could be read from any direction in the depot. "9:08," said the clocks. He checked his father's pocket watch and it was right on the money. It always kept perfect time unless Jed forgot to wind it. That happened often.

Well, I'll just have to wait it out, he thought. *I may've missed her but I have to be sure.* John Little Deer's morning would be undisturbed a little while longer.

Jed sat down on one of the long wooden, pew-like benches. It was far back from the staircase entrance into the depot but had an unimpeded view. If she were still on the train she'd have to pass this way.

Jed picked up the front section of the morning *Kansas City Times* left by someone on the bench. But his lack of sleep, the warmth of the depot, the constant rumble of trains below, the combined echo of train announcements and mingling passengers; it all affected Jed like a sedative. He would doze—then awaken as his chin fell to his chest. He focused on the top of the stairway from the trains, determined not to miss Erica.

...read a sentence—
...check the stairway—
...read a sentence—
...*dooozzzze,* and the chin drops to the chest—
...head snaps up—
...shift position and start the routine all over again.

But finally the night before, overcame the morning after. His chin dropped slowly to his chest. He still heard the sounds around him. He would've sworn he was awake—but this time he slept.

Jed would've missed her entirely except for the sound; a sound that cut through the mind-numbing ambience of the room. Deep inside his consciousness he heard it, but still he slept. It came from out in front of him, from the direction of the stairway.

Click! click! click! click! It passed off to his right ten yards away. *Click! click! click!* It receded behind him. The sound was almost totally gone when Jed jerked wide-awake. He *knew* what he'd heard. He jumped from the bench and looked toward the large revolving doors at the depot's street entrance.

There! Ten feet from the doors was a woman walking away from Jed. She wore a sleek gray wool coat and matching hat. The *click!* of her gray high heels was now barely audible.

Was it her? That particular sway to her walk; it *had* to be her!

The woman entered the revolving door and upon exiting, turned to wait for a porter, carrying luggage. She was fifty yards from Jed but he could see clearly. She wore fashionable dark glasses like a movie star. But the mass of red hair framing her face, forced there by her hat brim and turned-up collar, was unmistakable. It was Erica!

Jed sprinted after her, vaulting across an entire five-piece set of faux-alligator luggage by Samsonite. Her name formed on his lips and in his throat, and oblivious to the throngs around him he started to yell it out.

However, Jed did not see the small duffel bag that had fallen from a passing baggage cart. The toe of his right Tony Lama caught it, and he sprawled forward like a powerfully launched horizontal projectile. His suitcase and Stetson rocketed out in front of him, racing him toward the doors. It cannot be said that Jed ever fell—not completely. But it can be said that he fell *continually* more than he walked; the amazing spectacle of it all made it seem an interminable distance across Union Station's Grand Hall to the revolving doors.

Jed's arms and legs flailed wildly as he attempted to regain balance. He was aware that people were staring, transfixed at the scene. Somehow he managed to grab the handle of his suitcase with one hand and his Stetson with the other. Fortunately an open section of the revolving door toward which he stumbled came around at exactly the right second and Jed slammed into the glass and brass rail, accelerating the door's revolution three times its normal speed. He landed outside, miraculously on his feet, but sure he'd given the elderly lady about to enter Union Station a coronary. Her mouth was open, her face pale, lips as purple as death—unsure whether to cry or curse. She looked as though she thought him insane and expected his attack at any moment.

Jed put his Stetson over his heart, bowed in a chivalrous manner, and said, "Sorry, ma'm. Please excuse me!"

The woman's eyes narrowed to slits. She said not a word but decided it safe to enter the revolving door.

It appeared to Jed that every citizen of Kansas City was intent on leaving town by train at that exact moment. People were everywhere, most of them coming toward him and he stood on tiptoe looking for Erica.

He saw her gray coat and hat twenty yards away. The driver of a Yellow Cab had exited the car to open the back door for her.

"Erica!" he yelled.

She turned as though she heard something—but apparently didn't see him. She bent down and crawled into the '49 Plymouth.

Jed wormed his way through the crowd toward the cab. *"ERICA!"* he yelled even louder.

She looked up again, saw Jed through the window and touched the cabbie's shoulder signaling a halt. Erica rolled down the glass as Jed approached.

"Erica, I was afraid I missed you. May I have your number? Can I call you this evening? And *why* are you wearing sunglasses? It's cloudy."

A slight smile crossed Erica's face. "Because my eyes are bloodshot, Jed—but no, I—I don't think the number is a good idea."

"Why?" Jed's voice was a whisper and he knew he was begging but didn't care. There wasn't much time to persuade.

"Look, Jed, last night was fun, OK? But I've had time to think this morning. There was—well, there was a lot of wine, and scotch—and I think we should just leave it there. To tell the truth, Jed—the rancher; I think it might be serious."

"Do you always call him *The Rancher?* Does he have a name?" Jed was trying to be funny and sarcastic but it didn't work.

"Of course, he has a name," she replied haughtily. "It's Bill—William. William Jenkins."

Jed leaned down to the window, his face just four inches from Erica's. He smiled, in what he hoped was his most fetching manner. "Well, Erica, what ol' Bill don't know won't hurt him."

"No, Jed." Erica was firm. "No. I've said all I'm going to say. It was fun. I'll always remember"—a little smile flashed briefly—"but, no." This time it was her voice that was a whisper. She briefly touched Jed's hand through the open window, then gently tapped the cabbie on the shoulder.

The Plymouth pulled away from the curb and Erica rolled up the window. She did not look back.

"I'm at The Muehlebach!" Jed yelled. "Please call!" He hoped he got it out before her window completely closed.

Jed was still surrounded by throngs of people but he felt completely alone under the cloudy Kansas City sky. He walked to the next cab in line. "The Muehlebach," was all he said.

The cab pulled away from Union Station with driver and passenger both silent. The car's engine hummed smoothly. The radio was playing Tommy Dorsey's Orchestra; the melodic "I'll Never Smile Again." Jed knew the words without their being sung. He was glad this was the instrumental version. Sinatra's lonesome lyrics would be too much to take at this moment.

Several blocks later the cabbie spoke. "Don't blame ya fer bein' bummed out. But ya gave it a good try."

Silence.

"Mm-mmm," the cabbie continued, "I wouldn't even know what to say to a woman like that. *Mm-mmm.*" The man fell silent again for several long seconds and the music played on.

Finally, *"Man,* she *ssuurrre* was sumpin'!" the driver concluded.

Jed took little comfort in the cabbie's excellent taste in women or his sincere attempt at solace. And at this moment Jed didn't give a damn who killed Claude Stickett.

CHAPTER 13

Jean was watching for Erica's cab and ran from the house to embrace her kid sister.

"It's raining, Jean. You'll catch your death!" Erica scolded. "Get in the house."

"Just a drizzle, I won't melt." Jean waited while Erica paid the driver. "I'm sorry I couldn't pick you up but Tim just *had* to have the car. He has to run errands all day, maybe all night for Truman's boys. The President, of course, is in Independence."

"Oh! Of *course* he would be. I'm a history teacher," she chuckled, "I should have thought of that." Behind her sunglasses Erica hadn't noticed the security detail as she left the train. "But I *did* vote absentee. I think the dean would fire any history professor who *didn't* exercise the franchise."

When Erica's cab pulled away from Union Station she had fought an overwhelming desire to look back for one last glimpse of Jed. *But why should I?* She steeled her determination. *I know I did the right thing. Of course, I did!* The blustery gray clouds began to shed a light cold rain on Kansas City. *It's over—forget it.* Erica stared out the cab's misty window. *Over? Hell, it never began!* The cab moved slowly because of the rain and Erica thought she'd never get to Jean's. She needed to talk to someone. She needed companionship and felt an unexplainable loneliness.

Erica didn't even notice the fashionable homes they passed. Ward Parkway was one of the most coveted addresses in Kansas City, much too exclusive for Jean and Tim. They rented a homey little bungalow just two blocks off the Parkway.

Jean's husband, Tim Roland, was an assistant (a rather

lowly assistant), to the mayor of Kansas City. Jean met him when they both worked in Denver but upon their marriage they moved to Kansas City. It was Tim's hometown.

"We'll never be rich," Jean once told Erica, "but we're happy. Tim doesn't press his luck with ambition. He says with politicians, it's the ambitious guys they fear. *Those* types get knocked on their ass and they're out of a job." Jean shrugged. "Tim prefers being a staff man; he doesn't like the limelight." She suddenly laughed. "Quite frankly he doesn't think he could 'blather on' like a politician. They're all full of shit!"

Erica often recalled that conversation. Jean had been knocked on her own ass a few times and was content with Tim's philosophy.

Jean gave Erica a quick tour of the house. She was proud of the highly varnished hardwood floors in the newly remodeled living room and bedrooms, and more proud she convinced the landlord they'd move unless he paid for the remodeling.

"Did you vote for Harry?" Jean asked the question as she walked to the kitchen to perk a fresh pot of coffee.

"Of course I did, won't you?" Erica couldn't imagine her sister voting Republican. In Colorado Springs some called Jean the *wild* Harlan girl. "I mean—Harry Truman has stepped up to the plate," Erica explained. "He's risen to the task far better than I would have imagined. On the home front, he wants to continue the best of the New Deal; but he stands up to the communists. I *like* the Truman Doctrine."

"That's hard to disagree with; at least the part about the communists. But the New Deal? Or *Fair* Deal—whatever he calls it—I don't know." Jean was serious. "You know," and she paused for a second, "the older I get the more I agree with Dad." Another moment of contemplation and Erica said nothing.

"I'll walk down to Ward Parkway Presbyterian to vote in a few minutes," Jean continued. "Guess I'll make up my mind by then. You can tag along if you like unless you think *you'll* melt."

"That's enough, Sis, unless you want another reason to slap me." The sisters laughed loudly at Erica's remark. "I see you remember," Erica concluded.

"Of course, I remember." It had been the only time Jean ever laid a hand on Erica; and now, Jean looked at her younger sister as though ready to reprimand anew. "No eight-year-old little sister of mine is going to look me in the eye, and say, *'Screw you!'*" They erupted in laughter again.

"The funny thing is: I don't remember *why* I got mad at you," Erica said.

"Nor I. But seriously"—and Jean returned to the previous subject—"I'll never tell Tim if I vote for Dewey. Did you tell Dad you voted for Truman?"

"Heavens, *no!* Are you crazy?" Erica laughed. "But I think he suspects it."

The percolator was bubbling and the coffee's robust aroma filled the house. Jean got cups and saucers from the cabinet. She looked at Erica with a curious smile.

"By the way, dear girl,"—Jean handed Erica the steaming china cup—"you've been in the house ten minutes now. Why the dark glasses?"

Erica laughed as she removed the glasses, "I forgot I was wearing them."

"That doesn't answer the question. Why?"

"Well, to be honest, Jean," and Erica walked to a mirror, "the ol' eyes were a little bloodshot this morning." She checked her reflection, seemed satisfied, and put the glasses in her purse. "An elderly gentleman bought us—uh, bought me—a bottle of wine in the dining car last night."

"I *caught* that," Jean said gleefully, "does Bill know about this elderly guy who makes it 'us'?"

"No, no, he just bought it."

"*You* drank the *whole* bottle?" Jean had never known her sister to be a sot.

"No," and Erica paused, "I had help." She didn't know how far to go with this.

"Was this, uh, 'help' also elderly?"

"No, quite young really." Erica was a little miffed at the sibling interrogation but decided to tease a little on her own. She'd always enjoyed making Jean *drag* information from her.

"Okay, does Bill know about this young 'Romeo'?" Jean never took her eyes off Erica as she sipped her coffee.

"No, there's nothing to know—or tell," Erica added, "just a guy on the train; a nice guy, but just a guy."

"Was he good-looking?"

"Yeah." Erica swallowed and was enjoying the conversation a little less.

Jean didn't respond for a long moment. She just looked at Erica, straight and unblinking. But to Erica, Jean's gaze was accusatory and she felt her face begin to flush.

"Ooohh myyy gosh!" Jean chuckled. "You like him, don't you?"

"No! Well—oh, I don't know." Erica hated that her feelings were so transparent *and* that she wasn't more in control; and she hated Jean for being so persistent. "But he's just a guy on the train. It was *nothing."*

"Did you give him our phone number?" Jean would not let up.

"No, I did *not!"* Erica exclaimed as though that should end all questions on the topic.

"Mm-hmm." Jean was unconvinced. "What's he do?" she asked.

"He's an attorney."

"A successful one?"

"Not yet but he probably will be. *Why* must you persist?" Erica laughed nervously and was still somewhat miffed. However, Jean *was* her best friend and Erica knew sooner or later she'd tell everything—or almost everything.

"Hmmm. Lemme think." Jean was relishing the moment, "If it were me here in Kansas City; would I rather be the wife of a rich attorney, living in a big house on Ward Parkway, or would I rather herd cows on some ranch? Ooooh, *tough* choice!" Jean's tone dripped with sarcasm as she took her empty cup to the sink.

"But it's nothing," Erica insisted. "I'll never see him again, end of story." She took another sip of coffee, hoping Jean didn't notice the lack of conviction in her declaration. "And by the way"—Erica tried again with a stronger defense—"it's not like I'll have to *work* on Bill's ranch. He can afford help for that stuff."

"Well, gotta go vote." Jean walked to the front hall closet and pulled out a raincoat. "Wanna go?"

"No, I'll use the time to un-pack."

"Suit yourself; back in about twenty minutes."

But before Jean reached the door the telephone rang. "Hello?"

Erica heard the one-sided conversation from the guest room where she began sorting and hanging clothes in the closet.

"Well, I dunno, my sister's here. Mmmmm, oh, that sounds good, she'd enjoy that. M—mm. Well, hold on, let me ask."

Jean appeared in the doorway. "The hotel needs me to work this evening. Would you mind? Mrs. Benson is sick. It'd be just three or four hours to cover the phone and front desk. You can come along and have a hot mineral bath. I've told you how *great* those are!"

"Sure, sounds wonderful! But how do we get there if Tim has the car?"

"Mrs. Benson lives just around the corner. She's offered her car since she can't go."

Jean returned to the phone to say she'd work and with a "Back in a minute," was off to vote.

When Jean said "the hotel," Erica knew she meant The

Elms in Excelsior Springs, Missouri, forty minutes away. It was how Jean made extra spending money—not a steady job, just on call to help out in emergencies. They used her mostly on evenings and weekends and it was easy work. It was a quiet hotel so Jean took a book to read or found a magazine in the lobby. And it provided nice perks for her and Tim.

"The wages aren't great," the manager had told Jean, "but anytime you and Mister Roland want to come out and check in for the baths, a phone call's all we need. You can have any un-booked room we got."

For Tim and Jean, despite their modest means, it meant frequent romantic getaways; a touch of the life-style usually reserved for the wealthy.

Mmmm, a hot mineral bath, how relaxing. Erica closed her eyes in anticipation. Would a Swedish massage be available? She'd never had one but Preston Taylor bragged of indulging himself every time he visited New York City. Preston taught English Literature and Drama at Colorado College and was a devotee of Broadway musicals. He spent every spare penny on regular trips to check out the scene on the Great White Way. He would return, suitcase laden with new sheet music of the latest hits; or what he *predicted* would be a hit. There would follow an intense lobbying effort (Preston as the chief and sole lobbyist) to talk the music faculty into using their most talented students to do a college fundraiser singing Broadway tunes.

"Give Bach and Beethoven a rest, for Pete's sake." Preston was both pedestrian and persuasive on the subject. "The kids will love it!" he'd proclaim. "Kids, hell! The whole *town* will love it." And he was right. The town *did* love it.

Preston had been to New York last month and heard rehearsals for a new show about to debut. He'd sat down at the piano and banged out a couple of the tunes, singing at the top of his lungs. He wasn't great but he wasn't bad. There was one song in particular Erica thought catchy. She struggled to remember. *A show set in the south Pacific during the war, wasn't it?* Like a flash the words came back and Erica danced around the room, singing the title over and over: "I'm Gonna Wash That Man Right Outa My Hair!" *Maybe the mineral waters of Excelsior Springs will rinse away any thought of Jed.* And that silly thought brought a smile to Erica's face as she collapsed on the bed. But it wasn't a happy smile. She didn't feel happy.

CHAPTER 14

The Same Day—
11:40 a.m.—

The shower and shave were precisely what Jed needed; along with four cups of black coffee delivered by room service. He felt quite normal now except—there was something. It was like a cold gray storm cloud hanging quietly o'er the left side of his chest. Was that real? Did one's heart really feel sorrow, or was it merely from childhood you *heard* of the "heavy heart"? So, that's where your brain placed the feeling. Jed didn't know which theory was correct—or what the hell good it did to even consider the question.

"This is your lucky day," the desk clerk had told Jed as he checked in. "The ol' Muehlebach is full, full to the gills. One room left and you got it."

"Well, thanks." Jed was cordial but unimpressed. "I sure don't feel lucky."

The clerk looked at him closely from under his green eyeshade. "Was she a brunette or redhead? One or t'other; blondes will leave ya but they leave ya feelin' much better than *you* look."

Jed chuckled at the man's discernment but wasn't in the mood for chit-chat. "My key?" He hoped he wasn't overly curt.

The clerk was in no hurry. "I don't talk much about this but The President's staff is in the seventeenth floor penthouse." He paused for effect. "You're on sixteen. Hope they don't keep you awake tonight."

Jed by now had divined there was absolutely *nothing* this hotel clerk would *not* talk about, but had to admit the last revelation piqued his interest.

The clerk pulled his eyeshade lower and leaned close, his manner conspiratorial. "Wouldn't be a'tall surprised to see ol' Harry in here tonight; not surprised a'tall."

"Really!" The news excited Jed. He would love to get a glimpse of Harry Truman. He'd never seen a President of the United States.

"Course, he stays at the house out in Independence." The clerk was not about to shut up. "I know him well, quite well. He used to come in here for lunch often, before he went off to Washington."

Now, following his shower and shave, Jed tipped his Stetson to the eye-shaded clerk as he crossed the lobby and stepped through the entrance to Baltimore Street. The blustery and drizzly day added to Jed's loneliness but the wind in his face felt good. He decided to walk the five blocks to Stedman, Swift, and Jones. He ducked back into the Muehlebach newsstand to purchase a cheap umbrella and a couple of cigars.

The law firm was in a well-appointed office building on Wyandotte Street. Jed consulted the occupant roster in the exquisite lobby and took the elevator to the sixth floor. The hallway was a little dreary, but as he stepped into the reception area of Stedman, Swift, and Jones, the surroundings were again comfortable and elegant.

The pretty blonde receptionist was checking her lipstick in a compact mirror.

"May I help you?" She looked at Jed with flirtatious eyes.

"Thank you, ma'm, I'm here to see Mister John Deerman."

"May I tell him the nature of your visit?" Her hair fell just below her shoulders in curls; natural curls, Jed thought.

"Uh, I believe we have a mutual acquaintance," Jed answered.

The receptionist gingerly placed small headphones over her hair, messing the curls as little as possible, and hit a toggle switch on the intercom.

"Mister Deerman, a Mister Easton to see you. He says you have a mutual acquaintance." She paused to listen to her boss's response. "That's all he says, sir." Again she listens. "Yes, sir," and the receptionist removed the headset and rose from her chair. "This way, please."

As Jed followed the blonde down the hall he frowned. *What's wrong with me? This is one gorgeous dame.* She wore a white silk blouse (undoubtedly beyond her paycheck, Jed thought), and a black pinstriped suit that fit like a glove, especially the skirt. *Movie star hair—petite dynamite figure!* On her left wrist, swinging playfully at her side was a pearl bracelet. It matched the necklace. Jed noticed the cultured stones when he first walked in and wondered who bought them for her. *Crap, two days ago I'd be inquiring as to Blondie's dinner plans. But here I am mooning over some other gal who won't even see me.*

"Here we are." Blondie held open the office door and again gave Jed the flirty look.

Did she intentionally stand in the doorway—so I had to brush against her? He couldn't resist turning to watch Blondie's retreat to her desk. *Very nice!* However, Jed thought Erica could give Blondie pointers on how to walk in a sexier fashion—more model-like. He turned, a little embarrassed to find the man he was there to see, staring at him.

"I'm John Deerman, Mister Easton." The lawyer, about forty, walked from behind his desk and extended his hand. Every inch of his six-foot five-inch frame displayed Navajo ancestry. But his impeccable sartorial presentation was Brooks Brothers all the way except for the black cowboy boots. "Have we met before?" Deerman's accent was polished and urbane, as stylish as his Countess Mara necktie.

"Haven't had the pleasure, sir, nice to meet you." Jed took

the offered chair and reached in his pocket as Deerman returned to his desk. "Like a cigar?" Jed asked. "I picked up a couple of fine Cubans at the Muehlebach."

"No, thank you. I love the smell, even the taste. But they give me a sore throat. Help yourself."

Jed took his time lighting the cigar. Deerman waited patiently, suave and unperturbed. Jed took a long puff. "I'm from Raton, New Mexico, Mister Deerman."

Jed detected no change, no hesitation or fear in Deerman's eyes, just the steady smile.

"Really," the lawyer responded, "I grew up on the reservation near Gallup."

"I know." Jed took another long puff.

"In fact, I went out for a visit just last month," Deerman volunteered.

"Do tell!" Jed coughed. The cough was brought on by his quick intake of breath, which pulled the strong cigar smoke deep into his lungs. He hoped his shock at John Little Deer's ready admission wasn't overly obvious.

"Did you say we have a mutual friend?" Deerman was still pleasant but getting curious.

"Not a friend," Jed chuckled, "an acquaintance; a mutual acquaintance."

John Little Deer waited.

Through the blue haze of cigar smoke Jed fixed his eyes on Deerman's face. He wanted to catch the precise reaction as he mentioned the name.

"Did you ever meet Claude Stickett?"

"Stickett—Stickett—mmm," Deerman's countenance gave no hint of prevarication. "I don't believe so, Mister Easton, name doesn't sound familiar."

Jed reached into his pocket and pulled out a newspaper clipping. The *Raton Range* report on the Stickett murder included an old snapshot of Stickett taken years before. He was leaning against a big pine tree, a shotgun over his shoulder.

"Never seen him," said Deerman, "at least not that I recall." He silently scanned the story, "So someone did him in, eh?"

"Mister Deerman, I believe you had a cousin out in Gallup," and Jed again watched for reaction, "by the name of Morning Star."

Genuine sorrow came to John Little Deer's eyes. "Yes. Yes, I did," he said. "Is there a connection?"

"Mister Deerman, I'll just tell you man to man why I'm here. I'm the assistant D.A. in Colfax County and we've heard rumors that maybe somebody was certain—thought they knew for a fact—that our Claude Stickett killed Morning Star. And that this, uh, somebody..decided to even things up on his own."

"Oh. Oh, I see." The dawn of recognition was on Deerman's face. "So *that's* what this is about?" He leaned across his desk and looked steadily at Jed. "I want you to hear me well, Mister Easton. If I knew for sure that this ol' bastard, or any ol' bastard did what was done to Morning Star, you can be damn sure I'd gladly kill him!" Deerman halted abruptly and leaned back in his chair. He smiled at Jed. "Sorry. Strike that. Instinctive human reflex; but I never met your Mister Stickett and I sure as hell didn't kill him!"

Deerman stood up, a signal the interview was over.

Jed stood as well but kept talking. "I have to ask, sir. Can you account for your whereabouts last October fourteenth?"

Deerman picked up his appointment book from the desk and flipped through the pages in an irritated manner. "Here! See for yourself!" Deerman pushed the book into Jed's hand and Jed saw a full week of appointments starting Monday, October 11, 1948. It was an impressive act: that of a man who had nothing to hide; one who would lay out his appointment book to an *inquisitor,* who was also a *stranger.* And John Little Deer was an attorney, no less.

"When did you say you were in Gallup?" Jed asked.

"I believe I returned to Kansas City on Sunday—what would that be, the tenth?" Deerman was still icy.

Every appointment for the week noted the meeting place as "SSJ" (Stedman, Swift, and Jones) or some other Kansas City address. Jed returned the book to Deerman's desk but not before memorizing three of the names. "Mister Deerman, no offense intended. I'm just doing my job and if it makes you feel better, I believe you." Jed knew the last part was fifty percent lie but it seemed to make Deerman relax and he managed a smile.

"Anytime, Mister Easton, if you need anything else give me a call," and he picked up a calling card (using his left hand) from a small silver holder. Jed accepted the card, holding it by the edges. (He didn't know whether ol' Sheriff Emwiler had dusted the murder weapon for prints but it was worth a shot).

"Mister Deerman, are you a pilot?" Jed had just noticed a cartoon-like sketch at the top of the card. It showed a man in an open-cockpit bi-plane. He wore goggles, and a neck scarf flapped in the wind, trailing far behind the plane.

"Have been for years," Deerman responded, almost jaunty now. "Great hobby, I love it. And I have a small spread out in Colorado near the Kansas line; been drilling for oil and gas out there. The plane makes it much quicker to check on things. In fact, I flew out over the weekend; got back late last night, very late. If I'm irritable, I guess I'm just a little tired."

"No apology necessary," Jed smiled. "Do you own an airplane?"

"Well, more or less. The law firm does, a couple in fact—small single-engine models. We do a fair amount of practice throughout the states of Missouri and Kansas, so if I'm available I'll fly an attorney who needs quick transportation. In return I have access to a plane about anytime I want it; a good trade-off for me."

Jed eased John Little Deer's card into an inside pocket of his suit jacket, the one with the silk lining—the one he never used.

Jed's hand was on the doorknob but he had to ask one more question.

"Mister Deerman, again I hope you won't take offense—"

"You want to know how I got here." It was as though the New Mexico Navajo expected the question. "That's okay. Everybody does," and with the last two words Deerman was downright friendly again. "I love to tell the story but it takes awhile; better sit down."

Damn, why did I ask? Jed returned to the chair because he had no choice. *This guy's gonna write the great American novel right here, right now, just for me.*

"I was twenty years old," Deerman began. "You know, a hundred years ago that was prime age for a young Navajo—but on the reservation of 1928 or even today; well, you're just an 'injun' to most of this country. No future, it seemed. I did my share of whiskey and 'ladies of the night' in Gallup. One night I tarried a bit too long with one of the ladies," Deerman paused and smiled, "and missed my ride home."

However, Deerman said that was of little consequence. He'd walked the ten miles from his family's hut to Gallup and back many times.

"*Run* would be a better word. I guess it's in the genes," he chuckled. "A four-minute mile was a gentle lope for me, as easy as breathing. If I couldn't hitch a ride I ran."

On this particular night, about one o'clock in the morning, Deerman was five miles out of Gallup running along U.S. 66, thumb outstretched (but never breaking stride) to any rare vehicle that passed. A brand new Packard touring car sped by. "Had to be doing seventy-five," Deerman said.

Just after it passed, fifty yards in front of him, a front wheel came off.

"The car rolled three times. I counted, I could see in the moonlight." Deerman spoke somberly now. "I ran to the car. The three occupants were all thrown out. A lady was unconscious; a gentleman had a deep gash on his forehead. He couldn't move his right leg but was cognizant."

Deerman paused as though he had trouble continuing. "The little girl, nine years old; she was in bad shape, blood gushing from her mouth; a long severe cut on her shoulder. She was lying ten feet from her father and he was crying, 'Save my baby, save my baby!'" Deerman swallowed hard. "The Great Spirit was with me, Mister Easton. I said only four words to the gentleman: 'St. Mary's Hospital, Gallup.' I cradled the little girl in my arms and ran!"

Now Deerman smiled again. "The gentleman's watch was broken by the wreck; stopped at 1:07 a.m. Well, the old grandfather clock in the hospital lobby is 'burned into my brain', Mister Easton. When I carried the little girl through the door it read 1:20." There was another long pause. "Mister Easton, do you think Jesse Owens could've done that?" Deerman obviously loved comparing himself to the gallant Negro Olympian of 1936 and Jed smiled approvingly.

"Did they all survive?" Jed asked.

"The mother and father were hospitalized for four weeks, pretty banged up. But yes, they survived. They are Mister and Mrs. Benjamin Harrison Swift—as in Stedman, Swift, and Jones!" And Deerman's face revealed the deep satisfaction he felt at telling the story.

"It's an inspiring story, Mister Deerman."

"Yes, indeed—thank you," Deerman said gratefully, "but I took nothing for granted, studied hard, and finished in the top five percent of my class; college and law school."

"Wish I could say the same," Jed chuckled.

"But it still stands," Deerman concluded, "that I'm here, thanks to the gratitude of the Swifts."

"And the nine-year old, the little girl?" Jed asked cautiously wondering if she'd been incapacitated by the accident.

"Ah, the best part of the story!" Deerman responded.

This guy should be an actor, Jed thought, and couldn't help but admire how Deerman had honed the telling of his story to an art form.

The Navajo lawyer picked up a small, framed snapshot on his desk for Jed to see. "That's her on your left."

A gorgeous dimpled blonde, late twenties, with a Veronica Lake hairstyle smiled out at Jed.

"She's now Mrs. John Deerman!" and Deerman finished the story with a theatrical flourish worthy of Orson Wells.

Jed would be eternally grateful that Deerman revealed the finale in such surprising fashion. It gave cover for the shock, which Jed knew was showing on his own face. The shock came not from the picture of the scrumptious young blonde whom John Little Deer managed to assign permanently to his boudoir, nor from the handsome man beside her; a tall white man with a big smile. He looked like Ronald Reagan, the movie star.

But Jed's shock was brought on by the third person in the snapshot: a strikingly beautiful dark-haired woman. She appeared to be somewhere around thirty, possibly older, and bore an *uncanny* resemblance to Erica! For a split second Jed thought it was Erica—but her face was slightly longer.

"What a story, Mister Deerman!" Jed's mind was reeling. How could he frame the necessary question without appearing the nosey persistent gumshoe all over again?

"Who's the good-lookin' couple?" was all Jed could come up with.

"Just some very good friends." Deerman stood up again and again Jed sensed the signal for him to leave. "We went to Swope Park a month ago for a picnic. I snapped the picture."

Jed didn't know how hard to press and there was an awkward silence.

Fortunately Deerman continued, "Tim works for local government. He's a good guy," and he paused again.

"From around here, I suppose?" Jed tried his best to be casual.

"Yes, Tim's a Kansas City native. But I think he met his wife out west."

Jed couldn't stop now. The trail was hot and he had to know. "What did you say her name was?"

"I don't believe I said," and Deerman eyed Jed suspiciously. But he apparently concluded there was no harm in telling this visitor (who was wearing out his welcome) the name of his friend's wife. Perhaps it would hasten his departure.

"Jean—Jean's from Colorado I believe. Denver or Colorado Springs; *our* part of the world, Mister Easton." Deerman gave Jed another big smile.

Jed left John Little Deer's office happy with his detective work: possible progress on the Stickett case, progress definitely (and surprisingly) in his quest for Erica. Was it fate or Providence? *What are the odds?* Jed was betting on the latter. *The guy I came to Kansas City to see has a picture of Erica's big sis on his desk, for Pete's sake!* But at the moment Jed was just grateful for another shot at finding Erica while still in Kansas City.

As he waited for the elevator Jed jotted down the three client names he recalled from Deerman's appointment book. That's when it hit him; he didn't get Tim and Jean's last name. He wouldn't dare ask anything further of Deerman—but Blondie was another matter.

"By the way, miss,"—Jed stuck his head back in the door of the reception area, then walked all the way in—"uh, I'm sorry I didn't get your name."

"It's Penelope," the receptionist smiled, now even more coquettish. It seemed to Jed that her long lashes, dark with mascara, curled up almost to her eyebrows; then they would brush her cheeks as she shyly lowered her gaze. "But everybody calls me Blondie. I like that better."

"You're kidding!" Jed laughed, and sat down on the edge of her desk. "I've been thinking of you as *Blondie*. Really, I have."

The girl giggled and blushed.

"Uh, Blondie, I don't want to bother Mister Deerman again but he told me to call some guy who works in local government here. I failed to write the name down; Tim somebody, I remember that much."

"Oh, that would be Mister Roland, he works for the Mayor. Here, I have his number," and she thumbed through a three-by-five card file. "AMherst3744 at work—or, uh, COlgate2654 at home."

"Thank—you—Blondie." Jed spoke haltingly as he jotted down the numbers and feeling a little cocky at his success decided it was time for *him* to flirt a little. His fountain pen still in hand, he leaned in six inches from her face. "I can't promise what my schedule will allow," he whispered, "but when possible I like a cocktail about five o'clock. And I hate to drink alone." Jed handed Blondie his pen.

She looked down the hall to make sure no one was watching and with more eyelash flutters and another blush she quickly jotted her phone number below Tim and Jean's.

Jed left the office almost convinced he was the same ol' carefree ladies' man. But he knew that was also fifty percent lie, probably more. No matter how he tried, his thoughts returned over and over to Erica. For Jed Easton it was a surprising obsession. He'd never been so smitten. *She's ruined my life! I should forget her.* Then his very soul reminded him of a question, for which he had no answer: *And just how would I do that?*

CHAPTER 15

Later the same day—

The silver Taylorcraft L-2A reached the end of the grass runway and turned into the wind. The pilot, the lone occupant of the plane, set the brake and revved the single engine to full throttle. The motor was smooth and quiet even at maximum revolution. He released the brake and the Taylorcraft headed down the grass strip, quickly gathering speed. At one hundred fifty yards the pilot eased back on the stick and was airborne.

The Taylorcraft was a faster airplane than the Piper Cub and this one was like new, less than forty hours. It was a tandem model, one seat behind the other. The plane had been destined for United States Army reconnaissance but the war ended before the Taylorcraft got its coat of olive drab paint.

Despite the blustery day the ride was relatively smooth at twenty-five-hundred-feet so he leveled off, heading southwest. He twirled the dial on the radio direction finder, locking it in on 770 kilocycles. He trusted the signal of Albuquerque's KKOB radio station would reach this far and was relieved to see the needle respond. The pilot touched the rudder pedals until the needle stood at twelve o'clock high and settled back for the long ride.

Since the night two weeks ago when he finally took matters into his own hands, he tried to keep constantly busy. It was not in his best interest to have time on his hands. Solitude and reflection were no longer things to be treasured. He had hoped—he had believed—the act would bring peace. Shouldn't justice accomplished bring serenity? Instead nagging questions, doubt, and guilt—heavy guilt—had replaced his previous anger.

As much as he loved to fly, it had drawbacks. As long as things went well there was little to do but think. So now he had to look for distractions.

He pushed the stick forward and descended through the bumpy air to seventeen-hundred-feet. There it again seemed calm, and fixtures and movement on the ground were more easily discerned.

He saw the plume of smoke two miles to his left and moved the rudder to take him there. The Santa Fe fast freight was just that. It was boiling down the mainline, also heading southwest, the black trail from the steam locomotive drifting back over the entire length of the mile-long train.

The pilot touched the right rudder pedal and brought the Taylorcraft parallel to the freight's caboose, now comfortably visible through his left window. Cruising speed for the Taylorcraft was ninety-five to one hundred miles-per-hour; but with a prevailing headwind it would take miles and moments to overtake the train.

Some twenty cars were loaded with coal. There were also many closed boxcars and the pilot could only guess at their contents. The rest appeared to be empty cattle cars headed back to the ranches of the West and Southwest, to be filled once again for the slaughterhouses of the Midwest.

Whether it was the thought of the slaughterhouses or mere coincidence, a wave of nausea hit the pilot in the pit of his stomach. The sudden attacks came daily now. They had occurred less frequently prior to October fourteenth.

He quickly reached into the plane's glove box and pulled out one of the heavy paper bags stored there for this very purpose. He wretched into the bag and found his thermos of water under the seat. He rinsed his mouth thoroughly before spitting again into the bag.

A blast of cold air hit him in the face as he opened the window to drop the bag outside. For the moment he felt refreshed and renewed.

His eyes again settled on the freight train he was ever so slowly passing by. And with the passing, as the train fell farther and farther behind, his mind again returned to the nagging questions: would he be found out, and if so, when; or would he live to be an old man, his secret buried within? There was another possibility, another question that haunted: within a few short weeks, might he die in the electric chair—in the Penitentiary of New Mexico at Santa Fe?

The pilot reached again for a paper bag.

CHAPTER 16

Independence, Missouri—
4:03 p.m.—

The only sound in the small study was the ticking of the old clock ensconced in hand-carved wood. It sat on the fireplace mantel, the varnish of its ornate frieze reflecting the reading lamp by the over-stuffed chair.

Outside the drone of voices steadily increased. Harry Truman for the fifth time this afternoon put down the book he was reading; yet another volume on Andy Jackson. He cautiously pulled back the front window curtain, just an inch, to look at the growing crowd on Delaware Street.

Well, we'll all soon know. I'll do well by my fellow citizens here in Independence—or I'll be the town goat! The President's eyes landed on a group of chain-smoking men, neckties askew, lounging around a tree. A few had a big SpeedGraphic camera in hand or strapped to the shoulder. *Now, the press there—that bunch o' horses' asses; they think they know. They think I'm history. Well, we'll see.*

Harry returned to his book but had trouble concentrating. *We'll just see. I think there's a big surprise in store.* In fact, at that moment he'd have bet five bucks he'd be the hero. But there was no one to bet with. No one else was in the room.

For weeks he'd told everyone in America—everyone who would listen—that he and Senator Barkley were going to win this election. Of course he didn't know that. He *thought* so but he couldn't *know*. Everyone else including the experts said he would lose.

But the crowds; my, my, he thought, the crowds had been great. Something was afoot. And no matter the outcome, the whistle-stop campaign had been a good idea. The President thought it would help the Democrat Party—maybe not him, but the party.

Today there was little to do but wait. The clock's pendulum swung to and fro. *Tick, tick, tick.* It was the waiting that made him antsy.

The President put his book aside and went to his desk. He took out an envelope, a clean sheet of paper, and reached for his fountain pen.

As he scribbled a brief note the door to the study opened. Bess walked in.

"Harry, don't you ever get tired of writing letters?" she asked.

"Well, my dear, this is one no one will ever read. Well, maybe Margaret," he added.

He stuck the note in the envelope, sealed it, and marked the envelope with a big "X".

"Bess, Rowley and his boys will be here in a few minutes. Shift change," he said. Jim Rowley was in charge of the Secret Service detail on this trip. "I'm gonna get outa here. Those guys out front—the press—they're gonna be pesterin' me all night for a statement and I'm in no mood to make any damn statement."

"Well, just don't answer the door, Harry!"

"Nope, won't work. I don't want you and Margaret disturbed all night. Now, I'm putting this envelope with the 'X' right here." Harry opened the top drawer of his desk. "Don't open it unless you absolutely have to get in touch with me; then you won't have to lie all evening. You truly won't *know* where I am." Harry knew that Bess's Episcopalian sensibilities bothered her when telling even white lies. He also knew Margaret would read the note—and not care a whit to fib to the press.

"Whenever you get ready to go to bed," The President concluded, "go out and tell 'em ya don't know where I am." He chuckled, "That oughta get Merriman Smith's hackles up."

Like most presidents, Harry S Truman had a love-hate relationship with the press. United Press's Merriman Smith was a good reporter but sometimes he was too damn good *(bother*some would be the word) for Ol' Harry.

The President kissed Bess on the lips (he did that often when no one was watching), and walked to the back door where he could see down the alley. He stood there, watching for Jim Rowley and the relief bunch from the Secret Service.

CHAPTER 17

"Hell, this is November," Jean said, "there'll be no more than three guests in the entire hotel." As they pulled onto the long bridge over the Missouri River, Jean slowed the big car so Erica could get a good look at the long barge loaded with coal, passing directly beneath them. "You and I will have the run of the place."

The Elms was one of the hotels built in Excelsior Springs, Missouri following the discovery of mineral springs there in the late nineteenth century. Many people believed bathing in the waters was beneficial to good health and over the years some famous names were patrons: John D. Rockefeller, Franklin Roosevelt, even Al Capone.

"If they all go to bed early," Jean continued, "I know where they keep the key to the liquor cabinet." Their girlish giggles were the same as those that filled the Harlan residence years earlier. Erica turned up the radio and snapped her fingers to the beat of Glenn Miller's "In The Mood."

The drive from Kansas City to The Elms was relaxing and picturesque; out across the big river and through the rolling countryside. Mrs. Benson's car was a brand new Chrysler New Yorker. She had told Jean of her new possession just a few days earlier.

"I drove it off the showroom floor forty-eight hours after it arrived," Mrs. Benson exulted. The 1949 model was a black coupe and its shiny paint glistened like the coat on an Arabian stallion. It floated along the highway as though on air.

"How can an elderly widow, working as a hotel desk clerk,

afford a car like this?" Erica wondered aloud.

"She has a boyfriend," Jean smiled, "and who says she's elderly?"

"What do you mean?"

"Mrs. Benson is a widow but she's extremely gorgeous—*and* she's thirty-seven years old."

"Wow! I had no idea," Erica exclaimed, "who's the boyfriend?"

"Never seen him." Jean glanced at Erica, eyebrows raised. "Some suspect he *also* has a wife."

"Oh, my! And why does she still call herself Mrs. Benson?"

Jean shrugged her shoulders and waved a hand toward the dashboard of the luxurious coupe. "I don't know—but it seems to be working." They laughed again like teenagers.

Erica shook her head, "I just couldn't handle that—the 'other woman' thing, I mean."

"Nor I," Jean agreed, "not anymore.

Jean eased the Chrysler up the wide driveway. The huge timber and stone lodge, imposing yet inviting, beckoned them for an evening of rest and relaxation.

"Gosh, Jean! This is beautiful!" Erica suddenly felt she was a world away from any genuine concern about anything. "Do you have to work? Can't we just play?"

"It's hardly work, Erica, I mainly relax and read. Enjoy yourself—go soak as long as you want. Then, I'll let *you* answer the phone and I'll grab a bath."

"Who are those guys?" Erica pointed to three men, neatly dressed, standing by a late-model Ford sedan, black like the Chrysler.

"Never seen them," said Jean.

"They look like some of those riverfront gamblers; the Kansas City mob types you wrote me about."

"Naw," Jean responded, " too neat. The mob guys dress,

uh—questionably *flashy.*"

With a few moments left before she had to take over the desk, Jean gave Erica a quick tour: the huge dining room just off the kitchen, the outdoor springs, then the huge gender-segregated bathrooms, with tubs twice the size of any Erica had ever seen. Jean also took her to one of the premier suites where she and Tim had whiled away a few hours on several occasions.

"Oh, my," Jean deadpanned, "if these walls could talk!"

"Spare me, that may be more information than I need from my big sister," Erica laughed. They returned downstairs to the front desk.

"Go soak awhile, kid." Jean pointed down the hall to her right. "Go through the dining room to the kitchen. Immediately to your left there's a closet full of bathrobes and towels. Grab anything you need. Enjoy!"

An hour and twenty minutes later Erica returned to the front desk.

"You're positively *glowing!*" Jean was admiring as well as envious. "I'm sorry the masseur was already booked for one of our guests; but you don't seem to have needed him, anyway!"

"The bath was wonderful!" Erica had never felt so relaxed in her life. "Go, Jean. Sit in a tub, unless you think I'll mess things up?"

"Are you kidding?" Jean was already walking from behind the desk. "The phone has rung once; wrong number. Grab something to read or you'll fall asleep," she called over her shoulder and was already down the hall to get towels and a bathrobe.

Erica found a *Life* magazine; an issue from last month dated October eleven. She recognized the sexy young actress on the cover but couldn't remember her name. The article was a rundown on starlets in Hollywood who were discovered through the new medium of television. She found the article. Rita Colton was the actress's name and Erica recalled how she first heard of her. Preston Taylor, returning from one of his New York trips, had said, "Erica, sweets! You know whom you look like?"

"Who, Preston—and are you serious, or is this a joke?"

"Dead serious. Rita Colton is her name."

"Never heard of her." Erica was unimpressed.

"Well, you will if she gets the breaks. She's a dynamite young actress and model in New York." Then he'd paused as though uncertain whether to say what was on his mind. He threw all caution to the wind. "You especially remind me of her—because of that sweater you're wearing today."

"Well, I trust that's a compliment," said Erica.

"Oh, it is. *Trust me. It is!*" Preston's smile was more leer than smile and Erica blushed.

Now, at The Elms, she turned the page of the magazine and blushed all over again. There was the lovely Miss Colton in a scene with Dean Jagger. Her sweater-covered bust was more akin to twin Pike's Peaks than the human anatomy.

Erica looked up from her magazine as two men entered the room, men from the black Ford. They did not sit down but merely looked around the room, then looked out the window.

"May I help you?" Erica was her cheerful best.

"No, thank you, ma'm." The tall one who spoke was very pleasant but all business. "We're just waiting for someone." He touched his hat brim but didn't remove the hat.

Odd, Erica thought. She went back to *Life* and the television starlets.

Three minutes later she sensed more than saw a man in front of the desk.

"Excuse me, ma'm, I'm so sorry to take you from your story."

Even before Erica looked up something in the back of her

mind awakened. The voice; it was so familiar.

"No problem, sir, what can I"—Erica was stunned into silence. She could not find her voice.

There at the desk was a smiling gentleman, about sixty years of age. He looked distinguished even in an Elms Hotel terrycloth bathrobe. His eyes twinkled behind thick eyeglasses. "Truly sorry to bother you, young lady—".

"Not at all, Har—*Mister President!*" she said, her voice barely audible. Erica gulped and scrambled to her feet. Her hand covered her mouth in embarrassment at the breach of protocol. "I apologize, sir, I do know better than to call The President of the United States by his first name. I'm just so *shocked!* I had no idea you were here."

"And that's just the way I want it, ma'm," Harry chuckled, "and don't worry. Harry's one of the nicest things I'm called these days. Bess even calls me worse than that," and The President laughed aloud—then added with a wry smile: "'Course she usually says that sorta stuff under her breath!"

In a matter of seconds Harry Truman had made Erica completely comfortable.

"How can I help you, Mister President?"

"Dear lady, I'm a bit hungry. Doesn't seem to be any help in the kitchen; do you think you could scare me up a sandwich?"

Under her breath Erica thanked all the angels in God's vast heaven that Jean had given her that little twenty-five cent tour.

"I'm not regular help here, Mister President, but I did spot a huge cooler back in the kitchen. Let's see what we can find."

Erica introduced herself en route and swung open the white enamel door of the commercial-size Frigidaire. She breathed a sigh of relief to see a large platter stacked high with something, covered by tin foil. Erica pulled back the foil and yes!—it was half a baked ham, mouth-watering in appearance, and already sliced.

"Oh, this looks good, Mister President! And isn't that a

box of cheese? Pull that out, would you?" Erica couldn't believe she'd just ordered the President of the United States to help fix his own dinner.

Harry pulled out the cheese, "And lookee here! Just what the doctor ordered!" The President was holding up a quart jar of yellowish white liquid already frosting over from the heat of the room. "Unless I'm badly mistaken that's cold fresh buttermilk! My favorite." He unscrewed the Mason lid and passed the jar briefly under his nose. "Yes, indeed. Buttermilk! Where would I find a glass?"

"Maybe the shelf, Mister President, over the sink." Erica was manning a spatula, building a high stack of sliced ham on a plate. "But don't close the cooler, there's surely some lettuce and mayonnaise in there somewhere."

Harry's head was already stuck back into the Frigidaire. "Here's some Miracle Whip," he said, "close enough for me."

Then began, one of the most memorable and enchanting twenty minutes, of Erica's thirty-two years. She summoned all powers of concentration; she didn't want to forget a single second of the experience. She knew she'd tell the story to every freshman class for the rest of her professional life.

"My dear young lady," The President smiled at Erica, "this is going to be a long night for America—but not for me. When I finish this sandwich I'm goin' to bed."

With three Secret Service men standing in the hall, Harry sat down in a simple kitchen chair, a wooden one. The chair's green enamel paint was spotty from years of use. He sat at a long table, the opposite end of the table stacked with sparkling pots and pans, already spiffed clean for the tasks of tomorrow.

"I hope you voted today." There was a hint of the schoolteacher in his voice.

"Yes, but a few days ago, Mister President. I voted absentee. I live in Colorado Springs—and if you're wondering, I voted for you."

"Thank you, uh—Erica did you say?"

She nodded and The President continued. "Colorado; I fully expect that state to be in our column tonight. Why are you here? Is this a working vacation for you?"

Erica explained she was visiting her sister who was the hotel employee, and that she (Erica) was a professor.

"Ah, a history teacher," The President said longingly. "Now, if I could've gotten to college that's what I'd have been; been a much better history teacher than politician," he chuckled. "Are your parents teachers?"

"No, sir, Dad's a retired physician—and, I'm sorry to say, a Dewey man."

"Oh, that's OK," Harry smiled. "We all make our cases and let the people decide. That's America." He paused for a moment. "You know, for better or for worse most people get their politics—and religion too, I suppose—from their parents. You're to be commended for giving it a little individual thought."

Out of the corner of her eye Erica saw Jean pass the doorway, do an abrupt double-take, and stand now with her mouth open, staring at the two. Erica suddenly realized the front desk had been unattended for a half hour or more; but could not care less. And she couldn't resist putting on a little show for Jean.

"Jean, darling," she called, "come meet my friend. Mister President, this is my sister, Jean Roland; Jean, President Truman."

"I'm so sorry, Mister President," Jean blurted, "I voted for Dewey today," and immediately wondered why she'd revealed that fact to Harry Truman.

Harry chuckled and stood to shake Jean's hand, "Don't give it a second thought, I understand it runs in the family. But I also understand you live in Kansas City. Right?"

"Yes sir."

"Then no harm done. My gang will go to the Electoral

College here in Missouri if nowhere else. By the way, I like your little place here—The Elms, I mean; been here many times off and on over the years."

The President picked up what was left of his ham and cheese sandwich. "Thanks, Mrs. Swanson,"—he had noticed Erica's gold band—"this was a gourmet delicacy. You make a fine sandwich," and he swallowed the last bite. "I'm takin' the buttermilk to my room. Gonna get some sleep. Nice to meet you both." And he was gone, following a Secret Service agent down the hall. Two more fell in step behind him.

Erica and Jean walked slowly back to the front desk, a dazed look on their faces. They said not a word. They were too busy pinching themselves.

CHAPTER 18

7:10 p.m.—

Jed looked at his father's pocket watch for the eighth time in five minutes. Then, he looked at the phone for the eighth time in the same five minutes. He'd been sitting on the edge of the bed in the Muehlebach for two hours—except when he paced the floor. He reached for the phone a hundred times; but would hesitate. What would he say to Erica? Would she be mad; or worse yet, frightened at his hunting her down? Would she think him the classic "unwanted admirer," *or* just a plain creep.

He spent an infinitesimal amount of time thinking about the Stickett case. One moment Jed believed that John Deerman was a sincere, honest, hard working straight shooter; the next moment he thought Deerman, aka John Little Deer, the best damn liar he'd ever seen. But there was nothing he could do with the investigation tonight.

Jed picked up the phone. It was time to do something! "Operator, COlgate2654."

The number was ringing and Jed was sweating. He prayed he'd find the right words if Erica answered. It rang and rang—four, five, six—on the eighth ring Jed gave up.

Dear lord, I need a shower. Six minutes later, sitting naked on the bed, a towel draped over his still-soaked hair, he tried the number again. Ten rings this time but still no answer.

Jed put on a fresh white shirt and his brown silk tie. It was the tie great-aunt Martha sent him last Christmas and boasted a small hand-painted bright orange stallion, dead center. He checked his suit jacket; it had hung out nicely. He was heading downstairs to catch some election returns.

Upon his return from Deerman's office Jed noticed the Muehlebach had pulled up extra chairs around the big floor-model radio in the lobby. Coffee tables and chair-side lamp tables were stocked with heaping bowls of salted peanuts, cashews, almonds, and English walnuts. Strains of Glenn Miller, Benny Goodman, and Frank Sinatra poured from the radio, and even at that early hour the adjoining bar was jumping.

Just before he headed up to his room, a new Christmas song blared from the radio speaker. Jed had never heard it before. "Here Comes Santa Claus" *had* to be the title. The twangy voice sang the phrase over and over. Jed thought it was Gene Autry but wasn't sure.

Now, Jed toweled dry, dressed, and pulled on his Tony Lamas. He looked at his Stetson on the bedpost but thought better of it. Some of these downtown Kansas City gals might think him a hick.

Since he couldn't find Erica—Jed would find a party. He stepped into the hall—*should I try one more time?* He checked his father's pocket watch. *Hell, no, it's quarter of eight. They're probably out on the town*—(he slammed the door hard)—*out in some fancy restaurant; Tim, Jean, Erica, and some handsome jerk they'd invite to keep Erica company.* Jed was surprised at how mad the thought made him.

The elevator arrived and the old Negro operator looked at Jed expectantly.

"I'm sorry, sir, go ahead. I forgot something," and Jed returned to his room. *Well, why not?*

He picked up the telephone. "Operator, get me CHelsea5241." Jed read from the small card he pulled from his pocket. It was the third number on the card written in a dainty feminine hand.

"Hello?" Blondie answered on the second ring. Her voice was soft and breathy.

"Blondie? I'm sorry I'm so late, I just got caught up." It wasn't much of a lie.

"I knew you'd call," she breathed, "I've just been waiting."

"Well, *did* you now? Uh, look, I still haven't had time for that cocktail and, uh, I'll happily spring for dinner."

"Sounds nice, where do I meet you?"

Good gosh! he thought, no wonder Deerman has this girl answer the phone. *I'd call up to hear her read a recipe.*

"I'm at The Muehlebach," Jed answered. "Gonna be a little crowded here tonight; but we oughta be able to find a dark corner somewhere." He grimaced, wondering how she'd take that last line.

"Great!" (Blondie didn't seem to notice). "My apartment is just seven blocks. I'll walk over."

"No! No dinner date of mine is walking on a chilly, November night. What's your address? I'll send a cab."

"If you insist, but don't send one," Blondie replied. "There's a cabstand right across the street from me. I'll see you at the Muehlebach in a bit."

"I'll meet you at the front door of the lobby and pay the cabbie," Jed responded. "How soon?"

"Fifteen minutes," she whispered. Her voice sounded more sexy with each syllable. "I told you—I've been waiting." Click.

Damn! I've hit the jackpot! Jed headed again for the elevator and every time he thought of Erica, did his best to push the thought away.

CHAPTER 19

The moment Blondie stepped from the cab Jed found it somewhat easier not to think of Erica. As the pretty receptionist slid from the back seat her rayon lavender dress slid past the tops of her shiny nylons. Blondie had marvelous legs. The same exquisite pearls he saw in the office swung elegantly from her neck and from her wrist.

"Aren't you cold?" Jed put his arm around her as they hurried the few steps to the revolving lobby door. She wore a lightweight shawl, sparkly white, across her shoulders.

"No, I only wear a coat if it's really cold. I'm hot-blooded," she giggled and looked up at Jed in her flirty way.

Jed surmised she didn't even own a coat. *The guy who bought the pearls should've sprung for a coat as well!*

As they entered the lobby, Jed (for the second time in as many days) saw heads turn to gaze at the lass on his arm. That always gave him great pleasure. He had friends who got mad as hell when other guys looked too closely at their ladies. Jed never understood that.

"Why would you wanna go out with someone, no one wants to look at?" Jed asked. He found the idea absurd. His buddies usually responded with the middle-finger salute.

Blondie's dress had a short cap sleeve and a hemline shorter than current styles, striking her just above the knee.

Maybe Stedman, Swift, and Jones need a <u>swift</u> kick in the butt. If they've got the girl on the front desk they oughta pay enough to keep her fashionable. Not that Jed minded; he loved the shorter skirt. So does she, he thought; she knows she has great gams!

And her legs looked even longer because of the tall black pumps. The shoes made her seem much taller than five-feet, which is what Jed guessed her to be.

"I'm sorry, it'll be at least an hour," the *maitre d'* told Jed, "but if you're in a hurry try the bar; same food, same kitchen."

Jed looked at Blondie.

"I'm starving," she whispered.

"You poor kid!" Jed suddenly felt a surge of compassion for Blondie. He put his arms around her tiny waist, lifted her off the floor, and set her down headed in the direction of the bar.

"Thanks, pal," he called to the *maitre d'*, "I gotta get this gal some chow," (and to Blondie), "I'm so sorry I made you wait."

"That's okay, you warned me. Besides, I know your type," and there was the coquettish smile and eyelid flutter again.

"What type is that, Blondie?"

"Well, your type has to check everything out, look over the field; just to make sure there's not a better deal out there." There was no derision in her tone. She was merely stating a fact as she saw it.

"Oh, come on, Blondie, I'm not like that." Jed felt more ashamed for telling that lie than any he'd told in a long time— *because* he knew her words were on the mark. "And hey," he continued, "you told me on the phone you knew I'd call."

"Of course," Blondie smiled up at him, her sea blue eyes sparkling, "I knew you wouldn't find a better deal!"

Jed chuckled as Blondie laughed hilariously at the little jab she'd landed home. Her laugh reminded Jed of a small brook gushing over a waterfall.

"*Touche*, kid." (Cary Grant said that to some gal in a movie, and Jed had always wanted to use the phrase. However, he usually thought of it after he took his date home).

There were two empty places at the far end of the bar, up against the wall. The management had crowded in extra stools for the big night and Jed and Blondie enjoyed a few self-conscious laughs as they shifted back and forth, so as to face each other in the tiny space. They finally made their nest; then Blondie crossed her legs. Jed was certain Blondie didn't realize the extreme angle demanded of those gams! The rayon dress slid again above her hose—way above; a titillating sight for Jed and he felt a familiar stirring deep, deep down; the stirring that assured mankind would father a next generation, and a next, until the end of time. Blondie had to be unaware—or, *perhaps she knows precisely what she's doing!*

The bartender stood before them and Jed raised his eyebrows at Blondie.

"A glass of sherry, please," she told the barkeep.

"Beefeater on the rocks, here," Jed said. "And some menus. I could eat a horse."

"Then you'll love our steaks," the bartender said dryly. Jed rolled his eyes.

The bartender smiled wanly in apology. "Sorry, old joke. But seriously, the steaks are really good here," and the man turned to fix the drinks.

Jed ordered a T-bone, Blondie the meatloaf.

"Don't you want a steak?" Jed asked.

"They're too big. I've seen them before."

She was right. Jed's T-bone covered an entire platter. The vegetables came on a separate plate.

Again there were leg tangles as they readjusted to eat. Blondie's left leg actually wound up atop Jed's right knee but she seemed comfortable with it. Jed sure as hell didn't mind.

The music suddenly stopped as the radio announcer interrupted. Election returns were beginning to filter in and the bartender turned up the volume. The news commentator made a melodramatic theatrical presentation of the nation's first complete precinct tally, which had been known in the early morning hours. It was Hart's Location, New Hampshire:

Truman 1, Dewey 11.

"What the hell difference does that make?" Jed asked of no one in particular and signaled the bartender for another drink.

"I don't know much about politics," Blondie said.

"Me neither, really, I just like ol' Harry." As Jed spoke he took his first bite of the most juicy, tender steak he'd ever eaten. ("And no wonder ol' Harry ate *here!*" he interjected). "To be truthful about it, Mister Truman seems to feel the government can solve a helluva lot more problems than I think it can. But I still like him." He took another swig of his gin. "Most people I know out West don't give a flyin' rat's ass—uh, sorry, I shouldn't talk that way 'round a lady."

They both giggled and Jed continued. "Folks out my way don't really care what they do in Washington so long as they stay out of *our* hair."

Interestingly enough (and the commentator seemed confused by it), Dewey was leading in New York and Pennsylvania—key states—but Truman led the popular vote across the nation.

"Does your father like Harry?" Jed asked between bites of T-bone and hot rolls.

Blondie put down her fork and smiled, but barely. "I don't—I don't know my father." Her voice was just a whisper and she took a sip of the sherry.

"I'm very sorry," Jed mumbled.

"Momma says its best that way," and she took another sip. "I think she knows where he lives and—I don't know—I think…" her voice trailed off. "I *think* I'd like to meet him some day." Blondie took a bite of potato before concluding. "He—he wouldn't marry Momma."

A few bites in silence, accompanied by the flirty smile; then, "Momma says most men are pigs."

Jed couldn't help it. He chuckled, softly at first, then louder and louder. Finally they were both laughing uproariously. It was precisely the icebreaker needed.

"Well, Blondie," and Jed nodded his head slowly, "all too often—I'm afraid your momma's right."

"You're not a pig, Mister Easton."

"I hope not, Blondie. I truly hope not."

And so the night went: enjoyable conversation between two new friends, interrupted of course, by election reports. Each time Jed was ready to call it a night (or get on with the next part of it), the race would tighten up. They were caught up in the excitement and neither wanted to leave.

Jed thought Blondie complete vixen *and* sweet innocent. Her sensuous manner was a strong attraction. *Sorely tempted!* (Jed often went to sleep at night with the radio on. There was some preacher on XERF, Del Rio, Texas, who took to the airwaves at three a.m. Sorely tempted was the preacher's favorite phrase).

Do I want her? Hell, yes! But she deserved better. If Jed allowed himself the carnal luxury—could he live with himself? As for those sentiments, Jed was rather amazed he'd suddenly become so—so scrupulous.

They moved to the lobby and grabbed a couple of comfortable, just vacated chairs. They again arranged to face each other, close together, till their knees touched. She told him stories—funny stories—from her childhood and about her current roommates. From the vivid account the two other girls, a dime store clerk and an apprentice telephone operator, were a weird duo.

Blondie occasionally waved at friends in the crowd, pretty young girls. "Some of the gang I run around with," she explained. Each was often on the arm of a man much older than she. Blondie also waved at a handsome man or two. She did so subtly, as though embarrassed for Jed to see.

"An old boyfriend?" Jed hoped to put her at ease.

"Oh, you saw that?" Blondie blushed. "Yeah, I date, uh, quite a bit."

"I'm sure you *do!*" Jed teased.

The lobby waiter passed by again, Jed looked at Blondie

and she nodded. He hadn't been counting but was sure the drinks were eating into his bankroll in a considerable manner. *If Colfax County's gonna pay for this I'd better ask something about Deerman.*

"Do you always stay up this late? When do you go to work in the morning?"

"I don't go in till one on Wednesdays," Blondie responded, brightened by the thought. "I work nine till two Saturdays. In exchange they give me Wednesday mornings off."

"Well, great!" Jed took their next round from the waiter. "If you're game we'll just stay right here and see this election through, unless"—Jed thought she might be bored. "Would you rather go to a club? Do you like to dance?"

"Yeah, I love it—but I'm happy right here, Mister Easton. I love talking to you. Most guys I, uh—most guys I'm with..they don't wanna talk much."

"Yeah, I suppose not." Jed thought he caught her meaning and hoped he was mistaken.

"In fact," she added, "I was just about to thank you, Mister Easton."

"For what? And please call me Jed. We can drop the Mister Easton stuff."

"Okay, Jed. Thank you for—for not asking me to your room."

Jed was taken aback by the comment, not that the thought hadn't crossed his mind. In fact he figured Blondie knew the thought had crossed his mind.

"I don't know what you think of me, Jed." She spoke so softly he leaned close to hear. "Some guys think I do that, uh—you know what I mean. But I don't. Momma says I flirt too much but I don't mean anything by it. It's just my way. I've come close—uh, to doing the wrong thing." She gave an embarrassed laugh and Jed was uncomfortable. But it was obvious she wanted to make a statement. "I'm waiting for the right guy,

Jed. So, I would've said no—a *sad* no—but no. Even if you'd asked."

"And then?"

"Well, then,"—there were tears in her flirty eyes—"then I would've gone home and cried. Li'l me, lonely again." She smiled at her attempt at self-deprecation—"and I'd have been disappointed in you."

To hell with the Stickett investigation tonight, Jed decided. If Colfax County refused to pick up the tab for the evening, he'd just have to swallow it.

"Come here, Blondie." Jed took her by the hand and led her to an empty leather sofa, a big one; the kind that swallows you up. "If we're not goin' dancing let's get a little more comfortable." The sofa faced the front window of the hotel but was shielded from the lobby by a huge pillar and several large potted plants. However, they could still hear the high volume radio just fine.

"This is more like it," Jed sighed. The network was still interspersing segments of music between the election reports.
"Ya know, Blondie—we could dance right here on the marble floor. No one would notice—or care."

"May I rest a minute?" she asked plaintively.

"Of course, sweetie," Jed laughed, "me too. Dear lord, the room is spinning. Too much gin."

Blondie snuggled next to Jed, held tight to his hand, and put her sumptuous blonde curls on his shoulder. It was as though she trusted him with her life.

And right now, I guess she can. In sixty seconds, the noisy room notwithstanding, they were both sound asleep.

CHAPTER 20

Jed was awakened by the commotion. People, mostly men, were pouring into the Muehlebach lobby through all doors. The gray light of dawn was outside and the clock over the registration desk said ten minutes to six. The smells of fresh perked coffee and bacon frying wafted in from the coffee shop.

"What's happening?" Blondie's eyes were even more sexy when half shut and half asleep.

Jed helped her off the couch. "I don't know but it must be something big."

The room was getting more crowded; Jed and Blondie were shoved against the huge front window, scarcely able to move.

"I can't see!" Blondie wailed. Her petite figure was indeed surrounded by towering men.

At that moment Jed heard motorcycles and the shriek of sirens. A big black Ford sedan, accompanied by the cycles, came to an abrupt halt at the lobby's front door. Several men piled out of the Ford, one of them—*could it be?* Jed wasn't sure. Then the man strode through the revolving door and the instantaneous cheers were deafening. The whoops, hurrahs, whistling and applause reverberated off the walls. It was *The President of the United States!*

"I can't see!" Blondie cried again.

Jed looked down into wide pleading eyes. She needed a rescue and Jed could think of only one way.

"Hike your skirt and spread your legs!" Jed yelled in her ear. Blondie's mouth opened wide, a look of shock on her pretty face. *"Excuse me, Mister Easton?"*

"I'm sorry!" Jed was giddy with weariness and excitement. "That sounded horrible." His words sputtered out through delirious laughter. "I didn't mean it that way. I just mean—if you get your skirt out of the way I'll set you on my shoulders. Cheerleaders do it all the time."

Blondie's suspicious smile said she questioned his motive; but it quickly gave way to a mischievous little smirk. She got into the moment and hiked her skirt high.

Jed moved behind her and placed his hands on her tiny waist. "And upsy-daisy!" he said. Jed saw a flash of bare thighs, a black garter belt, and pink lace.

Blondie locked her legs around his neck and squealed with delight. *"Harry!* Mister President!" She waved one hand and with the other tried valiantly to cover her thighs. As to the latter she failed miserably.

The cheers and applause continued for Harry S Truman, the thirty-third President of the United States. He stood quietly, nodding his appreciation.

Jed noticed that The President was a snappy dresser, more so than black-and-white news photos were able to reveal. After all, Harry had been a haberdasher. He wore a crisp white shirt, double-breasted blue suit, and blue polka-dot tie. Mister Truman was moved by the crowd's display of affection. Jed saw tears behind The President's thick eyeglasses.

"Mister *President!"* Blondie squealed again.

Truman caught sight of the pretty face (Jed hoped that was all he caught sight of) and tipped his dove gray hat, a Stetson Open Road. Then he raised his arms and brought them down slowly, signaling the crowd he was about to speak.

"Boys," The President began, "and girls,"—(Truman again tipped the Stetson to Blondie, bringing a burst of laughter from the crowd)—"folks, we got 'em beat and they know it! They just won't admit it."

Again the room erupted and again Truman signaled for

silence. "Don't you worry, just hold on and this'll be over in a coupla hours."

Before the crowd could cheer again Truman waved at the desk clerk, the same "green eyeshade" who had checked Jed in. "Hey, Eddie, send up a barber. I haven't had my shave." And with that The President and his entourage entered the elevator.

The jumbled sound of multitudinous conversations started immediately—but it was somewhat hushed. That was because everyone including Jed and Blondie stood almost reverently, watching the indicator arrow above the elevator door. They watched until it stopped at floor seventeen.

The crowd was evaporating and Blondie, suddenly self-conscious, slid down from Jed's shoulders. There was no way to do that delicately and Jed was again aware of the attention this perky secretary attracted. (He was fairly confident that Blondie was also aware).

"Want some breakfast?" Jed was now wide-awake.

"You eat a lot, don't you, Mister Easton?"

Jed laughed loudly. "Yes, I do, Penelope. If you insist on calling me Mister Easton, I'm gonna call you Penelope."

Blondie snuggled close as they walked, and Jed could understand why any mother would think this daughter a flirt. They sat down at the coffee shop counter and ordered bacon, eggs, toast, and coffee.

"Oh, Jed." Blondie grabbed his hand and held it tightly. "I've never had so much fun in my whole life."

Jed looked at her. "I've had fun too, Blondie," but as he spoke his heart ached. *Dear Lord, why is life so difficult?* Just as Blondie grabbed his hand—he was again thinking of Erica.

I must be nuts! Here I am with one of the sweetest, sexiest little gals in the world—but I'm obsessed with some dame who never wants to see me again! Jed wished he could tell Erica he saw Ol' Harry. *That* would damn sure impress Miss Prissy Green Garters—her and her hot-shot rancher!

Jed couldn't believe how angry it all made him—or the devastation he felt at the very real possibility..he'd never see Erica again. It almost took his breath away.

Was Erica *the one?* Jed felt he was too sensible to actually fall in love with a girl he'd spent mere hours with aboard a train, particularly since a fair amount of alcohol was involved. But he couldn't shake the feeling.

Breakfast arrived. Jed and Blondie ate like waifs, with only small bits of chit-chat between bites. Jed finally looked at Blondie and was surprised to see big tears welling in those sea blue eyes.

"I'll never see you again, will I Mister Easton?" She bit her lip to keep from crying.

Jed put his elbow on the counter, his chin in his hand, and looked into Blondie's eyes. It seemed he could almost see her soul, and he had to acknowledge he felt something for her. She so wanted to love; and be loved—as did he. But he would not lie to this sweet girl—not now.

"Blondie, I don't know whether I'll see you again. But probably not." He was at a loss for more words.

"You're in love with someone, aren't you, Mister Easton?"

Jed hadn't expected that. "Why? Why would say that?"

"Because—when"—Blondie was also searching for words—"when you touch me it's—it's so tender but you're just not—you pull back. You can't really give yourself."

Jed gently placed his hands on her face and touched her lips with his fingertips.

"Mister Easton, are you in love with Mrs. Roland?" Blondie blurted the question as though she couldn't contain it any longer and she seemed about to cry a river. "Mister Deerman says your murder investigation was just a ruse; that you're probably one of Mrs. Roland's ex-husbands."

"Mister Deerman says that, does he?" Jed wasn't sure how much he should explain.

"Look, Blondie, Mister Deerman is way off base there. The murder story is no ruse, and I've never even *met* Mrs. Roland."

Blondie remained silent.

"But"—Jed was uncertain what he'd wind up saying—"Yes, I *am* in love. But not with Mrs. Roland." Jed drained his coffee cup. He'd said aloud, what he felt inside.

Jed was delivered from the awkward moment by a jubilant eruption. Neither could see what was happening but they heard the clatter. It came from the kitchen and sounded like a big spoon or fork clanging on an empty cooking pot.

"Awright, Brother Harry, my *good* man!" came the Negro shout and the cook stuck his joyous face out of the kitchen. "The ol' sonuvagun won!"

A second man appeared also, this one taller and older but he too wore a smile of victory. "Truman carried Ohio!" said the second man, his voice eloquent, his English perfect; and that caused Jed to recognize him. He was the distinguished black porter who'd been so kind and polite at Union Station. "That's it!" the porter continued. "It gives The President two-hundred-seventy electoral votes. Two-sixty-six are all he needs."

It was a spontaneous reaction for Jed and Blondie as they hugged in their longest embrace yet. Jed lifted her by the waist and pulled her close—as close as possible while sitting on coffee counter stools. They could not stop hugging—and didn't want to. For whatever reason, even as Blondie smiled and wept at the same time, at this moment they were a great comfort to each other.

Maybe this would be a good point for time to freeze, Jed thought—to stand still forever. He wouldn't have to worry about the future, with or without Professor Erica Harlan Swanson, of Colorado Springs. It wasn't exactly a romantic setting: a bright white room, bluish florescent light glaring down. Jed hated that kind of light. But right now, he didn't care. He kissed

Blondie's petite little nose and again caressed her face.

Over Blondie's shoulder Jed saw a well-dressed man, a country club type, sitting five stools away. At the celebration by the kitchen staff the man stopped reading his *EXTRA!* early edition of the *Kansas City Star*. He mumbled something too low for Jed to hear but the man's countenance suggested it was something his mother (no son's mother) would approve of. He got up and walked by Jed and Blondie, shaking his head. There was the *hint* of a smile on the gentleman's face, and he halted to speak more or less to Jed; but really to no one in particular.

"I just can't believe it," he muttered, "and it makes me sick. But ya gotta hand it to the little guy. He's sure got guts!" He walked out the door leaving his *Kansas City Star,* with news that was no longer news, on the counter. His breakfast was untouched.

Twenty minutes later—

The coffee shop was almost empty, the morning rush over. Jed leaned over and again kissed Blondie's nose. "Blondie, there's some guy out there for you. I know it! There has to be. And when he finds you he'll treat you like a queen." Jed paused. "If he doesn't, just call me. I'll come cut off his—uh, sorry," he chuckled, "there I go again. A gentleman shouldn't talk that way to a lady. I think I'm a little giddy from our all-nighter." Then, he couldn't resist. "But I'd come cut 'em off, anyway!"

It was too crass, and Jed knew it; but it seemed to do the trick. It was language Blondie understood and she laughed while dabbing a coffee shop napkin to her eyes.

"Thank you, Mister Easton. I need to go home now. I need some sleep."

As they left the coffee shop Jed nodded to the distinguished porter behind the counter. "Hello, there. Thanks again for your help yesterday."

The man seemed puzzled, but only for second. "Oh—yes sir. I see you found your lady."

It was not the response Jed expected and he turned with embarrassment toward Blondie. Fortunately, she was momentarily distracted by a *Radio Mirror* magazine someone had left on the counter.

"Uh, yeah," Jed said softly, hoping Blondie would take no notice—then more loudly: "When do you head out again?"

"Ten twenty-five tonight, on the Rock Island line. *The Golden State Limited.* Going all the way to Los Angeles this trip."

"Have you been up all night like most everybody?"

"Oh, yes sir. I couldn't sleep, it got too exciting. When it looked like Mister Truman would win, I just had to come down and celebrate with my brother. He's the early morning cook here."

"Well, he's a good one," Jed smiled. "Breakfast was wonderful." He took Blondie's hand and they walked slowly through the lobby; as though they didn't want to part but knew they must.

Blondie crawled into the cab, and in the process, Jed caught one more glimpse of luscious white thighs. And as the cab pulled away from the canopy he knew his last sight of Blondie would stay with him forever. She looked at him, a forlorn stare; her blue eyes wide and unblinking. She pressed her fingers to her lips; then to the taxi's window glass.

Dear Lord, why is life so difficult? Jed concluded he'd always have a lot of questions.

CHAPTER 21

The same morning, many miles to the west—
9:15 a.m.—

The silver Taylorcraft L-2A came in low from the west. The wind rarely blew from the east but this morning it did. The landing was perfect. The two front wheels touched down smoothly, not even a bump. Seconds later the tail wheel dropped to the runway.

Liberal, Kansas is farm and ranch country. Sixty-five miles to the west is the Colorado line. Travel a mere two miles to the south and you're in the Oklahoma panhandle. Keep going another thirty-five miles and you cross into Texas. Take a hard right from that point, and one hundred thirty land miles later you're back in the state of New Mexico, the Land of Enchantment.

For mile after mile around Liberal, at any degree of the compass, you fly over rolling prairie; section after section of grain fields, the hard winter wheat now lying dormant. Come spring, given enough moisture, it will burst into a lush green carpet and grow tall enough to wave in the gusty winds that sweep the high plateau. Then, as the searing sun of June and July mercilessly bakes all beneath it, the lush green turns to golden straw topped with a wispy beard. And inside that beard is enough whole grain to feed the world.

Beyond, and mingled with the miles of wheat, are more miles of grassland. Herds of cattle, mostly white-faced Herefords, graze contentedly. They move slowly across the prairie from day to day and unless nature has withheld its rains from heaven, there is always more to munch.

Since the years of the Dust Bowl other fixtures dot the landscape. From the air some resembled giant insects on wheels, which drew water in the warmer months from deep, deep wells. The insect-like irrigation equipment inched along, spraying a broad mist across cropland that Mother Nature had temporarily forsaken.

And there were the oil derricks—phallic symbols of the newly rich, or those who *hoped* to be newly (and forever) rich.

It was the oil business that brought the silver Taylorcraft to Liberal; a tip from the pilot's major benefactor that sounded like a sure thing. "Check it out. But don't get involved unless it's on the up-and-up," came the advice.

Any investment with the possibility of a quick and heavy dividend should not be overlooked—particularly in his circumstance. It was a lesson of life in these parts: as clouds turn dark on the horizon the expediency of rainy-day funds becomes a given. If his crime were discovered would he run or face the music? At this point he wanted options, and that took cash.

The tall brown-skinned man taxied the Taylorcraft to the gasoline pump and walked into the small Quonset hut that passed as an airport terminal.

"Look who's here," smiled the nineteen-year-old behind the tall counter with the short wave radio and microphone.

"Better top 'er off, Jack," the pilot responded, "these prairie headwinds really suck the gas out of it."

"You got it, but can it wait a little? I'm just headin' to the house for a bite. I overslept and missed breakfast this morning."

"Fine, I'll be in town a few hours. If you don't mind, I'll hitch a ride."

Jack dropped him off at the Blue Goose Café. The tall man took a stool at the counter just as the pretty dark-haired waitress emerged from the kitchen. Two plates of bacon and eggs were balanced on her left arm and the fingers of her right hand were linked through the handles of two mugs of steaming coffee.

"Well, if it ain't the hot-shot lawyer," she said as she passed. Light freckles dotted her nose. Smooth olive skin surrounded deep blue eyes. Her tone and smile suggested more than mere recognition of an acquaintance. The tall man loved, yet hated, how weak she made him.

"I'll be right back," she whispered and headed for the table by the front window. Two hungry businessmen wanted their breakfast.

"Here we are.'" She gracefully eased all the food and beverage into place, spilling nothing. She smiled warmly at each man and her fingertips brushed theirs and lingered a second— but not so long as to *necessarily* suggest the touch was anything other than accidental. The customer could believe what he wanted. She just knew it got big tips.

"What can I getcha?" she asked the tall man as she returned. She teasingly raised her eyebrows making the innocent question pleasantly provocative. Her pencil was poised above the ticket pad and she appeared to be "all business"—except for the knowing smile she gave the handsome Navajo.

"Why do you always make fun of me?" His tone was curt, his smile half-frozen.

"I'm not making fun. You *could* be a hot-shot lawyer if you'd ever seize the moment. Look, you're the one always tellin' me I can do better."

"Well, Lois, of course you can. Hell, with *your looks*— what are you still doing in this cowtown, anyway?"

"We are just a little grumpy this morning, aren't we? I'm sorry," she smiled. "I didn't mean to piss you off; just havin' some fun."

"No, it's me. *I'm* sorry. I'm not feeling well. Tell the cook to fix me a couple of poached eggs and dry toast—no coffee, just ice water. I can't seem to keep anything on my stomach."

Lois walked to the kitchen and attached the ticket to the silver whirl-wheel. She returned and leaned seductively across the counter, the top button of her white uniform straining against its contents as the neckline revealed more than a little.

"Maybe a *special* little pick-me-up would do the trick. I get off at one."

The tall man smiled, suddenly feeling better. The eggs and toast arrived and he slicked up his plate for the first time in days. He left twice the money necessary on the counter.

Lois was behind the cash register as he left.

"One-fifteen?" he asked.

"Well, aren't we feeling better? Two o'clock," she whispered, "I wanna take a bath first," and Lois swayed away with a hot pot of coffee to refill the bottomless cups.

With a few minutes to kill he stopped by the drug store for a new safety razor and a bottle of Old Spice cologne. Across the street was Ravenscroft's Men's Store where he bought a white Van Heusen dress shirt for his rendezvous with Lois.

She liked him in white shirts. "Shows off that 'red man' tan," she teased.

The tall man arrived at the First National Bank of Liberal at ten twenty-eight, two minutes early for his appointment. A young vice-president waved from his glass and wood cubicle at the back and arose nervously to shake the pilot's hand.

"Look," the banker said, standing close to speak quietly. "You were never here today! Understand? I don't have to tell you this would be big trouble for you—and *heap* big trouble for me." The banker gave a self-satisfied smile at his lame attempt at ethnic humor.

The Navajo didn't smile. He was in no mood for such jokes today, particularly since the banker's words had just revealed the deal was *not* on the up-and-up. However, due to his situation (advice to the contrary), the pilot would not be picky.

"I understand, Mr. Gorson. What's the story?"

"Oklahoma Panhandle Pipeline; no matter what the official word is, the stock will split in two to three weeks, guaranteed. It will probably split again a month later."

"Sounds good."

"Can you buy a thousand shares?"

"Yeah."

"You still use that broker in Denver?"

"Yeah."

"Wire him today, tomorrow at the latest, but not from here; from anywhere, *anywhere* but Liberal. And," the banker added with a sly smile, "we're agreed on fifteen percent for me when you sell, right?"

"Right," and the Navajo turned to leave. "By the way," he turned back with a cold smile, "how many 'fifteen percents' you got lined up?"

"None of your business." This time it was the banker who didn't smile. "Get outa here! I've never met ya."

Lois's apartment was a block down the street from the Blue Goose, across the street from the Rock Island Depot and the Cimarron Hotel. But they never, ever met at her place.

"I have a reputation to maintain," she explained. "It's a small town."

The first time, the tall man asked why she thought it better for her reputation to meet a strange man across the street in a hotel, than to invite a guest (with the knowledge of no one else) to her own apartment.

"My aunt lives in the Cimarron. I visit all the time. No one will know the difference."

The tall man nodded but didn't reveal his suspicions: namely, that if it were such a small town, someone—maybe the

Cimarron desk clerk, maybe even Lois's aunt—*someone* would connect the dots, and notice that Lois's visits to the hotel usually occurred when a Navajo stranger flew into Liberal and rented a room by the hour.

"I just need to shave and freshen up," he told the desk clerk as he took the room key. He could never think of anything more original and the clerk didn't seem to care.

He showered and shaved, and changed into the fresh white shirt. The laundry, just a half block from the bank, had agreed to wash, starch, and dry the garment in front of an electric fan—then they ironed the shirt, all while he waited. The rush service was a mere fifteen cents extra.

He opened the door to Lois's knock. She immediately ran her fingertips across the crisp cotton Van Heusen. "Feels like glass," she said, then pushed her fingers between the buttons to softly caress his chest. He loved that.

"Sit down, I'll fix you a drink," she invited as she removed her coat. She wore no dress, just an expensive-looking slip.

He took the tall glass of Smirnoff vodka over shaved ice. Lois sat on the bed in front of his chair and tucked her feet under her hips. She was drinking a frosty six-and-a-half ounce bottle of Coca-Cola.

"Want some of this in there?" he asked.

"No, you know booze just makes me sleepy."

"What's wrong with that?" he questioned with a sly smile.

Lois stood up and standing on tiptoe, stretched her slim arms toward the ceiling as though she were already sleepy. The action caused the pink silk slip to slide up her tan thighs. He now could see the slip was all she wore.

"How do you stay so tan?" he asked. "It's November, for Pete's sake."

She gave him a startled look; then burst out laughing. "That question from *you,* of all people. I have Indian blood; a little—an eighth, a sixteenth. I forget, but my mother told me."

"You never told *me*."

"You never *asked*," came her pointed reply.

"Come 'ere, baby," he responded hoarsely and took another sip of the cold vodka.

She sat on his lap and kissed him. "Mmm, that was good," he said.

"It's been too long," she breathed.

He set the glass of vodka on the dresser next to his chair, lifted Lois in his arms, and gingerly laid her on the bed. As he settled in beside her he was completely calm, no hint of apprehension, no hint of upset stomach.

Lois waited a full ten minutes to make sure he wouldn't return. She picked up the phone and asked for the First National Bank. "Mister Gorson," she requested; then when the banker picked up his extension, "It's okay," she told him.

The vice-president recognized her voice. "Did he say anything?" he asked, the tension obvious.

"Not a word. I *told* you I was good at picking people to do this; people who *won't* spill their guts. I think we're safe."

Lois hung up the phone and snuggled deep into the room's only chair. She stretched her long legs straight out in front, her petite feet resting on the footstool. The pink slip slid all the way to the top of her tan thighs.

She reached to the dresser, drained the glass of vodka down her throat, and promptly went to sleep. On this day she did *not* visit her aunt.

CHAPTER 22

Kansas City, Missouri—

Jed slept until three p.m. He was completely worn out from the all-night election vigil—groggy from too little sleep, groggy from too *much* gin. As always when exhausted, his sleep was fitful. He dreamed. But they were confusing dreams.

He saw Erica's face but her hair was not red. Instead it was a luxuriant mass of long blonde curls. He was with her atop a Pullman bed, the upper bunk, and she was on her knees. She wore *only* green garters and he pulled her to him for a long, deep kiss. But when the kiss ended the nearly naked girl was not Erica—she was Blondie.

Jed was awakened by an abrupt loud snore—his own. He struggled to focus his eyes on the bedside clock. It was a cloudy day, but in his state the glare from the afternoon daylight through the hotel window was blinding. He thought the clock said seven past three.

His shower and shave were quick and perfunctory. He donned his last fresh shirt, a pale blue one with a maroon stripe, and decided to skip the necktie. He threw his belongings into his new suitcase. *Damn you, 'case—you and that little mix-up. You're why I feel so lousy.*

Just twenty-four hours ago Jed would've sworn his life could get no more complicated. But it had. He yearned to see Erica; but was also battling a strong desire to call Blondie.

Don't do it. It's not good gumption. In his head Jed heard his mother's voice speaking the words "good gumption" as clearly as though she stood by his side. Whether Mrs. Easton used the words correctly, Jed didn't know; but he knew what she was talking about: plain old common sense. He presumed she coined the phrase because he heard no one else use it so often, and always with the assumption it would solve every problem.

Jed paid his hotel bill with a grimace. When Mrs. TJ called, before he left Raton, she'd told Jed that TJ offered to send expense money. Jed, in youthful pride, said no. He told her he'd handle it himself and get reimbursed upon return—yet another lesson learned the hard way. It did no justice to the King's English to now call his wad of cash, a wad.

As Jed walked across the lobby "good gumption" lost out to male ego and desire. He closed the door to the phone booth and dropped in a nickel.

"Stedman, Swift, and Jones." Blondie's voice was virtually *all* breath today.

"Good morning, Blondie, guess who?"

There was a brief silence from Blondie, then hesitantly, "Stedman—Swift"—(she cleared her throat)—"Stedman, Swift and Jones."

"This is Jed, Blondie."

"I know, Mister Easton." She sounded forlorn. "Why are you calling?"

"Well, Blondie, I just had a hankerin' to call you."

"Please don't do this, Mister Easton," she whispered, "you said we'd never see each other again. You're in love, remember?"

Guilt and confusion swept over Jed. He hadn't anticipated such a reaction. "Gosh, I don't wanna hurt you. I thought we could still be friends," and Jed scrambled to redeem himself. "I—I really called to speak with Mister Deerman, just for a moment." *And what the hell am I gonna say to him?*

Jed was relieved at Blondie's response. "He's not here, Mister Easton. Gone flying again I think, I'm not sure. He left right after you did, yesterday."

Now, what's that sly sonuvabitch up to? "Blondie, is he gone a lot in the middle of the week?"

"Not really, Mister Easton, not until recently. He really loves to fly."

Jed was more convinced he needed to verify John Little Deer's whereabouts in mid-October. But first he brought his attention back to the lovely lass on the other end of the line. "Blondie, I wouldn't hurt you for anything in the world. Just because I said we wouldn't meet again, well, that doesn't mean we *won't.*"

"Yes it does." There was a resigned sadness, but finality in Blondie's breathy tone. "Don't do this to me, Mister Easton. I'm going to hang up now," and she did.

Jed felt like a first-class jerk. In his mind he could see Blondie at this moment at her desk, dabbing her eyes with a white lace handkerchief some cad had bought her. In the process of making himself miserable he'd turned it into a communicable disease.

Jed headed for the Muehlebach coffee shop. He needed a cup of their "hottest 'n' blackest." Whether from heartache or hangover he wasn't sure, but for the first time in a long time he wasn't hungry.

En route to the coffee shop he passed the hotel newsstand and laid down two cents for the hot-off-the-presses Kansas City Star.

STARTLING VICTORY FOR TRUMAN! screamed the banner headline.

—Crowds At The Hotel Muehlebach Cheer The
President On His Victory—
—Wild Scene At Hotel—
—Chief Executive Back Again To Excelsior Springs
Where He
Had Spent The Night—
—Presidential Party Will Depart At 8 O'Clock Tomorrow
For Washington—

The paper brought back fond memories from last night. Jed wished Blondie were here right now. For a second he even contemplated calling her again. Maybe he could talk her into dinner tonight. Pursuing Blondie was probably more sensible than chasing after Erica—but that wasn't saying much.

Jed knew one thing: if he could see neither girl he was ready to go home. He would first attempt to check out John Little Deer's alibi; make a couple of calls about the three names he'd memorized from the lawyer's appointment book. Unless there was a startling revelation he'd return to Raton and pursue the existence of fingerprints on the murder weapon.

Jed took the Santa Fe schedule from his pocket. The next train for Raton was the westbound *Chief* at ten-fifteen p.m. He checked his wallet to make sure he had money for the extra fare train. He did, but barely. A hamburger (maybe two) would have to suffice as dinner since he'd have to reserve a roomette. *The Chief* was all Pullman, all sleeper cars westbound from Kansas City.

If he could see Erica (or even Blondie) he'd gladly wait for the cheaper *California Limited* at ten forty-five the next morning.

"I shoulda made TJ buy me a round-trip ticket in the first place," Jed grumped aloud. But there was no one there to hear it. To be honest, he hadn't known what he'd find in Kansas City. The investigation might've taken him elsewhere before his return home. He was trying to do one simple step at a time.

"I just didn't know," he mumbled. "Prices are *high* in the big city."

At least he'd get a good night's rest. The schedule pegged *The Chief* for arrival in Raton shortly after nine o'clock, Thursday morning. He called Santa Fe reservations from the phone booth in the hotel lobby. A roomette was available so Jed returned to his black coffee and newspaper. He tried to read the sports page but nothing piqued his interest.

His father's pocket watch said four-fifty p.m. Might as

well walk to Union Station, Jed thought; plenty of time and I'll save cab fare. His war wound was a little sore from yesterday's drizzle but nothing he couldn't handle. If he found the guts to call Erica or Blondie, he could do so from the depot.

Union Station was inundated in its usual hubbub but Jed delighted in its warmth. The walk from the Muehlebach was invigorating to say the least. Kansas City's November wind is brisk and bone chilling.

Jed decided he could spare a dime for a suitcase locker and wandered around the cavernous building unencumbered. An inveterate people-watcher, he never tired of wondering where this or that person was going, and why. Would someone be there to greet them on arrival? Would that someone be happy to see them? Would a husband welcome his wife back to his bed or lament the passing of a window of independence? Was the traveling wife warmly anticipating the return to her husband's arms; or was she returning from an exciting and secret rendezvous? Her husband merely *thought* she was visiting her cousin. And was she still excited? Or did she just feel shabby?

And why do all my thoughts eventually wind up on women and sex? Jed laughed loudly at the inward acknowledgment of a base appetite. His face turned red as four or five people turned to stare.

Moments later a gorgeous statuesque brunette walked by, headed for the departure tracks. *Wow! She should be in the movies!* Dressed in a form fitting, solid black gabardine suit, the woman's thick hair fell around her face to her shoulders. Her eyes were a startling bright blue. She passed just six feet from Jed and smiled at him; a let's-get-acquainted look as blatant as any he'd ever seen.

A red fox coat was draped over her arm *(can't blame her for showing off that figure),* and two thoroughly scrubbed and powdered Airedales strained at their leashes in front of her.

"Easy, Muffin..easy, Reggie," the brunette cooed while

tugging gallantly on the leashes.

She walked on toward the trains, and just before disappearing turned again to smile at Jed. He gave her a little wink.

Thank you, God, that's she's not on my train. I've got all the woman problems I need for the moment.

He headed to buy his ticket—but what if he talked to Erica and she agreed to see him? He knew for her, he'd delay his return—and he'd need his cash for their evening.

In that case, he'd just have to swallow his pride and call TJ for ticket money home. He abhorred the thought. His conscience would demand that he tell his boss it involved a personal matter. But Jed thought he could handle the hypocrisy until he got home. He'd repay the county with interest.

At long last, proving there was still *some* normalcy to his life, Jed was hungry. The morning breakfast with Blondie was wearing thin. He found a stool at the Harvey House counter and ordered two hamburgers and a cup of coffee.

As he ordered, six men walked in and settled into a large corner booth. A well-dressed gentleman seemed to do most of the talking and four others were scribbling in small notebooks, taking down every word he said.

"So, Mayor Kemp, are you actually saying, The President's victory came as *no surprise to you?*" one of the scribblers asked, his tone sarcastic and incredulous.

"Absolutely, Joe, I knew the polls were wrong all along, just ask the Missus—she'll tell you. I said it all along."

The mayor and the press! Politicians are the same everywhere, Jed thought. For that matter, so is the press. The sixth man in the group said not a word. His back was to Jed but something about him seemed vaguely familiar.

Jed's hamburgers arrived and he turned to the pleasant task of wolfing them down. He'd never been so hungry, probably because he was out of money. He glanced back at the mayor's group just as His Honor told a joke and everyone laughed. The sixth man threw back his head in mirth and turned to glance around the restaurant. That's when Jed saw his face. *The Ronald Reagan smile!* It was Tim Roland, Jean's husband. Blondie had said he worked for the mayor.

For a split second Jed had the impulse to rush over and introduce himself. But what would he say?

"Hi, I'm Jed Easton from Raton, New Mexico. I'm in love with your sister-in-law and your best friend is a murderer!"

The mayor and his entourage would call the "white-coat boys" immediately and Jed would be calling TJ from the sanitarium—if they'd let him use the phone.

Long after Mayor Kemp and the newsboys left the Harvey House Jed sat staring at the grounds in his coffee cup. *Enough of this bullshit!*

He paid his tab and headed for the bank of phone booths. He closed the door behind him. His breathing was quick and jerky. *Get hold of yourself, man.*

He dialed the Rolands' number. One ring, two rings—

"Roland residence." The voice was soft and feminine. It could be Erica. But of course Jean would probably sound much the same. Jed was caught off guard, too stunned to say anything.

The feminine purr came again, "Roland residence, this is Erica Swanson. Who's calling?"

"Erica?" Jed grimaced. The tension made his voice sound like a kid. Anyone on the other end would conclude he was twelve years old.

"Yes, who's calling?"

"Erica, this is Jed"—(silence on her end)—"Jed Easton." He'd now gained some control and sounded like an adult.

"How did you get this number?" Erica didn't sound angry but a little cool.

"It's a long story, Erica, but in no way devious." This was no time to quibble over *yet another* little white lie. "I've finished with my business here in Kansas City and am about to head home, but—I'd, uh, gladly wait till tomorrow..if you'll have dinner with me tonight." There! He'd said it.

"Jed, uh"—Erica was whispering now and Jed heard laughter and tinkling glasses in the background. He wondered if there were always parties at the Roland household while Tim was away being attentive to the mayor.

"Jed, please," Erica continued in a soft whisper. He wasn't sure she meant it to sound sexy—but to Jed it sounded sexy because he *wanted* it to sound sexy. He wanted to reach through the phone line and pull her to him.

"Okay, I'll admit," Erica started over, "I'm just a little tempted but what I said at Union Station still stands. I can't, I really can't. I don't think I *should*. It's—it's just pointless."

"Well, what would it hurt? Just a little dinner."

"Goodbye, Jed." There was determination in Erica's voice. "It was sweet, silly fun—but goodbye."

"Well, could I call you in Colorado Springs? May I write you?" Jed simply could *not* give up.

"No. Please, don't, Jed. *Please* don't. Goodbye." Click.

It was a full sixty seconds before Jed hung up the phone. He sat longer still in the semi-dark phone booth. The dim glow from the overhead bulb and the quiet whir from the cubicle's small rubber fan blade; to Jed it seemed he was inside a coffin—*but I don't think a coffin has a fan.* He just stared at the cradled telephone. There were no more thoughts of John Little Deer's October whereabouts; of the clients the Navajo had claimed as an alibi, or where the Navajo was off to now in his airplane. In this moment Jed forgot all that and the investigation. He didn't even think of Blondie.

Jed walked to the ticket counter. "One-way to Raton on *The Chief.* I have a reservation," and he looked at his father's pocket watch. It was nine-ten p.m.; still an hour to kill and he felt it would kill him.

Jed boarded *The Chief* at nine fifty-five, on the very first announcement. The porter pointed to the door of his roomette and Jed slipped the man his last four dollars, and whispered in his ear. He realized he'd just given the man an excessively healthy tip, but didn't care. It made no difference now.

When the porter arrived five minutes later with the half-pint of Beefeater, Jed was already undressed. He accepted the bottle through the barely open door and immediately downed all the contents, straight. He crawled between the crisp cool sheets hoping desperately to sleep.

And he did, but again fitfully. And again he dreamed. He stood at the top of the down staircase leading to the departure tracks in Kansas City's Union Station. Hundreds of people walked by. Then, Blondie walked by and she blew him a kiss. Then, the statuesque brunette walked by, led by the two Airedales. *She* blew him a kiss. Jed smiled and winked at both Blondie and the brunette—but felt no pain at seeing them go.

Then Erica walked by.

"Erica, Erica." In his dream, his voice seemed far away and no one could hear him. He must try harder. *"ERICA!"* he yelled, and this time his voice came out in a roar. Everyone in Union Station stopped dead still to look at him.

He stood frozen, and a sudden wind from nowhere lifted Erica's full skirt—and for a brief moment Jed again glimpsed the green tap panty and garters.

"*ERICA!*" He yelled her name as loud as he could, not caring who stared.

But she did *not* blow a kiss. She didn't even turn and look his way.

Somewhere outside La Junta, Colorado, in the cold gray light of dawn, the long mournful whistle of the Santa Fe *Chief* awakened Jed. He was embarrassed that the pillow was wet with his tears.

CHAPTER 23

Another look back—
Thursday, December 10, 1942—

"If you do this very special favor for me I'll promise to never tell a soul." There was a devilish twinkle in the eyes of Professor Arthur Aldridge, and his tantalizing sentence was Erica's first clue that today's lunch with her old teacher would be another adventure in "Arthur's World."

"Now, what have you got up your sleeve?" Erica's own eyes had a twinkle because she thoroughly enjoyed the older man's company. This was in no small measure because he delighted in surprises; such as the time he showed up at her office in a huge Mexican sombrero and announced they would luncheon at a new little restaurant he'd discovered.

The restaurant was really the home of a couple from Xalapa, Mexico. The man had been the editor of a weekly newspaper and was forced to flee, run out of town for publishing an expose of bribery by the city fathers; bribery condoned by Xalapa's police officials. All his money, a lifetime of hard-won savings, was used to purchase a quaint little house just outside Colorado Springs, near the Garden of the Gods.

With no income the old editor and his wife did what they could to make a living. They each were marvelous cooks and the word soon spread among The Springs' well-to-do that the best Mexican food in Colorado was available at their little white bungalow.

Service was by reservation only; lunch from eleven-thirty

to two, the hours strictly observed. Evening reservations were much more flexible; never before eight, but the professor said he once took a lady (Erica didn't ask who) to dine there at midnight.

There were four small tables for two in the dining room, four small tables for two in the living room. That was it. They could serve no more than sixteen people at a time; nor did they want to.

The Mexican newspaperman was a good businessman. He quickly realized his clientele would pay much more for dishes prepared with culinary authenticity. The couple made up for their small space by charging two or three times the going rate for Mexican cuisine. However, repeat business was guaranteed, in no small part, because the margaritas were gratis.

"And *I* will guarantee you they're seventy-percent tequila," Erica laughed after her first sip.

Meals with Arthur, as she now called him, were regular occasions. From the time Erica joined the faculty at Colorado College they managed a respite together two or three times a month—the "old professor" and his "star pupil."

Today, he picked her up after her ten-thirty class on the Founding Fathers. Like a proud old peacock he strutted off the campus with its youngest and most beautiful female instructor.

"Today, my dear Erica, it's the Broadmoor," Arthur proudly announced. "One must occasionally see how the other half lives."

Erica loved to visit Colorado's most exclusive resort. She always noticed an extra spring in her step when she walked into the place. They were escorted to the sleek lustrous barroom that gave off every indication of Arthur's suggestion: life by the "other half."

"And just exactly *what* requires such secrecy? Why spirit me away to this 'island of riches?'" Erica loved to tease the professor and he loved her teasing. Their relationship was not romantic. He was, after all, thirty years her senior. But they did flirt a little. Friendship and professional respect made them comfortable together.

"The brass up at Buckley Field has invited a few of us ol' WWI guys to their New Year's Eve soiree." Aldredge took another sip of the Broadmoor's wild turkey and rice soup. Erica thought she knew where this was headed.

"Guess they want the current crop of fly-boys to see us ol' infantry geezers," he continued, "to buck 'em up a little, or inspire them. Who the hell *knows* why they want us there? But they've invited a bunch of us from all service branches."

"And?" Erica was not going to make this easy. She would make the professor work for it.

"Well, since I'm the only *single* guy of the Battery D boys showing up, I'd love to make them all jealous as hell! You on my arm would do precisely that. Unless of course you're already booked," he added quickly.

"Oh, Arthur, how sweet! I'm not booked and yes, I'll be your date. It sounds like fun."

Erica knew the professor had been widowed for ten years and from all accounts the love affair with his wife had been genuine. She assumed that was the reason he hadn't remarried. He was very handsome for his age and she loved being on his arm.

"They've rented the ballroom at the Brown Palace Hotel and hired the best twenty musicians in Denver." Arthur's eyes gleamed as he finished his soup. "The band should really swing! They're even bringing in a USO songstress from Chicago." The professor touched the corners of his mouth with a white linen napkin. "I feel like celebrating *right now*. How 'bout a drink before we head back to the salt mine?"

"Arthur! It's ten past noon. I never drink this early."

"It's Christmas time! Good time to start," and the professor snapped his fingers for the waiter.

"But why the secrecy?" Erica asked as the drinks arrived.

"Oh, that. That was merely a gallant act from your titled

knight here, m'lady,"—Arthur made a theatrical bow—"in case you're afraid your reputation might suffer. So far as I'm concerned you can tell the whole world. In fact I wish you would. 'Twould burnish *my* reputation considerably."

They finished their drinks and the professor fell silent. He stared past Erica looking out the window at a Pike's Peak slowly being obscured by light snowflakes.

"Erica, this war! Dear God, war is horrible. But what choice do we have—what *choice* do we have?" He shook his head. "God only knows where all this will end up. I am sometimes very fearful." Aldredge swallowed some shaved ice from his glass before he continued. "Roosevelt is wonderful—for the most part, it seems to me—at keeping the nation confident and upbeat. But—I don't know. Best we live each day to the fullest."

Erica reached across the table and touched his hand. "You miss her terribly, don't you, Arthur; your wife?"

"Yes—yes, I do, Erica." He looked over at the polished mahogany bar, only half the stools filled at lunchtime. "She and I used to have cocktails here every Friday night."

"Oh, Arthur! This must be hard for you. Why come to the Broadmoor? There are plenty of other places."

"No, no, I love coming here," and his smile showed he was telling the truth. "You see, with the relationship we had there are no bad memories; only good ones." The professor pushed back his chair, rose, and reached for Erica's hand.

They passed the bar and Arthur paused as though something was left unsaid. "What bothers me—I can't help thinking about it. These young men from Buckley, on New Year's Eve," and he shook his head. "How many will we ever see again? What I really mean is—how many will we *never* see again?"

For security reasons there was never a public announcement, but Erica knew (at least it was rumored), that Buckley Field was a major training facility for bombardiers—those who would serve aboard the B-17 Flying Fortress and the B-24 Liberator.

As they left the Broadmoor the professor touched her arm. "Erica, I don't think I have to say this but just in case, I want to be clear. I expect nothing untoward in this. We'll stay at the Brown Palace but separate rooms, my treat."

"No other thought ever crossed my mind, Arthur." She kissed him lightly on the cheek. Perhaps it was the sherry, but for a fleeting second she was sorry Arthur was so old-fashioned.

"When is your next class?" Arthur asked.

"Today is Thursday, Arthur, I'm done for the day. *You know that.* Back to the salt mine," she added sarcastically, "just whom do you think you're kidding?" Erica wondered what was coming next, again tantalized by the possibilities.

"I'm kidding no one," he laughed. "We're going to The Bungalow for margaritas. I told them to expect us at one-fifteen."

"Great!" she exclaimed with a delightful squeal. Would Arthur step beyond his normal reserve? (Erica was scared to death she just might assent...) She concluded she'd best halt the thought right there.

Erica seemed in a mood for most anything—which made Arthur weak. They walked hand in hand to his blue Lincoln Zephyr. He straightened his shoulders. He was a gentleman. *God give me strength to remain so!*

Thursday, New Year's Eve, 1942—

"I'm sorry the Captain won't be able to make it." Save for that expression of disappointment Arthur was jovial as a young cadet on the drive from Colorado Springs to Denver. Erica loved hearing his stories, particularly when his mood was so light-hearted.

"That would be the Senator from Missouri, right?" Erica knew she was right.

"Indeed! Ol' Harry has his hands full ever since they gave

him that committee to look at our defense situation. Should've done it years ago. If they'd have done that, I'd be much less apprehensive now. But he's a helluva man. Nobody ever loved their Captain more than we boys of Battery D."

Erica was delighted that Arthur asked her to chauffeur. She loved to drive his car. The professor had bought the 1940 Lincoln Zephyr, a dark blue coupe, off the showroom floor when it was brand new. Aldredge babied the three-passenger car; it had one bench-style seat—no back seat—and the odometer on the classy dashboard showed barely four thousand miles. With a powerful V-12 engine, it did seventy-five miles-per-hour as easily as forty-five, and the beautiful snow-covered Rockies slid swiftly by on their left.

The ornate lobby of the Brown Palace was just as Erica remembered from her one and only previous visit. The occasion had been for a leisurely lunch with Jean and her friends. That trip to Denver was "big sister's" college graduation gift to Erica. She stayed a week with Jean and her roommate and they crammed every moment with the sights and sounds of the Mile-High City. Plus, they worked in a couple of picnics in the mountains.

Arthur and Erica had hoped to arrive in time for an early cocktail, sinking into those divine leather couches the Brown Palace was famous for, but a cattle truck accident just south of Denver tied up traffic for a half hour. "I wouldn't want you rushed, my dear." Arthur put his arm around her waist. "Plenty of time to talk at dinner. Go soak for a while. I'll tap on your door at seven-thirty."

"Thank you, Arthur. I'm so looking forward to this evening."

"I feel like a twenty-year-old," he replied, and Erica thought the light in his eyes made him look about twenty.

The bellman set Erica's bags on the varnished pine luggage rack at the foot of the bed.

"Would you like me to hang your clothes, madam?"

"No, sir, thank you. I'll do that." She tipped the bellman

and he left. Erica immediately began drawing a hot bath, sprinkling in the special salts provided by the hotel. She undressed and slipped into the soft quilted Brown Palace robe; brown in color, of course, with a gold "BP" monogram. She was in such an indulgent mood she decided to stretch out on the bed for a moment, but not before checking the tub overflow valve. A flooded bathroom and a drenched guest room below would not portend the kind of evening she hoped for. She dozed a little, a renewing ten-minute nap. The steaming water was precisely the right temperature when she submerged up to her neck.

Erica's choice for the evening was a low-cut black dress, a very light satin fabric. She'd worn it only once before—to her first faculty social two years ago. Meanwhile, the war had brought shortages of most everything. Make do and mend, was the patriotic catch-phrase. There had been editorials calling for shorter skirts to save material. Erica was somewhat suspicious of the *real* reason for such a call, (since it came from male newspaper editors), but here and there younger women were complying.

Erica was not displeased. It meant that she, by merely shortening the hemline of the black dress, had a flashy little number that looked brand new; not to mention quite trendy. *And* the style showed off her legs. She believed every woman should play to her assets.

Erica was dabbing perfume behind her ears when Arthur's light tap-tap sounded on the door. Even at his age, he was matinee idol material in his freshly cleaned and pressed uniform.

"Congratulations, Arthur, your uniform still fits you perfectly." Erica gave him a big hug, which turned into a very long embrace. Arthur was left wondering if Erica had deeper feelings for him, than he heretofore had imagined.

"You're wrong about the uniform, my dear," Arthur chuckled, *"now* it fits. In the Battery D days it hung like a sack."

As Arthur and Erica entered the ballroom the band was almost in place. The pianist was already playing Cole Porter, his touch on the ivories light and tasteful, very romantic. It matched Erica's mood perfectly.

They had just ordered cocktails when the bandleader gave the downbeat. The twenty-piece orchestra came to life with "Opus One." They were obviously using Tommy Dorsey charts and the rendition could not have been more authentic if the good man himself had been flashing the baton.

"Oh, Arthur, I can't wait," and Erica pulled him up out of his chair and onto the dance floor. "What fun! I know God loves me when I dance!" Erica squealed with delight and stepped out of his arms to do her very own solo twirls and steps. It must have been impressive because other dancers on the crowded floor slowed their own swing and sway to watch. She sashayed into Arthur's arms again and their feet were light as feathers.

"Gosh, Arthur, what a great band!"

"Didn't I tell you?"

"Opus One" ended, and *bam!* right into "We'll Git It."

Not a single couple left the dance floor. In fact, save for a few quick sips of their cocktails, Arthur and Erica danced for a solid hour. Not until he held her close for "I'll Never Smile Again," did Erica realize how exhausted she was. The USO singer from Chicago was no Jo Stafford; but she was no slouch either.

Miss USO took her bow and Erica fanned herself with her hand. "Whew, Arthur. Take me to the veranda. I need some air."

"Of course." But before they took three steps another Battery D buddy spotted Arthur and the war stories (literally) were underway. "Go ahead, Erica dear, I'll be right out," Arthur smiled.

Erica stepped outside onto the spacious second floor veranda. The Brown Palace had fires going in Navajo kilns here and there, so the chill of the mountain air was reduced to crisp comfort. You could easily get *too* warm if you stood too close to a kiln.

A young brunette standing next to Erica unsnapped her purse and took out a pack of Lucky Strikes. "Would you like one?" she offered.

"Yes, thank you, I would." Erica rarely smoked; but it fit the ambience of the lovely setting in the mountain air. As she put the cigarette between her lips a lighter snapped and flamed in front of her.

"Allow me," said a baritone voice.

She dipped her head to draw on the flame and gave the gentleman a polite, "Thank you." Only then did she look up at him—and into the eyes of the United States Army's Ronald Swanson!

"Lieutenant Swa—I'm sorry, it's now *Major* Swanson, I see. How are you? It's been years."

"Right now, I'm just fine, Erica—because I've been watching you all evening. You're even more beautiful than I remember."

Erica was glad the veranda was dimly lit because she could feel her face beginning to flush, her heartbeat beginning to rush. His words, particularly in such a straightforward manner, gave her a vibrant tingle of excitement and a shortness of breath. She remembered the same feeling six years ago, the night they first met. In her head, "One O'clock Jump" was playing just as it had then. She looked briefly into his dark eyes; he was *flirting* with her, just as he had in 1936—when he peered over her father's shoulder, watching her brazen dance.

The cigarette now seemed to have nervous tremors between her fingers. She seemed unable to look directly at the handsome officer.

Finally, Erica forced herself. She looked up at Major Swanson, drew slowly on her Lucky, and knew why movie stars like to smoke while shooting a scene. It's something to do—'til you remember your lines.

CHAPTER 24

Thirty minutes later—

"I apologize, Erica." Professor Aldredge walked hurriedly onto the Brown Palace veranda, took her hand, and nodded to Major Swanson. "I've been reliving days best forgotten, and lost track of time. I'm happy to see that one of our *finest* has come to your rescue."

"Professor Arthur Aldredge, this is Major Ronald Swanson. He's an old family friend, currently assigned to the War Department in Washington."

"But not for long I trust," said the major as he returned the old lieutenant's salute. "I'm off to the big brouhaha soon they tell me; just waiting for the papers to come through." The handsome young officer took a pack of Chesterfields from his shirt pocket and offered a cigarette to each before taking one himself. "Erica tells me you're her Rock of Gibraltar these days."

"If I were ten years younger," Arthur responded with a hearty laugh, "I'd push for more than that. But I'm a realist. If Gibraltar's the best I can do—I'll take it," the professor smiled.

There was never a day since that Election Night party in 1936 that Erica didn't think of Ronald Swanson. She'd summoned the courage two days later to tell sister Jean of their flirting *and* of her fears that she and the handsome officer hadn't been terribly discreet about it. She held her breath expecting a "Big Sis" scolding.

Instead Jean smiled. "Can't say I'm surprised." Her tone neither condoned nor disapproved. "I thought I noticed a little electricity between you two."

"You're not mad?"

"No, just a little concerned, Erica," and Jean brushed a strand of hair from her little sister's forehead. "He's thirty-five, you know—and he's *in the army, for Pete's sake!* Just because they ascribe the girl-in-every-port thing to sailors, doesn't mean the caissons are not right in lockstep."

"But Lieutenant Swanson seems different, Jean."

"He does? *How?*" Jean's laugh was derisive. "He was about two steps from propositioning you, while escorting another woman; his *fiancé* yet!" Jean was giving Erica her best sibling-as-parent routine.

"Well, I just don't think he's like that." Erica retorted, knowing it sounded lame. "And if he's so bad why is he *your* friend?"

This brought another laugh from Jean. "Good point, kid. I don't think he's bad, Erica, he's just—he's just a man." Jean concluded the sentence with a shrug of resignation.

Lieutenant Ronald Swanson did not call the pretty young coed immediately. It was two weeks later; and it was snowing heavily in Colorado Springs, a virtual blizzard. Erica was helping Mother Heather decorate the house for Christmas. They always started earlier than anyone else in town; unusually early. By Thanksgiving you'd expect Ol' Saint Nick himself to slide down the Harlan chimney at any moment.

Erica picked up the phone on the second ring.

"Long distance calling for Erica Harlan." The operator sounded thousands of miles away and there was constant static on the line.

"This is she."

"Erica? This is Ron—Ron Swanson."

Erica put her hand on her bosom as though that could keep her heart from jumping from her chest.

"Hello, Ron, so nice to hear from you. Where are you?"

"Much farther away than I wish, Erica. I'm at the train

station in Cincinnati." The line went silent for a moment.

"Are you coming west soon?" Erica asked hopefully.

At this, Mother Heather interrupted her mission to secure a cluster of bright red, tin foil jingle bells to an archway. She looked at Erica with raised eyebrows, stepped off the ladder, and quietly left the room.

"No—no, I wish I were," Ron continued." I'm headed for Washington. I'm waiting for my train and just—I just had a sudden urge to call." A surge of static left Erica unsure whether she missed something important, for when she heard Ron's voice again he was in the middle of a sentence.

"…too late if I didn't call now."

"What do you mean, too late, Ron?"

"My train doesn't reach there until three a.m., dear. I wouldn't want to awaken Doctor and Mrs. Harlan."

"Oh." Erica's tone showed her disappointment. "Well, I'm really glad you called."

"I should have called sooner. I could kick myself because I didn't. But I feared your parents might view me as a—as a—"

"As what, Lieutenant?"

"Well, as a cradle-robber. Please understand, I think you're very much an adult. But I know parents might see it differently."

"Well, I don't think that's anything we should worry about. You know, I *do* graduate college, come spring. And besides, Mother and Father consider you an officer and a gentleman—as I do." She said the last three words in a whisper.

"I wish I could touch you right now." Swanson's words, and the way he said them, called into question how *much* of a gentleman he wanted to be at that moment.

"I must confess, uh"—Erica was unsure how to proceed— "I—I do wonder about Miss Hamilton—and you."

"Erica, things are not always as they seem, "Swanson replied, "or more precisely, as people think they are. Uh," (the lieutenant was stumbling a little himself), "some friends thought we were engaged, but—well, Shirley and I aren't really there yet. At least *I* don't think of it in that way."

Erica felt a rush of relief but was still uneasy. "Do you know when you'll be back this way?" She knew the likely answer.

"Sadly, I don't, Erica. This assignment to the War Department has just occurred. I don't really know what's in store."

"Would you write?"

"Uhhh, yes. I hesitate only because I know myself. I'm not very good at letters but I'll really try; because I want to," and just as Swanson finished the sentence another surge of static was so loud and long Erica was afraid she'd lost the connection.

"Are you there? Ron? Lieutentant?"

"Yes, I'm here but I have to go. They just called my train. Goodbye. I—I really want to see you, Erica," and the line went dead.

Mother Heather heard the phone being replaced in the cradle and returned to the living room. "Was that who I think it was?" she queried.

"Well, Mother—that depends on *whom* you think it was."

"That was Lieutenant Swanson, wasn't it?" There was no scolding in Heather's tone or her expression—just a sense of accepting the inevitable.

"How did you know, Mother?"

"Erica, dear," (Heather so enjoyed her role as parent at moments like this), "your father and I"—and she paused for dramatic effect—"we were *not* born yesterday."

Heather and Erica returned to their Christmas decorating.

And Lieutenant Ronald Swanson, United States Army, did write to Erica Harlan. The couple corresponded two or three times a month, for six or seven months. His letters to Erica (and hers to him) were passionate—terribly passionate for people who, in reality, didn't know each other. She spent much time blushing as she read the letters; then made sure they were well hidden. Not that Erica expected her parents to pry, not at her age. But why risk it?

Then, the lieutenant's letters came less and less—there was more time between each letter. And each letter seemed shorter than the one before.

Ronald's last letter came to her in July 1937, a mere note about the hot Washington summer. She responded just as briefly and inconsequentially—and never heard from him again.

...until now—New Year's Eve, 1942—on the veranda of Denver's Brown Palace Hotel. As Erica stood between Arthur and Ronald, looking at first one then the other, she said little. She listened to these men of the world talk—and was lost in her own thoughts. The assorted memories: months of unfulfilled longing and desire for Ron, then years of his total absence from her life; no letters, no phone calls—nothing. Surely it was never to be.

In contrast was her recent companionship with Arthur; burning passion, no, but there was a certain deep affection. The relationship was comfortable, relaxing, rewarding, and fun. In the end Erica hardly knew how she felt, or how to react to the feelings she could divine.

"Look, I've taken enough of your time," and as Major Swanson spoke he stepped aside and extended his arm toward the dance floor. "Go cut a rug, you two."

But just then the band went into a song introduction and the Major recognized it immediately.

"Professor, please don't kill me," Swanson apologized, "but I beg this dance with Erica; it's my favorite. I heard Vaughn Monroe sing this song in Hollywood just three weeks ago."

"Be my guest," said the ever-gallant Arthur, and Major Swanson escorted Erica to the dance floor.

The singer from Chicago leaned close to the microphone. Her pretty face, framed in shiny blonde tresses, was bathed in the bright spotlight. She closed her eyes, and the lyrics of "When The Lights Go On Again All Over The World," filled the room.

With all its hope, it was still such a somber song, Erica thought; and for good reason. How long would Americans have to live behind heavily curtained windows at night, their auto headlights painted black at the top? She knew there was less danger of an aerial attack in the country's interior than on the coast; nevertheless, the thought made her fearful. She snuggled against Ron, and he drew her close.

The lights in the ballroom were now quite dim. The overhead chandeliers had been doused, giving way to dreamy romantic flickers from the tea candles on the many tables.

Ronald now held Erica so tightly she gasped for breath. But she had a growing sensation..that she wanted him *never* to let go.

"Can we get the hell outa here, go somewhere and talk?" the Major whispered.

"I'm sorry, Major, I'm here with Arthur. I just couldn't do that to him."

"Of course you couldn't. Forgive me for asking." The music stopped and Erica waved to Arthur as they walked in his direction.

"But I must see you," Swanson said quietly. "I'm expecting word any day as to when I leave here, and I promise—I'll come to Colorado Springs if at all possible before I head back east. ."

"Haven't I heard something like that before?" Erica's question came out slightly sharp and the officer grimaced.

"Oooh, ya got me there. I've been frightfully self-absorbed, haven't I?"

"No—*I'm* sorry", Erica replied, "I've no right to be bitchy. You have important duties." She shook her head sadly. "This war takes all our attention and the world is so screwy right now."

At this moment Erica would've loved another cigarette with Ronald, but could not be rude to her old friend, the professor. Fortunately, another old army buddy had just encountered Arthur, so she and the major talked on at the edge of the dance floor.

"Are you really off to the battlefield?" Erica could not disguise her concern.

"I hope. I want to see some action, Erica. I'm a soldier—a *career* soldier. That's what I do."

"I know," Erica replied with a sad smile. "It does not give me ease—but I understand."

"We don't have to worry about that tonight." Ronald gave her arm a tender pat. "That's a few weeks away; at least I think so. They'll likely send me to Los Alamos from here."

"New Mexico?" Erica wondered why on earth the War Department would send him there, but didn't ask.

"Uh, forget I said that," Ron whispered, "just—just forget I said that."

Erica assumed she'd just witnessed a small security lapse. "Said what?" she responded in her most nonchalant manner.

"Thank you." Ronald gave Erica a final hug as Arthur approached to take his turn with Erica on the dance floor.

As the Major walked out the door, away from the ballroom, the USO gal began to sing "You'd Be So Nice To Come Home To." The officer stopped to listen, wondering if there was any chance—any chance at all—that someday he'd have the pleasure of cuddling Erica..by the light of a romantic fireplace.

"God, make it so," Swanson prayed, "please, make it so."

Erica woke up abruptly. She didn't stir. Something had awakened her—a noise ever so slight. The room was not entirely dark. The glow from the streetlights outside the Brown Palace meant she could see, but dimly. Scarcely moving, she turned her eyes to survey the room. Nothing. She slowly sat up in bed. A single white envelope lay by the door. She presumed that was the sound she heard, someone slipping the envelope under the door.

She jumped from the bed and grabbed the envelope but immediately climbed back under the covers. Her thin negligee did not mask the chill of the room. She switched on the bedside lamp. The alarm clock said four-forty.

Erica's heart was beating rapidly as she unfolded the single piece of stationery:

This must be fate!

(The scrawl was masculine).

Erica, I couldn't sleep. I asked the hotel operator for your room number. I said there was a family emergency and I was your brother. Sweetheart, my room is across the hall from you; <u>right across the hall, can you believe it</u>? If you want a nightcap at any hour—room #704, just tap.

I love you,
Ron

Without a moment's hesitation Erica slid from the bed. She didn't think of getting a nightgown to cover her negligee, but opened the door and looked up and down the hall. It was deserted.

She tapped on the Major's door and he opened it immediately. The officer wore striped pajama bottoms, no top.

That's when Erica remembered she was wearing *just* a negligee—but she didn't turn back. She jumped into his outstretched arms and covered his face, his shoulders, his hairy chest, with her kisses.

The major lifted Erica off the floor, cradling her in his

arms and carried her effortlessly, as though she were a baby, to his bed. It was the first time in her life that Erica gave herself completely to a man, and their walk on passion's path was not hurried—not at first. Then, accelerating desire became all consuming.

They arrived at the zenith in a cascade of mutual ecstasy. Still in each other's arms, they spoke not a word for thirty minutes; save for the language proclaimed by tender kisses; scores of them.

"Erica," his voice was hoarse in her ear, "this war—God, I pray I'm wrong but there may be so little time. Will you marry me?"

"Of course, I will," she whispered as she stroked his hair. "Do you think I would be *here—in your bed*—had I not already made that decision?"

Their laughter was interrupted by another long kiss. Finally, they relaxed their embrace. Erica kissed him again on the lips, then the nose. She slid from the covers and again checked the hallway in both directions. She returned to her own bed but didn't sleep. She seemed to be lying on clouds. She was floating; she was happy. In some room down the hall, a radio played Artie Shaw's "Begin The Beguine"—and Erica knew her life would never be the same.

Not once in that eventful night—or anytime thereafter—did either ever mention Shirley Hamilton.

Mother Heather's response was precisely what Erica knew it would be. "But, Erica dear, it's so sudden!"

"Mother, I love him and there is so little time!" Tears glistened in Erica's eyes; a beatific smile adorned her face.

Doctor Harlan gently put his hand on Heather's arm, the only reminder she needed to carry this no further.

"You have our blessing, Erica." The doctor's voice trembled

with emotion as the parents simultaneously hugged their youngest daughter.

The radiant couple was married January 10, 1943, in Grace Episcopal Church, on Colorado Springs' Tejon Street. For an event put together so quickly it was magnificent. The only sad thing, Erica thought, was how few young men there were to escort the beautiful young ladies. She wouldn't linger on what she knew to be true: that her own escort would soon be absent from her life, and for how long no one could know.

Hilary Smith was the Maid of Honor, Judith Webster and Susan Carson the bridesmaids. Two young officers from Buckley Field, mere acquaintances of the major, were delighted to play groomsmen for Ron. His best friends were already in Europe. But it was Ron's idea with Erica's enthusiastic agreement, to invite Arthur to be Best Man. The four officers looked resplendent in their uniforms.

Major Swanson was due in Los Alamos the next evening. "Sorry I couldn't take you out of town, love—somewhere exotic! But that'll have to wait. I'm so sorry."

"Sorry?" Erica was incredulous. "Please! A night in the Broadmoor is exotic to me! Of all the times I've been here, I've never been an overnight guest."

"Whew, what a relief!" the major deadpanned. "I take great solace in that statement."

"Watch your mouth!" Erica retorted and gave his face a light playful slap.

They slept quite late in the morning—because they slept so little during the night.

The happy couple was having a late breakfast in the dining room when Western Union delivered the telegram. The major opened it slowly and bit his lip as he read. Wordlessly, he put the yellow paper in front of Erica.

Erica's eyes began to tear but through the haze she saw all she needed to see:

"DEPART FOR ASSIGNMENT IMMEDIATELY STOP
EUROPEAN THEATRE STOP
INITIAL FLIGHT DEPARTS BUCKLY 2300 HRS THIS DATE STOP"

Ron touched Erica's hand and walked to the telephone in the foyer. Making certain his groomsmen were still in town to provide transportation, he returned to the table and summoned the waiter.

"Send two bottles of your finest champagne to our room," he said, "and no calls unless it's a genuine emergency. We'll order some food later this evening." But they never did.

The door to their suite did not open again until eight-thirty p.m. That was as late as Ron dared stay. He had dressed quietly and quickly in the dark. The major then leaned over and kissed his new bride lightly on the lips. A tear—his tear—fell on her cheek. But she didn't stir.

While Erica slept, Major Ronald T. Swanson, United States Army, walked out the door and closed it silently behind him.

CHAPTER 25

Two years later—
Saturday, February 10, 1945—
10:13 a.m.—

It was not imagined. It was real.

As Erica poured herself a cup of coffee from Mother Heather's percolator, a disturbing sense of foreboding came over her; so much so she left the coffee in the china cup untouched, and walked tentatively into the living room. She shivered and pulled the lapels of her suit jacket together to ward off the chill. However, the chill came not from the room—but from inside her.

Seconds later, through the lace window curtains, Erica saw the car come into view and ease to a stop at the curb. It was an olive drab Ford sedan with a single white star emblazoned on the front door.

Two uniformed men got out of the car and started up the sidewalk. Sunshine bounced off a glimmering insignia on the older officer's pocket lapel. The insignia was a small gold cross. Erica knew what it meant. She bit her lip and steadied herself against the door jam, then opened the door before the knock came. But she maintained composure no longer.

Erica collapsed to her knees, sobbing. She wrapped her arms around the chaplain's legs and buried her face in his coat. The chaplain, eyes glistening, bowed his head in silent prayer and gently stroked Erica's thick red hair. Her shoulders shook as she cried and she tried unsuccessfully to muffle the moans. No one said a word and the younger officer stood immobile still holding the unopened telegram. He hated telegrams. There was no need to open this one. They all already knew what it said.

The wedding of Erica Elaine Harlan and Major Ronald T. Swanson had occurred twenty-five months ago this very day. As to how long Erica had been a widow she couldn't know. For that—she'd have to open the telegram.

CHAPTER 26

Antonito, Colorado—
Another story—
Back in time—
September, 1928—

*D*ora had come north from El Paso, to care for an aunt who lived alone and was in ill health. There was nothing to keep her in her native Texas. Her parents had died; and the man she had planned to marry was killed in a train accident. He was a fireman on the Santa Fe.

She was not wealthy, but better off than most single ladies. As the only child, she had inherited a comfortable bungalow from her parents. But at the time she was disconsolate from the losses in her life. Her means were not substantial enough to afford higher education; not that such would necessarily increase a woman's security anyway.

"My dearest cousin, Dora," the letter had begun. "I am so reluctant to write—but am at wit's end." The writer was Cousin Emma Whitley of Tucumcari, New Mexico. Dora Webb had met her only twice, but each had felt that instant bond that occurs when personalities are similar, <u>and</u> you know you're related. Over time they corresponded at least a couple of times a year.

Emma wrote that her mother, who lived in Antonito, was quite ill—congestive heart failure most likely—and alone. Tomlinson Whitley, Emma's husband, was the owner of Tucumcari's largest mercantile store and was financially quite capable of bringing her mother to live with them. However, all who knew the circumstances, thought it extremely doubtful the ill mother would survive the trip.

"I would gladly go stay with Mama in Antonito," Emma wrote," but as you know, my duties here do not allow it."

Dora did know. Tomlinson and Emma were the parents of seven children, ages one to thirteen.

"So, dearest Dora," the letter continued, "would you possibly consider spending some time with Mama in Antonito. If you're not comfortable with the prospect, I'll understand—but I remember your last letter; as to how lonely you are in El Paso, and thought you might entertain a change. Antonito is a beautiful little town, where you could garden to your heart's content. If you decide in the affirmative, come to Tucumcari as quickly as possible. We'll cover all expenses, and get you on to Antonito in short order."

Dora made her decision in less than twenty-four hours. She closed up the house, took the key to her banker, and boarded the Santa Fe for Tucumcari.

"Give Mama my love," said a weeping Emma. She hugged Dora tightly. "And I can't thank you enough."

"I'm so pleased to be of help," Dora responded.

"I hope the trip doesn't wear you too much—but it is _so_ beautiful, Dora. I'll never forget that train ride with Tomlinson, when we first married."

Dora was leaving with Tomlinson Whitley in the store's big mercantile truck. He and some business partners ran cattle near Chama, in the northern mountains of New Mexico, and he regularly took supplies. Since he could purchase such supplies wholesale it was good business all around, the trip notwithstanding.

At Chama, Dora would board the Cumbres & Toltec Railroad, the highest and longest narrow gauge railway in the country. Emma's enthusiastic description of the natural wonders to behold was not at all overdone. The spectacular and unspoiled vistas of the Chama Valley itself were breathtaking. From there the train steamed through Cumbres Pass and Los Pinos Valley; then, up over the continental divide of the South San Juan Mountains, and past the awe-inspiring Toltec Gorge. By the time the iron horse arrived in Antonito, Dora was ready to believe she had found her own little piece of heaven on earth.

She felt especially blessed to be of assistance to her aunt, in the last six months of her life. The woman died in the month of March, 1929. Emma and Tomlinson came from Tucumcari for the funeral. Friends had agreed to take turns looking after their children, while the couple was briefly away.

Kind businessman that he was, Tomlinson got right to the point. "Dora, you've been of immeasurable help and comfort to Emma and me at this time. If you like it here, you may stay. <u>And if that is your decision, fifty percent of this, my mother-in-law's house</u>—is yours at this moment. You can pay for the other half, over time, on terms comfortable for you."

Dora did not hesitate a second. "I'll write my banker tomorrow," she said. "He'll obtain a fair price for my house in El Paso—and you'll have your money shortly."

Emma had been prophetic in surmising how very much Dora would love this high plateau town in southern Colorado. She had never seen a more beautiful and bountiful garden, than the one Dora had grown in Antonito.

The banker in El Paso got more than a fair price for Dora's house. She paid for the other fifty percent of her aunt's Antonito home and had a nice nest egg left over.

The banker's advice for the residue, though well-meaning, did not turn out so well.

"Dear Miss Webb," he wrote. "Let's put it in the market. It's rip-roaring right now. And I'd suggest buying on the margin; more *bang for your buck!" The letter was dated September 20, 1929.*

Though Dora did not see it, (no one in Antonito saw it), the headline of October 30, in the <u>New York Times</u>, told the story:

"STOCKS COLLAPSE IN 16,410,030-SHARE DAY..."

By the spring of 1930, Dora Webb had tried in vain to resolve her financial problems. She sold her newly acquired Antonito house to pay as much of her margin debt as possible. In a matter of weeks she had gone from idyllic bliss—secure, comfortable, and confident—to crushing despondency.

She moved in with a nearby ranch family to cook, clean, and help take care of four children. Her wages consisted of room and board.

In her correspondence with Cousin Emma she never once mentioned her change of address—or her plight. The Antonito postmaster kindly forwarded her mail to the ranch house where she now worked—and lived.

CHAPTER 27

The day after the election—
Wednesday, November 3, 1948—

He loved to visit the Colorado ranch he had just left, and loved even more his visits to the Cimmaron Hotel in Liberal. But today he headed home with barely enough time to make it in daylight, which didn't help his already nervous stomach.

He was especially relieved to set the bird down this evening. He'd miscalculated again and the gas meter stood on empty. On such an occasion he was happy for the expanse of land behind the house, level enough and the grass short enough, to set the L-2A down gracefully.

She barely looked up and didn't smile at all when he walked into the house.

How does she know? he wondered. *She always knows.*

She'd never met Lois, had never seen Lois. She didn't even know the woman's name was Lois. But she *did* know Lois existed.

"Well, Truman showed 'em all, didn't he?" He tried to sound casual as well as pleased. "He was supposed to be gone—history."

Her response was a barely audible grunt as she flipped the pages of a magazine.

"Is there anything to eat?" he asked as he turned toward the Frigidaire. "It's been awhile for me. I'm hungry."

"I've already eaten and I'm tired. I'm going to bed." Those were the first and only words she spoke. She got up from the kitchen table and left the room.

He opened the icebox door but was no longer hungry. Instead he hurried to the small bathroom, the one he'd built just off the kitchen. He closed the door and turned the bathtub faucets open wide. He hoped the running water was loud enough to cover the sound of his vomiting into the commode.

CHAPTER 28

Friday, November 19, 1948—

"Why the hell didn't ya call these people while ya's in Kansas City?" TJ was never good at masking irritation. He looked at the three names Jed had memorized from John Little Deer's appointment book; all three from October fourteenth, the day Claude Stickett was murdered.

"Well," Jed sighed, "it's a long story, TJ."

"Seems like everything's a long story since ya got back from the big city." Disgust permeated TJ's gravelly growl. "'Cept ya never *tell* the story, long or short." There was a sound from TJ approximating the snort of a horse.

Jed was quite aware he'd been less than productive in the two weeks he'd been back from Kansas City. His concentration was shot. *Erica, Erica*—she was all he thought about.

"At least ya shoulda made these calls first thing when ya got back," TJ glared. "Didn't anyone ever tell you 'bout a cold trail?"

Jed stared out the window, no ready defense coming to mind.

"Who is she?" TJ's growl was barely audible.

"What?" Jed was startled by TJ's grasp of human nature.

"Ya didn't knock her up, didja?" TJ's question had a sarcastic lilt.

"No, of *course* not!" Jed whirled from the window, angry as hell at the question; but he heard his mother's voice: *"It never ceases to amaze! You young people are so surprised at how much we old folks know."*

"Well, it happens, ya know"—TJ would not quit—"and

don't get yer panties in a wad. Makes me suspicious."

"I know, but"—

"Most natural thing in the world, Jed." The old prosecutor warmed to his task, moving in for the kill.

"TJ, *I didn't knock anybody up!*" Jed wanted to punch his boss in the mouth. He sighed and walked to his desk. "Hell, TJ," (Jed relaxed a little and chuckled) "she won't even let me see her. Just how could I knock her up?"

"Ahhh, at last the truth." TJ had achieved a measure of victory. "There is a woman!"

Jed said nothing and doodled on a yellow legal pad. He was capable of two doodles: a Santa Fe FT engine (which he occasionally made into an E1 by sloping the nose angle), or a freight train caboose. He couldn't draw anything else worth a damn.

"You sonuvabitch!" TJ laughed, "yer just not gonna talk 'bout this, are ya?"

"There's nothin' to talk about, TJ," and Jed sounded as sad as he looked. "She won't see me. Hell, she even told me not to write."

Now it was TJ Johnson's turn to sigh. "I knew it was a woman; can't fool me. They beat all, Jed. Ya leave 'em alone—they hate ya. Ya love 'em—they *still* hate ya—least they act like they do. I'll never understand 'em,"—TJ paused for a full ten seconds—"'specially my own dear Mrs. Johnson."

TJ shifted his bulky frame in the creaky swivel chair. "Tell ya what—you head on over to El Portel and have yerself a drink. Yer no damn good here anyhow. I think I know how to work this out. I'll be over in an hour and fill ya in."

Jed was down the first flight of stairs when TJ bellowed, "Two drinks; no more than two drinks. Don't want no assistant D. A. of mine to be drunk in public." Jed smiled, wondering if the rule also applied to the head D.A.

Jed ordered his Beefeater on the rocks and was grateful the

bartender seemed in no mood to talk.

Jed *had* managed a slight amount of work on the case since his return. As he suspected Sheriff Emwiler hadn't yet submitted the hunting knife, found in Claude Stickett's chest, for fingerprint analysis.

"Sendin' it to Albuquerque this afternoon," the old sheriff told Jed, "yessir—this afternoon." Sheriff Emwiler repeated himself a lot.

Jed had gone to the sheriff's office immediately after disembarking from the Santa Fe *Chief* days ago. The FBI's incomplete results arrived in Raton two weeks later—just yesterday—and it left Jed no closer to a solution. The knife had a print—in fact three prints, but very faint. They were quite smudged and the FBI sent a communique saying they needed more time. They hoped a search of more files (perhaps those which local authorities hadn't yet forwarded to the FBI) would reveal a match. They believed the smudges to be prints of a thumb and the first two fingers of a left hand. Sadly, they said John Little Deer's business card had no discernible prints at all. Jed concluded Deerman touched only the edges when he handed it to him.

TJ arrived at El Portel ninety minutes after Jed. He took a sip of his Elijah Craig, neat. It was said that El Portel took care that a case was shipped special from Kentucky every couple of months; as a precaution that no one (TJ in particular) would mess with their liquor license.

"OK, here's the deal." TJ paused for a second sip. "D'ya know Emily Larson?"

"You mean Dr. Caldwell's nurse? Real pretty!"

"Yeah, her husband works for the FBI."

"Right, I went to school with her. But how's she gonna help"?

"She used to be a radio actress," TJ explained, "and was on a coupla 'soaps' outa Chicago. I fergit which ones."

"She was? I didn't know that."

"Jed, there's a lotta things you don't know, 'cause ya always got yer head up yer butt." TJ took another sip and continued. "Anyway, Emily is real good with voices. I assume John Little Deer has a secretary?"

"Yeah, the receptionist," Jed replied. "Blondie."

"Blondie?" TJ repeated the name with a sarcastic laugh and leering grin. "Lawdy, is that the little lady who's turned you into a no-good piece o' shit?"

"Hell, no!" Jed flashed—but that never worked with TJ. He smiled sheepishly—"Maybe under different circumstances, TJ; but no, not Blondie."

"Well, anyhow," the D.A. continued, "you go see Emily at Doc's office; ten o'clock tomorrow morning. Describe Blondie's voice—in fact have Emily call Little Deer's office in Kansas City so she can hear this gal. I'll bet a dollar to a donut li'l Emily can sound just like her."

"Then what?" Jed was warming to the project.

"Well," TJ explained, "Emily will call these three names ya brought back, give 'em some bullshit 'bout needin' to verify their appointment for billing purposes, and we just might learn if the Navajo was really *in* Kansas City..or outa town that day."

"Won't they know it's long distance?"

"Naw," TJ smiled, "Emily's hubby—I talked to him a few minutes ago—he'll arrange a patch through the FBI in Albuquerque. They can call direct—I dunno, leased lines or somethin'; it's like the radio networks use. They have 'em between major cities."

"And it sounds like it's local?"

"You bet, Jed. Emily's helped me a coupla times before. She's good!"

"What do we tell Doc Caldwell?"

"Nothin'." TJ said with a mysterious smile. "The Doc owes me big time."

Jed knew from TJ's countenance not to press the issue.

Emily Larson was even prettier than Jed remembered. Short, black hair; she looked a little like Susan Hayward. Deep brown eyes with little specks of gold, and her whole perky manner suggested someone who loved life and always made the best of it.

"Doc's ten o'clock cancelled," Emily explained, "so he went to Jody's. We should have an uninterrupted hour, at least."

"Well, just *what* do you think I'm *here* for?" Jed teased.

"Men!" Emily retorted as she feigned disgust. "You're all alike. Guess *you* haven't changed since high school." Her starched white uniform strained at all the appropriate points and Jed hoped his attraction to her didn't make him embarrass himself.

"How come you only did radio?" Jed asked. "You should be in the movies!"

Emily responded with a grateful grin and a glance that suggested she'd heard such lines before. "Now you're tryin' to sweet-talk me. Well, I went to Hollywood about ten years ago; even got a couple of walk-ons in a Henry Fonda western. But then I met Joe Larson—and here I am."

"Oh, come on! You could easily shed yourself of that ol' J. Edgar Hoover gumshoe." Jed was surprised at how much he was enjoying the harmless flirtation—a needed release, apparently. He'd had no appetite for such since his return from Kansas City.

"Naw," Emily shrugged. A look of true affection crossed her pretty face. "Joe's good to me and, well—I love him. Does that sound too old-fashioned?"

"Heck no," Jed said softly, "sounds perfect to me."

"But," Emily continued, (and here was the sense of humor Jed remembered from high school), "if I could actually trade him in for John Wayne"—and they laughed uproariously at the fantasy.

"Let's get busy," Emily said, turning serious, "TJ called to fill me in. What's this Blondie sound like?"

"Well, I've been thinking," Jed spoke slowly, trying to find the right words, "uh—the best I can come up with: it's a thin little voice like Gracie Allen but very soft, very breathy. However, she's not dumb; not like that ditzy character Gracie plays, not at all. Give her a call! If she's in today you can hear for yourself."

"Good idea." Emily looked at the number Jed had copied from John Deerman's business card and gave it to the operator. Jed leaned close to the receiver making sure it was Blondie who answered. It was.

Emily, speaking in her own voice, asked Blondie for information from the non-existent file of "John Q. Cedric." She listened intently as Blondie came back on the line to say no such person was a client.

"Is this the firm of Swifton, Kix, & Long?" Emily inquired.

"No, ma'm," breathed Blondie, "this is Stedman, Swift, & Jones."

"Oh, I'm so sorry," Emily fibbed, "I have the wrong firm," and she hung up.

"Mmm, a sexy Gracie—how's this?" Emily flipped open a *LOOK* magazine and read the first line of an Ivory soap ad.

"Close," Jed was gleeful. "But a little more breathy—and she doesn't talk that fast. Also, you'd better say you're Penelope Herron, of Stedman, Swift, and Jones. She'd likely use that instead of Blondie on a business call."

A little more rehearsal and, "That's it!" Jed exclaimed. He was astounded. Emily sounded just like Blondie.

"OK, so I'm giving these clients a line, uh, as to verifying their appointment the week of October eleventh, right?" Emily continued to talk like Blondie.

"Yeah, unless you think of something better," Jed replied. "Shall we write a script?"

"Naw, I'm better ad lib. The 'billing line' should work—

it's only mid-November."

There were two men and one woman on the list.

"Try the woman first," Jed instructed, "that's probably a divorce case—and she's probably home."

In a moment Emily had the FBI in Albuquerque on the line. "This is operative 74J3," she said, and after a brief pause continued, "290-23-1114."

Jed assumed they'd asked for her Social Security number to verify identification.

"Check for the residence phone of June Colson, in Kansas City, Missouri," Emily instructed, "and if you find it patch me through."

Seconds later Emily nodded with excitement. "It's ringing," she whispered, and holding the phone away from her ear slightly, she motioned Jed to lean in close and listen.

"Hello?" said a sophisticated feminine voice in Kansas City.

"Mrs. Colson, this is Penelope Herron at Stedman, Swift & Jones," and "faux-Blondie" was off and running.

"I wondered when I'd receive a bill," the woman responded, "just a moment. I'll check my calendar." Twenty seconds later— "Yes, here it is. I was there from two to three in the afternoon on, uh, on October fourteenth. That was a Thursday I believe."

"Thank you, ma'm, that's all I need," and Emily hung up the phone. "Isn't that the day Stickett was murdered?"

"Yeah," Jed replied quietly. "Do you think Deerman's coaching all these people?"

"Hell, Jed"—Emily bit her lip, realizing nice ladies in Raton didn't talk that way in front of men they weren't close to—"heck, I mean," she laughed, *"you're* more a gumshoe than Joe. Let's try the two guys."

The first man was a dead end—a Kansas City physician.

"I can't give out personal information over the phone," the doctor's austere receptionist said. "I'll have Doctor call Mister Deerman if you like."

"No, no"—Emily was quick on her feet—"here it is. I just found the time slip." She slammed down the receiver. "Close!" she giggled.

But number three was another confirmation for Little Deer's side. He was a down-to-earth manager of a wholesale plumbing house. "What's the matter with that Injun, he gettin' senile? Hell, he came to the house for poker that night. I took a-hundred-and-fifty bucks off 'im. Look's like he'd remember that! Gertie," the plumber was yelling at his secretary, "when did I go see the Navajo? Yeah, the lawyer," and there was another pause. "Gertie says it was the fourteenth of October, four p.m."

"Thank you, sir, that agrees with our records," breathed Emily.

"Tell that Navajo we're playin' poker again tonight," the plumber teased. "Sure like to have some more of his money." Click.

Well!" Jed straightened up from listening to Emily's telephone and walked to the window of the small office. "Where do I go from here? TJ's not likely to go up against a double alibi; especially a double alibi involving a fellow member of the bar."

He turned to Emily, "Thank you, dear, you were *great!*"

"Thank you, Jed." Emily gave him a shy smile.

"And it's always great to see you, Emily; *especially,* to see you!" Jed bent and kissed her hand. He seldom did such a thing but it was something else he'd seen in the movies.

Jed had reached the door when Emily called after him.

"Jed?"

He turned with his hand on the doorknob.

"You're *still* a big flirt!" Emily scolded, flirting a little herself.

"Yeah—yeah, I know." Jed smiled in resignation and closed the door behind him.

He walked down the three flights of stairs disappointed that no lead had panned out. But something else was making him sad. He couldn't quite put his finger on it. He'd heard

Blondie's voice—and Emily sounded exactly like Blondie. But that wasn't it. Then it dawned!

As Jed had leaned close to hear the phone, something stirred inside; something registered deep in his soul. Her fragrance—Emily wore the same perfume as Erica.

CHAPTER 29

Wednesday, December 15, 1948—

Christmas approached and Jed Easton dreaded it as never before. It had always been his favorite holiday—but that was before the winds of Raton revealed a certain work of living art. Erica Elaine Harlan Swanson, and that first vision of her, was never far from his mind. Jed asked himself the same questions over and over: how could a woman he scarcely knew, and hadn't seen since, consume and control his life? Why did a momentary glimpse (which seemingly occurred by pure accident) suck all the oxygen from his universe? There were times when the memory and the emotions it brought were so strong, he would bolt from his chair and walk outside. He had to. He needed fresh air. He couldn't breathe. Was he going crazy? He feared those around him thought it a certainty.

There were moments—a few moments—when he *wouldn't* think of her. But then something out of the blue would bring the memory flooding back. This evening it was the radio.

He drove slowly through the brisk snow flurries, headed home. He was listening to KOA in Denver, an NBC station. Morgan Beatty was reporting the news from Washington and buried in the newscast was the reminder:

> "The Electoral College convened in each of the forty-eight states today. President Truman and Senator Barkley were officially elected with 304 electoral votes."

The trip to Kansas City, Blondie, Ol' Harry, and Erica—especially Erica—it all came roaring back: those brief seconds on the loading platform of Raton's Santa Fe depot; he could see her standing there in the wind, her dress tail everywhere. Then, that first shy smile on her blushing face, their romantic dinner together, the intimate goodnight kiss; it cut to the quick to think he might never see her again.

He wanted so much to write her a letter but she'd begged him not to. Jed's parents raised him to be a gentleman, to respect a lady's wish.

But what the hell! The idea came suddenly and Jed executed a u-turn in front of Rexall Drug. His spirits were a little higher as he entered the drugstore and waved to young Ben Elliston behind the soda fountain. Jed had an urge for a chocolate soda.

"They ever tell you how to fix my special ice cream soda, Ben?" Jed could tell from the puzzled look on Ben's face they hadn't. Come to think of it, Ben might be too young to remember Jed Easton in his high school hey-day. "It's simple," Jed continued as he walked to the card rack, "just a regular chocolate soda, but add two tablespoons of vanilla extract. I'll drink it in a minute."

It was Christmas after all—and there's no law against sending a Christmas card. That's not the same as writing a letter.

He chose one with a Norman Rockwell painting: a man and woman in a horse-drawn sleigh slicing through pure white snow toward a gleaming and decorated country church; one with an extremely tall and slender steeple. There was no verse inside, just a place to write one. Jed took out his Sheaffer pen and was as direct as he dared:

> *"I think of you every day—*
> *heck, I think of you every minute.*
> *Merry Christmas.*
> *Jed Easton—"*

He bought a three-cent stamp and addressed the envelope:
>Professor Erica Swanson
>c/o Colorado College
>Colorado Springs, Colorado

He returned to the counter and downed his chocolate ice cream soda with vanilla extract. It was just as good as he remembered. Jed dropped the envelope in a street corner mailbox as he left the drugstore.

He drove home through the light snowfall; he even hummed along with "Silent Night" on the radio. At supper, Jed's mother thought his mood lighter than she'd noticed in weeks.

CHAPTER 30

Back in Antonito, Colorado—
The early 1930s—

"I insist you go to the dance, Dora. You need some fun in your life." The rancher's wife was persistent. "My husband has a cold. He's not up to takin' me, so I'll gladly stay with the kids. To be honest, I need the practice. You do such a wonderful job with them, I'm beginning to feel useless."

"But, ma'm—I'd feel awful funny going to a dance alone," Dora protested.

A sly smile crossed the face of the rancher's wife. "Trust me. I don't think that will be a problem. Just go to your room and freshen up."

"But"—Dora was shamefully getting to the real reason for her hesitation—"I..I have nothing fit to wear to a dance, ma'm."

"Now, you never mind. You look about my size to me—just go get your bath."

Just before Dora stepped into the galvanized tub of steaming hot water, there was a light tap on the door. She opened it a crack, and the rancher's wife handed her a wispy little rose-colored frock.

"I think this will be just perfect, Dora. And in case you're wondering, no one in this town has ever seen it."

And it <u>was</u> perfect. Dora Webb was not a stunning beauty, but the emotional lift of an unexpected night out, along with a brand new dress—it made her quite attractive; even radiant.

She walked into the kitchen, which doubled as a living room, and the under-the-weather rancher started applauding. Dora was embarrassed but flattered. The rancher's wife joined in the applause, as did a third person—a young cowboy Dora knew only as Johnny. He was much younger than Dora; she guessed him about nineteen.

"You look lovely, ma'm." Johnny stood up as he spoke. "The boss here has kindly offered me his truck to drive in to the dance—and if you'd oblige, I'd be most happy to be your escort."

Dora was pleasantly stunned.

But before she could speak, the cowboy continued. "You don't need to worry 'bout nothin'. My drivin' is good—I don't drink. I've tried," he laughed, "just can't stand the taste of the stuff."

"Thank you, Johnny," Dora smiled. "I'd love to go with you."

Dora could not remember the last time she felt so light-hearted. She and Johnny danced to every other tune; when they weren't dancing they sipped colas and chatted about everything, anything, and nothing.

"Ma'm"—Johnny cleared his throat and continued—"I wouldn't want to hog you from all these good-lookin' cowboys"—

"Oh, Johnny," Dora teased, "you don't have to apologize. I see all these pretty young girls lookin' at you. Go dance. I so enjoy just sitting here and watching."

"No—I'm serious, ma'm," Johnny replied. "The tall silver-haired man—in the black hat, directly across the dance floor. He's been eyein' you all night."

"I hadn't noticed," Dora smiled—knowing her smile belied her claim.

No sooner had Johnny started two-stepping with the prettiest young blonde in the hall, than the silver-haired cowboy in the black hat approached.

"Ma'm, my name is Charlie Starles," he said, "and I'd be forever grateful, if you'd tell me yours."

"I'm Dora," she smiled. "Dora Webb."

Charlie Starles was in his fifties. He worked on a neighboring ranch.

"Is your name Charles?" Dora had asked that first night.

"No," he laughed. "My momma thought 'Charles Starles' sounded awful; so she just named me Charlie."

Charlie had been a cowhand all his life. He grew up in New Mexico and the only other states he'd ever been to, were Texas and Colorado.

"I been saving what little money I could for a long time," Charlie told Dora. "Got my eye on a little place down where I grew up."

Dora wondered from time to time if Charlie had any thought of her in his future; but Charlie was not one to talk too much.

"Lotta people havin' tough times these days," he said, "but I been real lucky. I'm not afeared of hard work—and I always manage to find some."

They became a regular couple at the Saturday night dances, as Dora's employers, in appreciation for her services, started giving her that night off. If they also wanted to go dancing, they arranged for family or friends to watch the children—or took them along.

It was in the spring of '32 that Charlie announced, "Gonna be gone a few days Miss Dora. But don't you worry, I'll be back soon."

However, Dora did worry. She was not far enough removed from bad breaks in her life to do otherwise. She feared she'd never see Charlie again.

She was wrong. He showed up five weeks later at six p.m., a Saturday evening. "Hope nobody's beat me to askin' you to the dance tonight, Miss Dora."

"No, Charlie," she smiled, "no one else has asked."

"Well, if you'll pour me a cup of that coffee on the stove—I'll set right here and wait while you get ready."

That was the night Charlie gave Dora a ring. "It belonged to my dear late mother," he said. The ring was quite simple; a tiny emerald on a narrow gold band. "Hadn't told ya yet," Charlie went on, "but my bein' away—well, I been fixin' up my little place down south. It's all paid for now." He paused. "I..I guess this is where I'm supposed to get down on one knee—but ain't much room here in my old Model T."

Dora Webb began to weep.

"I'd be so proud," Charlie went on, "if—if you'd marry me, Miss Dora."

She was too emotional to find her voice, but nodded vigorously and smiled at Charlie through her tears. She placed the ring on the fourth finger of her left hand and threw her arms around his neck. She kissed him as she'd kissed no man before.

They were married a few days later in a seven-minute ceremony by the Methodist preacher. They left Antonito in the Model T pickup and Dora had never been happier. She had no token to give Charlie; nothing comparable to his mother's ring. Then, she remembered the gold coin she had carried for years in her purse; a gift from her father on her eighteenth birthday. She gave it to her new husband that night.

They were quite weary from the trip and glad to arrive at Charlie's little place. Dora was pleased and serene. The sunset was exquisite; extremely picturesque in this spot.

Dora Webb Sarles was quite certain she could make a good home for Charlie—here at their little clapboard house, a half-mile due north of the Santa Fe Railroad, near Dalies, New Mexico.

CHAPTER 31

Monday, December 27, 1948—

Jed Easton began this day at the office the same as all recent days at the office: his Tony Lamas propped up on the desk, as he stared out the window.

Christmas dinner had been pleasant enough. His mother had invited TJ and Mrs. TJ along with Professor Ramon Sanchez to the holiday meal. The conversation was lively, animated, and as always with this group, a mixture of wisdom and festive tomfoolery. Mrs. Easton's preparation of the turkey and dressing, and the traditional ham was (as always), first-class.

But there'd been no word from Erica. Jed had hoped for just a card; just an acknowledgment of his card to her. He anxiously went through the mail each morning at the D.A.'s office, even this morning. After all, with holiday volume Christmas mail often came late. But there was nothing—nothing from Erica. As much as he resisted, there was growing conviction he'd never see her again.

"I've got a very unpleasant task this morning, Jed." TJ made the somber announcement as soon as he walked in. "I promised myself I'd wait till after Christmas; and it's after Christmas."

"What are you talkin' about, TJ? Ya gonna fire me?"

"Hell, no," TJ laughed. "The widow Stickett—I gotta talk to her. Sheriff Emwiler will never get around to it."

"So, you really think she stuck the knife in ol' Claude, doncha?"

"I don't know who else. To be honest, I hope I learn

nothin'—least nothin' concrete. No Raton jury would ever convict her anyway. Dear Lord, Claude Stickett; he was one mean sonuvabitch!"

Without another word TJ left to perform the dreaded task. Jed, determined to extricate himself from the "Erica Blues," tried to do some work. His next day in court was still a week away but he thumbed through the thin particulars anyway: two drunken driving prosecutions, one public drunkenness case, and a liquor store hold-up. A cop, just off duty, stopped in the package store to pick up a pint, and he nabbed the kid before he left the cash register. All the cases looked simple enough so Jed placed the files back in his desk.

TJ had left behind the *Raton Range*, so Jed absentmindedly scanned the pages.

On page four, El Portel was advertising a big New Year's Eve bash, come Friday. *A date! That's what I need! Who could I invite?*

Since returning from law school Jed had squired a few of Raton's prettiest young ladies around town; and they were pretty. Had they not been, Jed would not have dated them. But most were looking for a husband (the sooner the better), and that was a road Jed wasn't ready to travel. He ticked them off in his mind: Julie Stone, now married; Beverly Hinson, married; Juanita Martinez, engaged; Georgette Smith—well, Jed caught her smooching another guy at a party; a party Jed had taken her to. Jed surmised that Jed Easton would not share a future with Georgette. And they were the cream of Raton's crop.

Just thinking about drumming up a date made Jed depressed. *I wonder if ol' FBI gumshoe Joe Larson is out of town New Year's Eve?* Jed scolded himself for entertaining such a ridiculous and lascivious thought. He felt the pang of conscience and made the sign of the cross. That reminded him he hadn't gone to confession in weeks. Jed's mother broached the subject often and he intended to go, but something always came up.

"Confessional visits should be regular, Jed." Mrs. Easton spoke firmly on such matters and Jed wondered how she knew he went so seldom. *He* knew he shirked but he sure didn't discuss it with his mother.

"I promise to do better, Mother." Jed knew now was time to make good on that promise. He'd go right after work.

His mind drifted back where it shouldn't. Even if Joe Larson were out of town Emily would never run around on him. It was such a stupid thought. She wasn't that kind of lady. *And* Jed would never ask. Raton was too small a town for such carrying on among respectable people.

Only forty minutes had passed when TJ came back to the office. "I guess we can close the Stickett file," he announced.

"Did she confess?" Jed jumped from his chair.

"No. She's dead!"

"What?"

"Neighbor lady found her 'bout an hour ago—in bed— no sign of foul play. Nothin' missin' that I can tell. Coroner got there same time I did. Sez most likely, a heart attack."

"Will they do an autopsy?" Jed asked.

"Pro'bly not," TJ sighed, "doesn't seem to be a reason for it."

"What a pitiful old lady," Jed said, mostly to himself.

"Yeah," TJ responded. "Would've liked to heard her story. Then again—maybe I don't wanna know."

Mrs. Stickett did have a story to tell; a story she very much <u>wanted</u> to tell. However, she faced a tremendous problem. She had no knowledge of legal niceties—but she knew enough to know she now was in jeopardy.

She knew she was innocent. But she also knew that her story, true though it was, could only serve to make her <u>more</u> of a suspect; to give her even greater motive.

This was the quandary she had faced for days; including the night she went to bed, went to sleep—and did not wake up.

Jed attended the Friday morning funeral service. He didn't know why, really; he scarcely knew the woman. It just seemed the right thing to do. And he was glad he went.

The Sticketts were not church people, to say the least, but the Baptist preacher agreed to do a service. There were only seven people in attendance counting Jed and the minister. And it reminded him he still hadn't gone to confession.

He walked the six blocks from the small Baptist church to St. Patrick's and spent several minutes with Father Kennedy. Jed even confessed his lust (however temporary) for another man's wife. He was glad there was no requirement to tell the priest her name; for as he left the sanctuary Emily Larson was kneeling in prayer at the back pew waiting her turn in the confessional. Jed couldn't help but wonder if their sins were similar.

He decided to take the rest of the day off. It was New Year's Eve—and he still didn't have a date.

CHAPTER 32

Monday, January 3, 1949—

The tall brown-skinned man stood at the window of the small ranch house near Holly, Colorado. It was a lonely house and he usually enjoyed the solitude. But today there was no joy anywhere in the world he surveyed.

The weather didn't help at all. The snowstorm sweeping down from The Rockies was setting in with full force. The snowflakes were like tiny beads of ice, blowing horizontal across Prowers County, northwest to southeast, driven by a steady fifty-mile-per-hour wind.

The storm was just beginning, but even at this point he could scarcely see the silver Taylorcraft fifty yards away. The old ramshackle barn had long ago been gutted so its roof could serve as some protection for the plane. The protection was a necessity, for with no shelter at all the snow and ice from these high plains blizzards could cling to the wings for days.

He'd invited her to come with him.

"You know I don't like to fly," was her quick reply.

He knew that was true. But he also knew she suspected his invitation was a mere gesture. She suspected he *really* wanted to see Lois, even though she didn't know Lois. And her suspicions were correct.

He flew first to Liberal to see the waitress at the Blue Goose. She leaned across the counter and looked longingly into his eyes.

"Honey, I'd like nothing more than to fly to that little love-nest you call a ranch, and lie in your arms for a week." The blue of Lois's eyes was a strikingly brilliant blue. The lust her eyes revealed was even more striking. "But you ever heard of Christmas? I'm broke. I spent all my money. Gotta keep this cute li'l behind, right here *behind* this counter—gotta work."

He was tempted to cash in some of his recently acquired stock certificates to give Lois money; but he knew it was too soon. He wanted to do nothing to raise suspicions. So, he'd flown on to the ranch alone and now, with blinding snow closing in all around him, he fought a feeling of panic.

It had been at least thirty-six hours since he'd kept any food down. He experienced brief hunger pangs but was still nauseous. He *had* to have sustenance. The wood burning stove in the tiny kitchen was already fiery hot. It also served to heat the place.

He cracked a couple of eggs into a black iron skillet but his quest for food stopped there. He felt faint and grabbed hold of the table to steady himself. Air—he needed air.

The blast of wind, sleet, and snow stung his face the moment he opened the door but it didn't help. Instead, it brought on more panic. He ran toward the Taylorcraft knowing full well he shouldn't fly in this weather. He'd tailspin into the high plains. But reason had left him. So what—at least it would all be over!

He was still ten yards from the silver plane in the barn when he lost consciousness. He fell to the ground face first, his head crashing through the winter's shriveled sagebrush—through the still thin layer of snow and ice. His head slammed against the hard-frozen, sandy and rocky soil of the Colorado prairie.

As the snow slowly turned bright red from the gash in his head, he felt nothing—nothing at all.

He first sensed the warmth. He was no longer cold. That must mean he'd been cold.

He was lying on a bed, the one he usually slept in. His vision was blurry but he could tell the man bending over him was a cowboy, somewhat small in stature. His ten-gallon hat seemed almost as big as he was. Drops of melting snow and ice dripped from the hat's brim.

"Can your hear me now?" The cowboy's voice seemed far away; and it didn't sound like the voice of a cowboy. "You had yourself quite a fall, there. I'm making some hot tea."

The brown-skinned man managed to sit up in bed and reached up to touch his own face. *Ouch!* His nose was terribly sore and he felt a large bandage on his right cheek, and one on his forehead.

The cowboy returned with a steaming tin cup of tea. "Be sure to grab the handle. This could burn and you don't need any more injuries."

He took a small sip of tea then sniffed through his aching nose. "Is something burning on the stove?"

"Done burnt," laughed the cowboy. "I guess those were your eggs frying—before you decided to take that swan dive outside. They're nothing but 'char' now."

Then the cowboy reached in the pocket of his long leather coat and pulled out a small flashlight. He shined it in one eye, then the other of the injured man—just as a doctor would.

"Are you feeling better?"

"Not much; course, I felt horrible *before* the fall."

"What do you mean?"

"I've been nauseous for weeks; can't keep anything on my stomach."

"Have you been to a doctor?" The cowboy reached in another coat pocket and pulled out a stethoscope.

"What kind of cowboy are you," the surprised patient asked, "a vet?"

"No," laughed the cowboy, "I'm not even a cowboy. I'm a doctor and I just feel insecure unless I keep some tools of the trade with me at all times." He moved the stethoscope over the man's chest and stomach, listening intently.

"Have you spit up any blood—I mean *before* this fall?"

"A little bit."

The doctor said nothing then put the stethoscope in his pocket and stuck out his hand. "Jim Grander—I live in Denver."

"What are you doing in these parts, Doc?"

"Holidays—my sister and her husband own a little spread near Hartman. I came down for Christmas and New Year's. I love to ride so I got up and took off early; apparently too early."

"Yeah, this storm came as a surprise."

"Danged ol' mare got us both lost in the snow; at least I'm lost. Where are we, anyway?"

"About seven miles east and a little south of Hartman. You're not very lost."

"Well, sonuvagun," the doctor said with a chuckle, "that ol' bitch mare knew her way home after all. I just gave her the reins hoping she'd get us there. My sis's place is three miles southeast of Hartman. Craddock—their name is Craddock. You probably know them."

The patient winced as he swung his feet to the floor. "No. I'm fairly new in these parts; don't know much of anybody, really. Do they herd cattle?"

"Mostly, they 'herd' cantaloupe," Grander chuckled. "They know some folks out around Rocky Ford who are doing quite well with truck-farming so they decided to try it." He paused with a suspicious look on his face. "I don't believe I got your name," he added and waited for an answer.

The brown-skinned man looked at the "cowboy doctor" and hesitated. "Most people call me—they call me Buck," he finally said. He didn't think the doctor believed him.

"Well, Buck, lucky for you the ol' mare came right through your place. I saw you lying there five feet in front of me. The snow was blowing so badly I hadn't even noticed the house or the barn. If I hadn't seen you, you'd be a block of ice about now, gone on to your reward."

"The way I feel I may go there yet." The nausea was returning.

"Lay back down, Buck. If you'll permit I'm going to check a couple of more things. Say, 'Ahhh.'" Doctor Grander shined the tiny flashlight down the man's throat giving an occasional grunt in the manner of most doctors, then looked again in each eye.

He put a hand on each side of the man's stomach. "I'm going to apply a little pressure. Does this hurt?"

"No."

"How about here?"

"Ouch!" the tall man cried.

"And here?"

"Ouch!" The cry was louder.

"Mmm-huh. Mmm-huh," then the doctor was silent. Finally, "Is that your airplane, Buck?"

"Not really, I fly it a lot."

"You do live here, don't you?"

"Not really, but I'm here quite a bit."

"Well, Buck, I'm not trying to pry. However, I have taken the Hippocratic oath. I'm bound to tell you the truth." He paused, a serious expression on his face. "I think you should see your doctor. You could have a problem; not from the fall, you'll get over that—but a problem that needs more examination. Where *do* you live?"

"Let's just say, I'm—I'm a native of New Mexico," the tall man answered haltingly.

"Are you Navajo, Apache—what?

"Navajo."

Doctor Grander picked up a notepad and pencil on the chest of drawers and scribbled on it. "Do you think you'll be able to fly to Albuquerque when this weather let's up?" and he handed the patient the note.

"I hope so." The Navajo wasn't sure he'd ever be able to fly again.

"Look up Doctor Samuel Lockman and give him this. He's a good man. We've done some research together."

"I'll think about it."

"Don't think about it. *Do it!* Now, I'm hungry. Have you got any bacon? I'll see if I can do a better job with some eggs than you did. And for you I'll need some baking soda, milk, and hooch, if you've got any. I think I can concoct something that might help you keep a little food down."

The Navajo followed the doctor to the kitchen, steadying himself on the furniture along the way. As he retrieved the requested staples, he wished this kind physician who'd already saved his life, had a prescription for the other cloud hanging over him—and he wasn't thinking of any medical problem that might be his.

CHAPTER 33

Five months later—
Friday, June 3, 1949—

The day dawned with a special brilliance in Raton. It was a day made especially for people with worries and cares—for one step into the outdoors would do much to assuage worries and cares. There was not even a hint of a cloud in the sky. The warmth of the sun spoke of summertime just days away, but the crisp air said it was still spring.

Jed Easton awoke early. He didn't do that often; largely because from childhood he'd get engrossed in a book, or find some far-off radio station on the Philco when he should have been asleep. His parents gave him the wooden table-model receiver on his thirteenth birthday. It had been on his bedside table ever since. But this all meant he was the perpetual sleepyhead.

However, on this morning the sun was so bright, the fragrance of the mountain air through his open bedroom window so fresh, he could not stay in bed. He bounded up, showered and shaved, and was out the door by six forty-five. Jed felt that just maybe he could get through one day; *this* day, with no more than one fleeting thought of Erica per hour. If he could limit it to that he might actually accomplish something.

It was busy this time of morning at Jody's Café. Jed glanced around the small room as he entered. The counter bar stools were full. They always filled up first. But there was still an empty chair sprinkled here and there among the half-dozen tables.

It was the diversity that Jed loved. Before him was a microcosm of Raton. Four men—men of the professions—sat at one table. Jed knew two of them, fellow lawyers. They smiled and nodded as the squeaky screen door closed behind him.

The other two Jed knew only by reputation: Solomon Smith was president of the Raton branch of New Mexico State Bank; Doctor Thomas C. Caldwell (Emily Larson's boss) had the small office above Woolworth's, downtown. Rumor had it that the good doctor once worked in a large Chicago hospital—but something happened. A patient died; a patient much too young, the story went—a patient who shouldn't have died. Jed knew nothing else of the story or whether it was even true—but the good doctor decided to seek his fortune somewhere other than Chicago. TJ's cryptic remark last November about the Doctor owing him "big time" made Jed curious. If he could get up the nerve, Jed wanted to ask TJ about that.

There were also a few store clerks, male and female, and a secretary or two—female of course. And hard-working men who truly earned their bread by the sweat of their brow: white, Latino, and Indian; truck drivers, carpenters, bricklayers. For them, a morning respite before the hard hours ahead was one of the day's greatest pleasures.

There was also Professor Ramon Sanchez, Mrs. Easton's Christmas guest. You couldn't miss the professor at the table in the back. Still dapper and refined at eighty-one, his suit always freshly cleaned and pressed. The black shoes gleamed from their daily shine by Carlos in El Portel Hotel. An exquisite silver and turquoise bola tie with silver-tipped black strings was the professor's only article of western clothing.

Ramon Sanchez was born and raised in Raton of an aristocratic family; Spanish ancestry, not Mexican, and if anyone failed to discern the distinction he told them posthaste. He was a dear friend of Jed's mother and his late father.

The professor's early education was in the local Catholic

schools; then Sanchez's parents shipped him off to Yale in 1885. He took to the academic environment, stayed on through his doctorate, and joined the faculty. Except for the occasional trip back to the Land of Enchantment he stayed in New Haven until retirement. That occurred about the same time General MacArthur accepted the Japanese surrender aboard the USS Missouri. Professor Sanchez returned to Raton to live for the same reason as Jed. It was home.

Jed loved to talk with the professor. If the old bromide were true (that a person could increase longevity by being curious about the world and everything in it), then Professor Sanchez would live forever.

Jed waited. He knew the unspoken rule. If Sanchez looked up, smiled and nodded, you were welcome at his table. If he were engrossed in his New *York Times* (it took each edition of the daily a full week to arrive in the mail by subscription), you sat somewhere else. Today Professor Sanchez's nose was buried in the Times' front page.

Jed walked to the edge of the counter and caught Jody's eye in the kitchen. "The usual, Jody."

Jody smiled and waved. He was the only Negro in the place. It was his café. His father, long before Jody was born, had been a slave in Mississippi. Freed by President Lincoln and the Civil War, and in need of a living, he came west and herded cattle on scores of ranches.

"He cowboy'd all over these parts." Jody loved to talk about his dad.

It was about the turn of the century that the ex-slave, approaching his biblical three-score and ten, came through Raton on a cattle drive to Denver. He went to a boot maker for a new pair of boots and the boot maker had a daughter; skin the color of coffee with cream and much too young for the old cowboy. But somehow it didn't matter. They hit it off, the cowboy never made it to Denver, and Jody was the result.

The old cowboy opened the restaurant cooking the simple plain food he'd known from his youth. When he died just twelve years later, Jody and his mother took over. They'd been there ever since.

Jed found an empty chair with two men wearing bib overalls; ranch hands maybe, feed and cream store workers more likely. Ralston-Purina had a place just around the corner. They nodded but said nothing. It's the damn necktie, Jed thought. If they only knew: Jed hated to wear the damn thing worse than anybody. But it was the only dress code TJ demanded—the tie, *and* if you were going to court, a suit jacket.

TJ always said it the same way. "Sorry, son, but ya gotta wear a tie. We're lawyers, ya know—gotta look professional. *(Beat, beat).* 'Course—*(beat)*—it's gonna take more than a necktie for some of us."

Jed picked up the *Raton Range*, discarded by an earlier patron. He seldom read the local paper because he didn't have to. Breakfast at Jody's, or lunch at El Portel, and a fifteen-minute saunter through the courthouse, chatting as you go; that provided all the local news Jed ever needed.

His breakfast arrived: two eggs, crisp bacon, fried potatoes, and toast. He was reminded of Mrs. TJ's story—as to how TJ got sick before the Kansas City trip.

"Hey, Jody," Jed yelled, "ya been keepin' these eggs in the cooler?"

Jody stuck his head out of the kitchen with a frown on his brown face. "Of course, I keep 'em in the cooler. Where you think I keep 'em?"

"Just checkin', Jody, just checkin.'"

Apparently TJ didn't tell Jody he got sick last fall.

On the front page of the *Range* Jed read of the Senate's ratification of NATO. There were rumors that Dwight D. Eisenhower, "Ike" himself, would soon become the organization's first Supreme Allied Commander. And Mao's forces were still fighting Chiang Kai-shek for China.

Jed discarded the front section of the paper. He'd heard Morgan Beatty talk about all that on KOA Radio, last night on the Philco. Wars and rumors of wars; the Good Book said it, and it knew what it was talking about.

He added more salt and pepper to his over-easy eggs. They were delicious. *Food poisoning from eggs, hell! TJ had one huge hangover! That was his problem.*

At this moment Jed's ears perked up. The conversation at the table from the two bib overall guys had taken a turn.

"Reckon they'll ever make an arrest in Claude Stickett's murder?"

"My God," came the response, "there's a thousand folk that'd like to've kilt that ol' bastard."

"Didja know 'im?"

"Barely. I played pool with 'im a time or two down at Chico's."

"He any good?"

"The best," the creamery worker laughed, "I quit playin' him. Lost too much money."

"Was he mean as ever'one sez?"

"Worse. Lemme tell ya what I saw: a bunch of us was standin' 'round outside Chico's one day, and a nun walked by. Now, I ain't Catholic—I ain't much of nothin'—but ol' Claude stuck his mouth 'bout two inches from her ear and yelled, 'Horseshit!'—just like that. Can you imagine? Beat anything I ever saw."

"God, that makes my skin crawl."

"Ya got that right. Ever'one was stunned. Ol' Claude jest kinda stared after the sister as she walked off. He looked like he'd like to kill her."

The two picked up their checks and headed for the cash register as the creamery worker concluded his story. "After that I never stood too close to ol' Claude," he said with a nervous chuckle. "I's afraid lightnin' would strike even on a clear day."

Good Lord, Jed thought, what possessed a man like Stickett? He wondered if there was any way to find out more of the man's background. The only people who spoke of Stickett—just said he was *mean!*

Jed would later consider: would his life have been better had he left right then; would it have helped if he'd read *only* the front page of the *Raton Range?* No matter. He'd have found out sometime anyway.

It was in the upper right hand corner of page four; a page of obituaries, births, weddings, and the occasional social item the editor thought worthy:

> *"Dr. and Mrs. William E. Harlan, of Tucson, Arizona, are pleased to announce the forthcoming marriage of their daughter, Mrs. Erica Elaine Harlan Swanson, of Colorado Springs, Colorado, to Mr. William D. Jenkins, of Maxwell, New Mexico. Mrs. Swanson is the widow of the late Maj. Ronald T. Swanson, who served with Gen. Anthony C. McAuliffe. Maj. Swanson lost his life at the Battle of the Bulge. The wedding is scheduled for one o'clock p.m., Saturday, July 9, at Mr. Jenkins' ranch, near Maxwell, where the couple will reside."*

Above the brief announcement were the smiling faces of a man and a woman: the gentleman with the Buick coupe at the train station last November, and on the gentleman's arm—the lovely Miss Green Garters.

With a word to no one Jed Easton walked out of the café. The delicious breakfast, which Jody so perfectly prepared, was suddenly inedible.

Jed couldn't recall the rest of the day. He barely remembered crawling into bed that night. He did remember fumbling on the bedside table for the half-pint of Beefeater; the second half-pint of the evening; the one he made it home with. He drained the bottle of its last dregs before throwing it in his small tin trashcan. And Jed remembered the horrendous clang and rattle as the small bottle careened round and round inside the can two, three, maybe four times. He was afraid the noise would awaken his mother.

Nevertheless, the stars shone again in Jed Easton's dreamland Milky Way. But this time they weren't so bright—no sparkle, no sizzle, no joy of love and life.

This night the stars, the green ones in particular, seemed to be weeping.

CHAPTER 34

Friday, July 1, 1949—

The engine of the brand new automobile hummed so quietly, Erica doubted she'd hear it even if the ragtop were up. As it was, she heard only the Colorado wind hissing over the smooth, rounded fenders; and that sound blended with the radio as it poured forth Frank Sinatra's mellow, sentimental phrasing of "Embraceable You." The classic Gershwin ballad was as fresh today, Erica thought, as when it first aired—*what, fifteen? twenty years ago?* It was one of her favorites. The lush presentation deepened her romantic mood as the foothills of the panoramic Rockies slipped by. For a brief moment the song brought memories of a night long ago. She had danced with Roscoe Squire at that election party—but had eyes for Ronald Swanson, the handsome soldier she eventually married. Erica pushed such thoughts from her mind. No need for nostalgia or second-guessing now. She was entering a new and exciting chapter of life.

The sky blue convertible, its white top glistening, had been delivered personally by Tom Cates, owner and general manager of Pike's Peak Kaiser-Frazer. He walked unannounced into Erica's small office at Colorado College just after her final class on June seventeenth, her thirty-third birthday.

"These here keys, my dear,"—and the car dealer dangled the keys aloft in triumph—"are from your Daddy and Momma. Happy Birthday!"

Erica knew her folks were financially comfortable but was

not prepared for the luxurious vehicle she was about to behold. It was a Frazer Manhattan, a four-door convertible, fit for any president, king, or movie star. Such extravagance for a mere birthday was out of character for Doctor and Heather Harlan. She could only surmise it was her upcoming wedding that caused their extreme generosity, and she was grateful. It gave her confidence that they were confident she'd made the right decision.

Now, the trunk of the southbound Frazer was packed with clothes. The back seat and floorboard were filled with books, paintings for the wall, and a couple of her favorite reading lamps. She tucked a heavy quilt around the back seat cargo, making sure all the blanket's edges were under a heavy item, so nothing (including the quilt) would blow away. To Erica it was unthinkable to drive a convertible with the top up on such a lovely day.

It had been Bill's suggestion: that Erica move to the ranch a week before the wedding and get settled in. She had no worry of improper appearances. There were five bedrooms and Bill's mother also lived at the comfortably furnished ranch house. This all meant the happy couple could return from their honeymoon on Mackinac Island, Michigan, with housekeeping set up and ready to go.

Erica had no need to move a lot of her belongings just yet. She was keeping her apartment in Colorado Springs, and would continue on the faculty of Colorado College through at least 1950 to avail herself of the long-awaited European sabbatical. Bill Jenkins insisted she do so and Erica responded to his open-mindedness by negotiating a shorter workweek. She would leave the campus each Thursday at noon for the four-hour drive to the Maxwell ranch, and would have no class scheduled until seven p.m., the following Monday.

Erica looked forward to being married again. She loved Bill Jenkins; she was certain she did. There were times when alone, in an introspective moment, she admitted that the tingling romantic spark she felt with the late Major Swanson—well, it wasn't quite the same with Bill. But could she—*should* she—ever expect that feeling again? Most people *never* experience that kind of love. And most who do, think it a one-time thing.

Bill Jenkins was a kind, sweet man. He obviously loved Erica and never arrived at her door in Colorado Springs without a bouquet of flowers. He could keep her in a fashion far beyond any she'd ever imagined. His ranch near the little town of Maxwell, New Mexico was mostly a hobby—hobby and residence. It was where he liked to live. He didn't have to make money with it. Bill Jenkins' financial security had been guaranteed long ago by the Texas oil fortune of his grandfather.

And there was something else: Erica *missed* being married. Her time with Major Swanson had been scant, a matter of hours rather than days. But she intuitively *knew* what she'd missed: cuddling in front of a fireplace in the cold winter or lying together on a blanket in the yard while gazing up at a million stars on a summer night. She wanted to wake up in the middle of the night and touch another warm body beside her.

There was also that other experience: the one that ostensibly causes a couple to go before a preacher in the first place; the one that so-called proper ladies didn't speak of—but Erica thought them prudish. "*Hell,* Jean," (on the other end of the long distance line Jean was jolted by Erica's outburst) "I miss sex! I've had too damn little of it."

"Well, sweetheart," Jean laughed, "ya know—you don't have to get married for that."

"Yes, I do, Jean," Erica answered softly. "You know I do."

Jean was silent for a long moment. "I know, Erica—I know. And that's wise. Some of us took too long to learn that lesson."

Since Major Swanson's death in the war there had been no relationship of note for Erica save Bill. She met him through a mutual acquaintance. A friend of Erica's mother was Bill Jenkins' aunt and both ladies delighted in playing matchmaker.

There was once a Colorado Springs bank president whom

Erica dated for a time. He was about fifty, a widower; very handsome and great company. He was conversant in the arts, theatre, politics, French wine—all of which Erica enjoyed. She even agreed to fly with him to New York City for a long weekend; but only after his solemn assurance she would have a separate hotel room. Erica had friends who were less scrupulous about such detail and she tried not to be judgmental. But her confirmation and Sunday school lessons had been augmented and expanded upon, by gentle hints from Mother Heather, all throughout her adolescent and teen years. And the teachings had stuck. Erica—for the most part—chose the straighter path for herself.

That New York trip was exciting and fun—but also the beginning of the end for Erica and the handsome banker. She had a strong sense all weekend (her own room notwithstanding), that the man anticipated she'd eventually throw aside her scruples, and a much more intimate get-away would develop. They dated rarely thereafter.

There had been absolutely no one else as a contender—unless you counted Professor Arthur Aldredge. Erica was never sure whether to count Arthur. He had been (and remained) such a dear friend. He was her strongest support in the immediate days and weeks following the news of Major Swanson's death.

"And what about the Raton lawyer?" Jean asked on the other end of the telephone.

Erica experienced an unexpected flash of anger at the question. She had called to Kansas City to happily announce her engagement. *"Jean! How could you?"* was Erica's sharp retort. "That was nothing. I scarcely remember the guy's name!" A lie, which momentarily, made Erica feel better.

"The lady doth protest too much, methinks!" came Jean's retort, and Erica laughed despite her pique. It was the only Shakespeare her big sister ever quoted. Jean admitted it was the only Shakespeare she knew—nevertheless, she used it over and over.

"*Puh-leeze,* Jean,"—Erica tried to fluff it off—"you'll *love* Bill. He's a dear. I don't even *know* that other guy." And that was the truth.

Erica had managed, with only an occasional lapse, to banish Jed Easton from her mind. She willed it so. She'd quickly tossed his Christmas card in the wastebasket. Wasn't that proof enough? She would scarcely acknowledge, even to herself, that she just as quickly retrieved the card from the wastebasket and put it in the beautiful little music box—a cedar one, on her office desk. The music box had been shipped from London, now years ago, with a brief note:

"*I miss you terribly—Ron.*"

It arrived two months *after* the chaplain delivered that horrible telegram.

Erica looked at the clock on the Frazer dashboard—2:25 in the afternoon. Then she saw the city limits sign—and a disturbing anxiety set in.

She had to know she'd pass through Raton en route to Maxwell. Of course, she knew—*I'm a geography teacher!* But the sign was somehow, disconcerting. It brought memories flooding back, memories she thought were gone.

She slowed the blue convertible even more than the speed limit required. She did this, she told herself, so as not to miss the road signs. But she was really looking at the sidewalks—back and forth, one side of the street then the other. Erica knew it was silly, utterly silly—but she hoped to see Jed.

The same day—
2:28 p.m.—

Jed walked to the window of the D.A.'s office. He looked down from the third floor to the traffic below, what little there was. The knot in the pit of his stomach felt like a baseball—a very nervous, electrified baseball. He couldn't sit in a chair for longer than two minutes. In bed at night, every thirty seconds, he tossed from one side to the other. At least it seemed like every thirty seconds. Nothing in his life, not even the death of his father, had hit him so hard. *I must be crazy! I barely know this woman.* The lines went through his mind constantly; but nothing gave him comfort.

On the street below, the mail truck was making its final pickup for the day from the scattered mailboxes on the street; a dairy truck, now finished with its route, was heading back to Trinidad; and there was a sky blue convertible with a sexy redhead at the wheel. The shiny new car moved slowly down the street. From Jed's vantage point he could tell the wind in the open car had blown the girl's skirt very high—and once again Jed, in his mind, was standing on the Raton depot platform. But then, these days, every girl reminded Jed of Erica. Blonde, brunette, redhead—*every* pretty girl, in some way, reminded Jed of Erica.

He found it impossible to concentrate on work and that made him feel guilty. Why, he didn't know, because there wasn't a damn thing he could do about it. He was in love with a girl he scarcely knew, and she was marrying someone else—end of story.

He *had* to get on with his life. It was time to grow up. Jed turned from the window to start that process—and the telephone rang.

Erica did not see Jed on the streets of Raton; and she was angry it made her so depressed, angry she was thinking of him in the first place. She knew it was asinine to even look for Jed. But she drove more and more slowly.

Five miles beyond the city she pulled to the side of the road. She opened her purse and searched for a hanky. She had to. She had to wipe the tears streaming down her face.

You goose, you idiot! were the words in her mind. However, "Ffffuck!!" was the word that escaped Erica's lips—half hiss, half whisper. Mother Heather would not have been pleased. (Nor would Mother Heather want to know that Erica, upon occasion, overheard the same hushed expletive escape Heather's lips). The dilemma in Erica's soul—angst, frustration, and an unexplainable loneliness—it all poured out in that one word.

She snapped the purse shut with a vengeance and tossed it on the floorboard. She yanked the Frazer into gear and tromped the accelerator so hard she bruised a perfectly painted big toe peeking from her high-heeled sandal.

In a cloud of dust and gravel, with a screech of rubber against pavement, she headed with new determination toward Maxwell, New Mexico, and her new life and home.

She didn't really think she'd turn into a pillar of salt—but just in case, she did *not* look back.

Jed picked up the ringing telephone. "Colfax County D.A." He was glad for even the slightest distraction.

"Calling for a Mister Johnson or Mister Easton," said the matter-of-fact male voice on the other end.

"This is Easton."

"Mister Easton. It's Jed, isn't it?"

"Yes, sir."

"Jed, this is Cedric Kozy—FBI, Albuquerque."

"Yes, sir."

"Sheriff Emwiler said to call your office direct—we may have a 'print identification for you in the Stickett case."

"May have?"

"Well, that does sound a little odd, doesn't it?" The FBI guy then gave his explanation. "As we told you earlier we found a smudged print on the knife—quite smudged. Four of our top guys in Washington have looked at it. One says there's not enough to go on but the other three say they believe it's a match. So on the basis of that, we thought it'd be worth an interview."

"Go on."

"As you know the Bureau doesn't get involved in a state murder case except to aid the local authorities, so I'll give you the name. You take it from there."

The possible suspect's last name was Begay and thought to be Navajo, from the Gallup area. His fingerprints were on file because of a technical infraction when he was sixteen: trespassing on a military installation. The authorities had finally concluded the episode was exactly what the kid claimed. He was taking a shortcut and didn't know he was on restricted property.

"Any idea where I find him?" Jed asked.

"Not now, the only address we have is the one he gave at the time of the trespassing thing. He lived then with his mother in a trailer house near Pine Tree Mission, outside Gallup."

Jed placed the phone's receiver in the cradle. *There's work to do!* At least for the moment he didn't think of Erica Swanson.

CHAPTER 35

Jed would've climbed into the '40 Chevy and headed for Albuquerque over the weekend, but he needed a new set of tires. He checked his bank balance—and decided to take the train. That was much cheaper than new tires, and offhand he could figure no quick way to get the county to buy new rubber. In the first place it was a holiday weekend, and such stuff took paper work; lots of paper work while the elderly Miss Garnett Figger, Colfax County Auditor, looked suspiciously over her glasses at anyone requesting an immediate requisition. Jed hated that. Besides, it had taken most of the weekend for Jed to get a clear plan of action.

Santa Fe's *California Limited* was scheduled to leave Raton at three-fifty a.m., Monday, July 4, the one hundred and seventy-third anniversary of the nation's birth. Jed went to bed at nine p.m., Sunday, but as was common in his current day-to-day life, he merely tossed and turned. From midnight to two o'clock he stared at the ceiling. He finally gave up, took a quick shower, picked up his already packed suitcase (the one just like *hers*), and headed for the depot.

If he could get ten minutes with this man Begay, that might be all that was necessary. If he had an iron clad alibi, then the *cautious* FBI investigator was right: the smudged fingerprint wasn't valid. *Or maybe I'll get a confession!* But Jed doubted that. Nothing had been easy in this case. And if the interview revealed nothing—then Jed was back where he started in the investigation: nowhere.

"Yeah, I know where his trailer is"—this, from a sheriff's

deputy in a Saturday telephone conversation with Jed. "'Bout fourteen miles south of Gallup, real close to Pine Tree Mission. Actually, it's more than a trailer now. He built a real house onto it."

Jed had called the McKinley County Sheriff's office Saturday morning and the deputy seemed anxious to get out of the office. "Want me to go out there? He don't have a phone, but I can patrol that direction as easy as anywhere."

"Does he still live with his mother?" Jed asked.

"Naw, his mother died three years ago. He lives there with his wife—well, I don't think it's really his wife, but"—

"Well, I don't want to scare him off," Jed cautioned, "he might run if he knows the law is after him."

"I'll take him out some coyote repellant. He raises a few sheep, I think. And he won't suspect nothin'," the deputy assured. "Coyotes are thick as fleas this year and we've been helpin' the USDA boys distribute that awful-smellin' stuff. Dang coyotes won't get within a mile of it."

Cy Smith, the overnight ticket agent, was listening to the dots and dashes of the telegraph when Jed arrived at the Raton depot.

"Mornin', Jed." Cy was a man of few words.

"Is ol' No. 3 on time, Cy?"

"Ya takin' the *Limited?* Yer early, my boy."

"Yeah, must be somethin' I ate," Jed lied, "couldn't sleep."

"Well, not a long wait; she was twelve minutes late outa La Junta. Want some coffee?" Cy moved toward the Warm Morning stove and a blue and white speckled coffee pot; at least it had once been blue and white. It was now scorched halfway up the side, just like TJ's.

"When did ya make it?" Jed didn't hide his skepticism about the coffee.

"Oh, 'bout midnight; just right, 'bout now. Make yer chest hair bristle. Might even stiffen up sumpin' else." Cy's laugh reminded Jed of a laying hen's cackle.

"Thanks anyway, Cy. 'Fraid it might make my damn belly-ache worse," and this time Jed wasn't lying. He had a vision of his stomach exploding with a mere half-cup of that stuff from Cy's coffee pot. "Gimme a ticket to Albuquerque."

"Round trip?" Cy was now behind the caged ticket window.

"Of course, Cy, ya think I'm gonna stay?"

"Jest never know 'bout you young people. Seems to me I remember you buyin' one-way when ya went back east 'while ago."

"Well, Cy, that was then; this is now." Jed wondered if Cy remembered every ticket he sold.

"Workin' on a case—or goin' to a big 4th of July celebration?" Cy was the curious type; nosey, to be precise.

"Oh, a little business, little pleasure." Jed thought that sounded as good as anything he could come up with. He wished the trip could be pleasurable but such prospects seemed quite remote.

Jed had heard from the deputy again, just yesterday. The aroma of Mrs. Easton's Sunday cookies, baking in the oven, filled the entire house. Jed rushed to the phone when it rang. He didn't want his mother getting in a long-winded conversation with a gossiping friend—then, the cookies would burn.

"Mister Easton, Begay's not home." The Gallup deputy was calling as an afternoon thunderstorm passed over Raton. Jed struggled to hear amidst the popping and crackling on the line. "His woman says he went to Albuquerque. He told her he was goin' to see somebody in the hospital. But she thinks he's the one that's sick."

"What hospital?"

"Bureau of Indian Affairs, I s'pose. That's where all the Navajo go up there."

Jed had a sudden impulse. "Sheriff, what does Begay look like?" Jed knew deputies love to be called sheriff.

"Never met him. I moved up here from Prescott, Arizona, just a couple of years ago."

"Really!" Jed was surprised. "Seemed to me you had a lotta info 'bout the guy."

"That's just jailhouse gossip," the deputy laughed. "Some days, that's all we got to do 'round here. But there was a picture on the lamp table of the woman I talked to; some guy was with her in the picture. I figure that's him."

"Well???" Jed waited. He could never understand why he had to pump police-types for information they'd eventually tell him anyway.

"Aw, 'bout forty, maybe forty-five, could be older—could be younger; a tall guy, six-three, six-four, I dunno."

Jed hung up the phone and walked into the kitchen to sample one of his mother's chocolate chip cookies. They were fresh from the oven and the aroma drove Jed crazy.

"Why are you grinnin'?" Mrs. Easton asked.

"Nothin', Mom, just business." Jed thought he was making progress. *Could Attorney John Little Deer (aka John Deerman, of Kansas City,Missouri)—could he have a double life going?*

Jed picked up three more cookies and went to pack his suitcase.

Jed heard the huffing and puffing before No. 3 came into view. The *California Limited* often used a steam engine on this leg of the run and Jed felt like a kid when the old 'Blue Goose' Hudson, No. 3460, chugged into sight. Before the diesels took over, this was the engine assigned to pull *The Chief.* It was his favorite and a chill of excitement ran up his spine as it hissed by. The train came to a halt with every brake screeching.

The conductor swung down from the car immediately in front of Jed, the step stool ricocheting off the cement. He motioned for Jed to board. No passengers were getting off and Jed was the only one getting on. But he knew it would be a few minutes before departure because No. 3 was as much mail train as passenger service. It took a little time to unload the overnight dispatches and freight from the east, and load the same for the west coast and points in between.

Jed settled into the big reclining window seat, checked to see that no one was behind him, and leaned the chair back as far as he could. To his surprise (had he been awake to notice) Jed was asleep before the *California Limited* left the station.

Jed awoke as someone settled into the aisle seat next to him. He glanced over long enough to know she was attractive but his eyes were still blurry from sleep. He pulled his handkerchief from his pocket and wiped his eyes, and the "travel oil" (he didn't know what else to call it) from his face. His father's pocket watch said it was three minutes to eight, still a good two hours from Albuquerque.

The sun shone brightly on the colorful vista that was New Mexico and he turned with a cheery "Good morning," to the peroxide blonde beside him.

Jeepers! Jed was glad he'd cleared his eyes. He tried hard not to leer because this gal was beyond attractive. She was a knockout!

"Good morning," came the happy response and as she spoke she opened her blue eyes wide. Jed thought she'd probably have trouble speaking without doing that thing with her eyes.

"Isn't it lovely out there?" The girl gazed past Jed at nature's handiwork. "Oh, I hope you don't mind my sitting here. I'm hungry but the dining car is full. I have to wait for the next seating."

"Not at all," Jed assured her, "be my guest. I'm a bit hungry myself."

"Well, you're welcome to join me," Miss Peroxide invited, "I hate to eat alone. They said a table should be ready in about fifteen minutes."

"Sure, delighted!" *Dear Lord, help me! Here we go again.*

Her breathy voice made Jed wonder if girls these days took lessons to talk that way. No one in Raton talked in such a manner, but everywhere else he went pretty girls seemed to gush when they spoke. *I sure know how to meet 'em—but just meet 'em, dammit! I never snag one.*

"The dining car is the next one back," the girl continued. "Thank you for not making me walk all the way to my Pullman. It's about ten cars behind us." As she imparted the information the 'Blue Goose' steam engine let out an exceptionally long, loud whistle and Miss Peroxide leaned close to Jed so he could hear. An ivory shoulder, bare in the boat line collar dress, was virtually on Jed's chest and when she turned her lips away from his ear, the outer tresses of her golden bob tickled his chin.

"Headed for the coast?" Jed asked and gulped slightly to get the words out. This dame was getting to him.

"Oh, yes, I spend most of my time there these days."

"Doing what?"

"Oh, this and that. I do some secretarial work and even model a little, but—well, I'd really like to act."

"You sure got the looks!" Jed told her.

"Thank you, but it takes more than that. I'm just not sure, uh..that I really have the talent. I've had some small successes but—I don't know. It's a heartbreak business."

The loud train whistle had long since ceased but the lovely young thing seemed quite comfortable resting on Jed's shoulder and made no effort to move.

"Miss Dougherty," the white-coated steward appeared in the aisle, "we have a table. Follow me."

"Oh, thank you, is there room"—and the girl placed her hand on Jed's thigh—"for my friend, uh, Mister—?"

"Easton—Jed Easton," and Jed nodded to the steward like they were being introduced.

"Anything you like, ma'm, of course," said the steward.

Curious, Jed thought. He couldn't remember a steward ever coming for a specific passenger. They would appear to announce, "BREAKFAST NOW SEATING!" to the entire car—but to one passenger?

Something about her was so familiar. She strode down the aisle in front of him, moving in an almost royal manner, and not surprisingly she drew the same close attention from others that Jed was giving.

They both ordered ham and eggs, a dollar forty in the Fred Harvey car. It was twice what Jed paid at Jody's, but there he didn't have such luscious company. The food arrived and they fell silent as they enjoyed each delectable bite.

Jed ate the last crumb of toast and looked up to find the voluptuous young lady staring at him. *How old is she—twenty-one, twenty-two?* Her blue eyes were wide, as her perfect chin rested on red-tipped and interlocked fingers, her elbows on the table.

"You're a happy man, aren't you, Jed?" Her question was one Jed had never really considered. He was especially surprised she'd arrive at *that* conclusion just now.

"Uh, usually yes, but here lately"—

"Oh, *my*, does Jed have a sweetheart problem?" Her blue eyes opened even wider as she put her hand on his, then reached up to lightly caress his cheek.

"I don't know how to answer that," Jed answered honestly.

"I'll bet she already has a beau, right?" The girl patted his hand, raising her eyebrows as a question mark.

"Worse than that," Jed growled, "how 'bout a husband within the week?" The comment came out more darkly than Jed wanted.

"*Oooh,* I'm truly sorry," Miss Peroxide cooed and Jed believed she actually was. She gently took his hand in both of hers. "No wonder you were hungry. I bet you haven't been eating much."

"No, I haven't."

"But see what a little companionship from the opposite sex can do? Here we are, both of us eating like *horses!*" and the pretty young girl laughed gaily, displaying ivory-white teeth, as perfect as those in any toothpaste ad. "Don't worry," she continued, "there is someone for everyone. I *have* to believe that."

"Hmmm, I told another young lady that very thing not long ago." Jed was suddenly a thousand miles away. "She was also a blonde," he added ruefully.

"Oh, *this* isn't my *real* color." The girl patted her hair and gave him a wink.

"Really? I had no idea." She took his sarcastic lie with the good humor intended.

"Well? Was it true?" Her face was now a querulous pout.

"Was what true?"

"The other blonde—was there someone for her?"

"Who knows? I'm sure there is."

"Listen to you—you *have* to believe. There *has* to be hope!" As she spoke she raised her slender white arms in the air. "Life is good—I'm a big girl now. I'm old enough to vote!" she concluded triumphantly.

"Ah, but *do* you vote?" Jed was glad to take the focus off him—even if it meant sounding like a schoolmaster.

"Oh, my yes," the girl said, "Abraham Lincoln is my *hero!*"

"Well, I know you didn't vote for him," Jed scoffed, and the smart-aleck remark brought a gale of laughter from the girl.

"*Oh,* but I would've loved to!" she gushed. "I have his portrait in my bedroom. By the way, this is *the 4th*—Happy Fourth of July!"

"Happy 4th to you." Jed struggled to picture the bearded

likeness of Honest Abe above this dish's bed. He quickly gave up and returned to her earlier assertion.

"What makes you think I'm happy?" he asked.

"I can always tell," and again her eyebrows went high. "I'll tell you something else I know about you." Now her chin was back in her hands, her elbows back on the table. She looked intently into Jed's eyes.

"Well?" Her directness made him slightly uncomfortable.

"You had a mother and father who loved each other—and you—and they raised you together, didn't they?" The question was more a statement of fact than a question.

"Well, yeah—sure." It was not in Jed's personality to sit around and philosophize about his childhood.

"I can always tell," Miss Peroxide cooed, "there's an aura of comfort and relaxation which surrounds such people."

"Well, *all* people have two parents!" Jed meant the statement as a lame joke; but was sorry he said the words the moment they left his lips. He saw her eyes moisten as she struggled with some deep emotional pain.

"They don't always stay together, though." Miss Peroxide fell silent for a moment. "Sometimes they don't even get together in the first place." She attempted a weak smile. "See, I—I've spent years now, trying to determine what—just what my name really is. That's no fun," she whispered, brushing a tear.

Jeepers, is this a blonde thing? The gal's story seemed so similar to that of Kansas City Blondie.

"They told me my name was Mortensen, then Baker," the girl continued, "..then recently I've come to believe my daddy's name was actually Gifford—but no one ever tells me for sure."

Jed handed the gal a napkin as a tear rolled down her cheek.

"So that's why I like Dougherty—my ex-husband's name," she continued, "even—even though we're no longer together. It's the first name I really *knew* was mine." She stared into space, recalling a pleasant memory. "Jimmie was a sweet kid. I really loved him and I'm sorry it didn't work out."

Jed noticed her eyes welling again and thought it time to change the subject. "I don't mean to be nosey but are you returning from a family visit, a photo shoot, er?—I'm just curious."

"Well, I even try my hand at singing a little,"—her faced turned sunny again—"I wish I were better. I have a friend in Kansas City who owns a club. He gives me a chance occasionally; usually when he can get no one else," she giggled.

Jed was now thoroughly enchanted by his dazzling breakfast companion. *A few more moments with this dame and maybe I'll forget Erica.* But it was not to be.

"Albuquerrr*QUEEE!*" came the porter's call.

The golden lass was (at one and the same time), shy and altogether fragile—yet confident and bold. Why could *this* encounter not have happened earlier? Jed wondered. *Before* the election week trip! Jed was getting fed up with unanswerable questions.

The *California Limited* rolled to a stop.

"I'm sorry, Ma'm, I've got to get my 'case, and get off the damn train." Jed stood and extended his hand. "What a pleasant time! Thanks for the invitation, uh, Miss—I'm sorry," Jed said, "I don't even know your first name!"

"Norma," said Miss Peroxide, "but my agent calls me Marilyn when my hair is this color." Her long fingers softly caressed the blonde tresses. "But I like Norma; Norma Jean, that's who I really am."

She stood up and moved close to Jed. "I won't settle for just a handshake!" Norma pressed her body against Jed, and reached up to kiss him lightly on the lips.

For a brief moment Jed Easton was severely tempted by an impulse completely foreign to his character: *to hell with the Stickett case, to hell with Raton, to hell with everything.* For an insane second he wanted to grab her and hold her tight; to ignore the uncomfortable silent stares of fellow passengers, and crush her against him. He wanted to inform Miss Peroxide he'd summon the conductor, pay the extra fare, and accompany her to Hollywood.

But as always with Jed, impulsive insanity passed quickly. "Well, Norma, if I ever get to the coast, may I look you up?"

"Oh, I'd like that, but my agent's very hard-nosed. He'd *kill* me if I gave my number to a stranger."

"No problem, Norma, I understand. If you ever change your mind call the D.A.'s office in Raton, New Mexico and ask for Jed. I'm your man."

Then, Jed couldn't help himself. For one more giddy moment, he strayed into the domain of the impulsive. He pulled her close, and kissed her on the lips—a 'silver screen' kiss! After all, that was her idea.

Conversation grew quiet in the dining car. Jed knew people were staring; he and Norma were making them uncomfortable. But he didn't give a damn.

Then, he felt the train begin to move. "Bye, dear."

"Goodbye, Jed."

He bounded for the car ahead with barely time to grab his suitcase and leap from the train. The *California Limited* was off to the coast.

Jed stood on the platform and watched the train depart. *Well, Norma, another time, another place.* He couldn't shake it—there was something so familiar about her. Those wide-open eyes; he could see them turning his way as though begging him to follow. *Where have I seen her?*

And her walk! *BINGO!* It hit Jed right between the eyes—he *had* seen her before. The hair color had thrown him.

Norma was the elegant brunette with the two Airedales who had openly flirted with Jed last November in Kansas City's Union Station. He wanted to run after the train to tell her. But the lounge car of Santa Fe's *California Limited* was disappearing from view, its red taillight a mere pinpoint.

Jed picked up his suitcase and headed for the cabs at curbside. *Norma, you doll. Poor kid!* From all he'd heard, Hollywood was one tough town.

In his now commonplace melancholy funk, Jed climbed into the taxi. Jed Easton was quite certain he'd never hear of Norma Jean Baker, or Gifford, or Dougherty *(Whatever the hell her name is!)* again.

CHAPTER 36

Jed needed exercise. He felt like crap. So, he walked up the three flights of stairs to the cancer ward. The pretty receptionist in the lobby of the Bureau of Indian Affairs Hospital had said Mister Begay could be found there. That was Jed's first inkling as to *why* the suspect was hospitalized. He'd confirmed that the man was a patient before leaving Raton, but pressed for no further detail lest someone alert Begay that questions were being asked.

"I'm not sure you can see him." A trace of sadness played across the receptionist's flawless face. "He's quite ill." The young lady's gleaming eyes (black was the only color you could call them) suggested Latin ancestry but her accent did not, and due to her light skin Jed surmised the "other side of the house" was white. He thanked her for her assistance. Her teasing glances revealed she was aware, that Jed liked what he saw. It was just as clear that she liked that he liked it.

Jed arrived on the third floor somewhat winded. *Been sittin' 'round starin' too much, gotta get with it.*

The nurse at the ward desk looked sternly at Jed. Suspicion exuded from every centimeter of her plump round face but Jed walked toward her anyway.

"Thinking of checking in, are we?" She uttered the question dryly as she eyed Jed's suitcase. Her tone was as icy as her visage.

"No, ma'm," Jed smiled, "I'm here to see Mister Begay; official business," he added quickly and slid his open wallet, badge visible, across the desk.

"You are Mister Easton?" She was looking at the identification card alongside the badge.

"That's right, ma'm," and Jed broadened his smile though quite uncertain any amount of charm would work on this woman.

"Mister Easton"—and the nurse cleared her throat ever so lightly—"I mean no disrespect but our first concern here is the patient. Mister Begay is a *very* sick man. There is a specialist from Denver with him as we speak. He'll be running tests, as the patient's condition allows, most of the day."

"I certainly understand, ma'm, but"—and Jed glanced at his suitcase while pulling out his father's pocket watch—"my train leaves at six-thirty this evening."

"Oh?" The nurse's voice dripped with acid-laced sarcasm. "The Santa Fe doesn't run tomorrow?"

Well, aren't you a ray sunshine? Jed was glad the woman couldn't read his mind.

"Ma'm," and Jed added a little official sternness to his own voice, "Mister Begay is the subject of an official murder investigation."

As impossible as it seemed, the woman's eyes became slits as her eyebrows arched. *How does she do that?* Her voice was calm and cold. "Mister Easton—sir—doctors, including Doctor Grander, a specialist from Denver, is with Mister Begay as we speak. Now, I don't care if he killed Abraham Lincoln. He is a *patient* in this hospital..and he is *unavailable.*"

"I'm sorry, ma'm. I'll check back later." He thought it odd that twice now, in as many hours, he'd heard the name Abraham Lincoln. *Are the history gods trying to communicate something?* Jed long ago stopped sharing such esoteric witticisms with people he didn't know, because the usual response was a blank stare conveying they thought Jed odd, if not downright insane.

He took the elevator, a very slow elevator, from the third floor to the ground level and walked across the flagstone floor of the lobby. He gave the pretty receptionist a wink and her penetrating eyes and snow-white teeth gleamed in return. Jet-black silky hair fell around her shoulders. Jed loved the Anglo-Hispanic mix.

He paused on the hospital's front steps and lit a cigar. He stood there for twenty minutes, maybe longer, comtemplating his next course of action. The man up on the third floor was apparently at death's door unless it was all a ruse. Was he really John Little Deer, aka John Deerman? Jed had to know. Besides, he needed to talk with Begay even if he *wasn't* the Kansas City attorney.

Finally, he stuck the cigar butt in the sand of a standing stone decorative ashtray and walked down the steps. But he didn't take the sidewalk leading to the street. Instead he turned right and headed down a narrow walkway along the hospital's front wall. Steps led down to a small covered parking garage. Six cars, nice cars: two Cadillacs, two Buicks, a Lincoln, and a Packard Clipper were inside. The doctors' garage, Jed assumed. And he spotted two other things that were helpful: a trash barrel (behind which he hid his suitcase and Stetson) and a doorway leading into the hospital basement.

He pushed the door open slightly and stopped to listen. There was nothing but the light hum of electrical appliances somewhere, and an occasional voice echoed far down the shadowy hallway.

Jed eased the door shut behind him and walked stealthily forward. He turned a corner and headed down a dimly lit hallway. There was a yellowed stairway sign above the door at the end.

He passed a room with the door open a mere inch, and the slightest sound came from inside; the unmistakable sound of a girl's soft laughter. Jed's curiosity was too great. Against his better instincts he slowly pushed the door open another two inches, praying it wouldn't squeak. He saw rows of clean hospital gowns hanging on racks, and large cardboard boxes stacked haphazardly. *TOILET TISSUE* the black letters proclaimed. Behind a rack of gowns Jed spotted a tall man wearing a hospital scrub cap. He was smiling down at someone, *whom* Jed couldn't tell because the figure was too short to be seen above the gowns. Jed presumed it was the girl he'd heard laughing.

Then all was made clear, as the doctor (Jed assumed he was a doctor) lifted the girl off the floor till her lips were even with his own. They locked in a passionate kiss, the girl's arms encircling the doctor's neck. The girl had long, black hair *(the receptionist!)* and although Jed couldn't see through the gowns, it was obvious from the sighs and physical motion he *could* see, that the girl's legs were encircling the man just like her arms— and with no less passion. Jed needed no instruction booklet to know what they were doing. *Using break-time in a hospital—to "play doctor." What a novel concept!*

Jed's plan was still a work in progress and the gowns seemed to fit in. Confident the doctor and receptionist wouldn't be easily distracted from their current "project," Jed slowly eased the door open, praying again it wouldn't squeak. It was now just wide enough to slip into the room. In a half crouch he tiptoed the three steps to the gown rack and cautiously reached up to lift a hanger from the rack. Fortunately a cap and a gown were pinned together. He backed out of the room in the same manner he'd entered—and moved on down the hall, a smile on his face. His mind had flashed back to the "play doctor" experiences he had as a kid. The doctor and receptionist were much less clumsy at it.

Once in the back stairwell, Jed slipped on the doctor's gown and pulled the scrub cap over his hair. He tied it in the back— then climbed the stairs to the third floor cancer ward. Peeking through the small window in the door Jed could see the desk at the end of the hall. The plump, oval-faced nurse-in-charge *(Miss Hospital Congeniality,* Jed thought) was still at her post.

A second later another nurse emerged from a room three

doors away and headed directly toward Jed. *Showtime!* He opened the door in commanding fashion.

"Excuse me, Nurse, I'm Doctor Smith." *(Wow, how original!)* "I'm here from Denver with Doctor Grander. What room is Mister Begay in?"

"Room 310, third door on your left." The nurse moved on past him with no obvious suspicion.

With a sigh of relief Jed walked toward the room, looking down and continually rubbing his forehead so his hand would obscure his face. He was sure that ol' drill sergeant at the ward desk had eyes like a hawk.

Through the half-closed door to Room 310 he spotted three doctors, uniformed exactly as he, bent over the bed—doing exactly what, Jed couldn't tell. *What now?*

Diagonally, another three yards down the hall, was a door with no number. Jed hoped it was a broom closet and he was right. Inside, with the door ajar a mere crack, he could still see the door to 310.

Ten or twelve minutes later the three physicians emerged with sighs and mutters of the mundane—"I'm sleepy…coffee…need a smoke." Jed caught only snatches of the subsiding conversation as the physicians moved on down the hall.

Jed knew he had to be fast. He peeked around the door. The one-woman Gestapo had her face buried in patient charts. With his face away from the nurse's station he walked quickly into Begay's room.

The patient was indeed a handsome Navajo but his finely chiseled jaw and smooth skin could not hide the ravages of disease. He was wan, his cheeks sunken. His lips had no color and his eyes were barely open. It could be him, Jed thought, but he wasn't sure. This man was so much thinner than the John Little Deer he met last fall in Kansas City.

"Haven't seen you before," the patient managed in a hoarse whisper.

"Oh, I believe you have"—Jed took a shot in the dark and removed his scrub cap—"I wasn't wearing this but we met in your office in Kansas City, Mister Deerman."

A puzzled frown crossed the patient's face.

"Remember now?" and Jed poked his badge a mere six inches in front of the man's eyes. "Jed Easton, assistant D.A. in Raton. I haven't forgotten you."

"You're a little confused, Mister Easton." The smooth baritone voice came from behind. Jed turned around—and had to agree he was confused. He was looking up at a very *healthy* John Little Deer.

CHAPTER 37

John Little Deer had been standing in the corner of the room all along, behind the door—and now he stood *between* Jed and the door.

Deerman's eyes were cold as steel and his words measured. "You're a pretty good cop after all, Mister Easton."

Jed liked compliments but right now wanted assurance it wouldn't be the last he'd ever hear. He fought back a flash of panic and wished he'd worn his revolver.

His mind was reeling. Was the sick man Deerman's twin, or double—or worse yet his hit man? Maybe he wasn't sick at all. Perhaps this was a setup, with Jed Easton as the next victim. He felt the creeping panic again. *For Pete's sake, get hold of yourself!*

Deerman took a step toward Jed—then extended his hand. "Relax, Jed," he smiled, "you look a little worn out."

Jed shook the attorney's hand and managed a weak smile. "So what's the story here, Mister Deerman?"

"Not here, Jed, as you can see this man is quite ill. He's not going anywhere. Let's you and I find a cup of coffee and let him rest."

Jed looked back at the patient who seemed almost asleep now. Deerman put a firm hand on Jed's shoulder and gestured toward the door. Jed tossed his hospital garb in the broom closet lest someone notice he wasn't supposed to be wearing it in the first place; but he didn't relax until it was clear that Deerman was indeed escorting him for a cup of coffee.

"We're brewing a fresh pot," said the man at the commissary cash register. "Have a seat. I'll send it over."

They took an isolated table in the back of the room, and within moments a waitress set two cups, steaming black, in front of them.

"Might I have some cream, please?" Deerman asked.

The woman pointed wordlessly to a small pitcher almost hidden by the sugar shaker.

Jed took a sip of the strong brew waiting for Deerman to speak.

"Mister Easton," the attorney began, "this may take a while. Got any of those cigars? I'll risk the sore throat," he said with a smile.

Jed pulled two cigars from his jacket and handed one to Deerman. But he was so eager to hear what his original suspect had to say, he forgot to offer a light—or to even light his own.

"As to the murder of Claude Stickett," John Little Deer began, "I've a story to tell, but I'm still not sure how *much* I should tell."

Jed finally remembered the unlit cigars, scratched a Swan match on the leather sole of his boot and fired up Deerman's smoke, then his own.

"Mister Deerman"—Jed took a couple of puffs to make sure his cigar was in operation—"uh, far be it from me to advise a man of your considerable legal talents; but do you think you should have an attorney; your *own attorney*—present for this?"

"Dear Lord, Jed!" John Little Deer laughed with more mirth than Jed had ever seen from him. "You are one *exuberant* cop."

Jed felt his face turning red but fortunately the Kansas City attorney kept talking.

"Jed, I'm not going to confess anything about *me*. I don't know how much you know—apparently not much, from that little scene upstairs. It's plain you've got some detective work still ahead."

"What are you getting at?"

"Mainly, that I consider Mister Begay to be my client. I

wouldn't be telling you *shit* but for the fact—which is plainly obvious—that it will soon be academic anyway."

Deerman's eyes seemed to moisten and he looked away. He cleared his throat and Jed took a long draw on his cigar.

"Your visit to my office in Kansas City got me thinking," John Little Deer began. "I correspond regularly with some of my people, on and off the reservation. My Aunt Tillie writes most often. She lives near Gallup and writes to all her nieces and nephews *in Navajo;* in Athabaskan, to give the language its true name," Deerman chuckled. "She took it upon herself to make sure we don't forget."

Deerman took a full fifteen minutes to tell his story and Jed was fascinated. John Little Deer said Aunt Tillie had expressed concern in recent letters over her oldest son, a bright boy who long ago graduated second in his mission high school.

"Jed, the sick man is my first cousin. He's eight or ten years younger and has always—well, looked up to me. Whatever I did, he wanted to do." A blue haze of cigar smoke surrounded Deerman's face and he coughed as though it was indeed making his throat sore. "He wanted to be a lawyer but could never settle down and do the studying. He wanted to fly airplanes and I *did* manage to teach him that."

Deerman said Begay was a man of serious nature. "He loves Navajo traditions and history. But as Aunt Tille puts it, 'He carries the weight of the ages.'"

Deerman said his cousin had become consumed with bitterness over the slights, offenses, and downright crimes against the Navajo—against American Indians in general, perpetrated by the white man.

"It really destroyed the deal we'd set up," Deerman continued. "As my own practice increased I had less time to pilot the other attorneys around. So, ten or eleven months ago I flew one of the firm's planes out to my little Colorado ranch and told my cousin to meet me there. I taught him the basics of flying and he was a natural. So I left the 'bird' with him so he could get solo time." Deerman laughed as he remembered something. "He got some good experience, all right—flew the damn plane out of gas one day and had to put it down on the prairie, south of Holly. He wound up walking back to the ranch to get the truck and a gas can."

Deerman said when Begay reached one thousand hours, Steadman, Swift, and Jones was going to hire him as a pilot and he could apprentice as a lawyer. If that went well they would get him into law school.

"So, why'd he screw up a deal like that?" Jed drew on his cigar, slowly exhaled, and realized for some dumb reason the cigar was giving *him* a sore throat.

"Well, as I said, your visit got me thinking. I recalled Aunt Tillie's concern. She wrote that the horrid murder of our cousin Morning Star—she was the daughter of yet another aunt of mine—that *deeply* affected her son."

"Were he and Morning Star close?" Jed asked.

"Very. He was a big brother to her. After the murder, Aunt Tillie said he'd disappear for days and tell no one where he'd been or what he was doing.

"Mister Deerman, let's cut to the chase." Jed wanted to make sure he was following the implications correctly. "Are you saying Mister Begay conducted his own investigation—then became judge, jury, and executioner? Did he kill Claude Stickett?"

"I told you, Jed—I'm his lawyer. You've still got to do some of this on your own." Deerman drained his cup before continuing. "Because of his health status now, I'll tell you this much: he doesn't have an alibi."

"Have you asked him directly if he killed Stickett?"

Deerman's response was non-verbal, a look of incredulity; not that Jed would ask the question, but that he would ask it of *him*.

Jed decided to ignore the professional disapproval. He kept talking. "What's the exact nature of his illness?" he asked.

"I have little understanding of medicine, Jed, but they tell me it's a form of cancer; blood cancer. They're seeing it more often these days. I believe it's called leukemia. I hope I'm pronouncing it right."

"How long does he have?"

"Not long—not long at all. You saw that for yourself." Deerman took another long pull on his cigar. "I've always tried to point him in the right direction—looks like it wasn't quite enough." He smiled as though remembering something else. "Although, I guess he took some of my *financial* advice. He's got a whole stack of stock certificates—oil, mostly—up there in his room. I think that came from a deal I told him to check out." Deerman smiled. "He's already told me to give half to the woman he's been living with; the other half to some waitress up in Kansas. I think her name is—Lou? Lois?—something like that." The Kansas City attorney shook his head. "I always suspected he had someone on the side—course he'd never talk about it."

Deerman ground out the cigar. "OK, Jed, let's go back upstairs. If he's awake, I'll give you a formal introduction to my cousin—to Buck Begay."

Deerman stood and reached in his pocket. "Oh—I almost forgot. Before I left Kansas City somebody picked up on the idea there was a slight chance I'd run into you—how, I don't know. They sent this."

Jed took the envelope and absentmindedly stuck it in his jacket. Something else was more important to Jed at this moment: a question simmered in his brain. "Mister Deerman, I have to ask."

"So, ask." Deerman's tall frame filled the commissary doorway as he turned, waiting.

"Buck Begay, your cousin—if he hadn't been ill, and I wound up filing charges, but he hired some *other* lawyer—would I have ever heard any of this from you?"

"Ah, Jed," and Deerman's words were accompanied by

that low rumble of a chuckle, deep in this throat. "You think there's ice water in hell, don't you? Besides,"—and now came the cold, John Little Deer stare again—"why in God's name would he hire some other lawyer?"

CHAPTER 38

"Mister Begay, I'm sorry I mistook you. To be honest, you and Mister Deerman look so much alike I thought you might be one and the same person."

Begay's response was cold silence but his gaze didn't shift from Jed's face for even a second.

Deerman stood silently at the foot of the bed. They had waited ten minutes while the doctors finished their final examination for the day, and with Deerman's concurrence Jed convinced them to allow a brief interrogation. Doctor Grander left one of his colleagues posted outside the door with strict instructions to "oust both of these ambulance-chasers if they go one second over fifteen minutes."

Deerman told Begay that because of the "particular circumstances of your physical situation," he would permit the assistant district attorney from Raton to ask some questions, "but I'll be right here and if things go too far astray, I won't hesitate to object. I've already told you, you don't have to tell the authorities anything you don't want to—but, Buck," (the attorney gripped the bed railing to steady himself), "you're family. You and I both know there are"—Deerman cleared his throat and swallowed—"there are considerations other than the here and now."

"Mister Begay, I'm investigating the murder of one Claude Stickett," Jed began, "I think you've probably heard the name."

No response, just the cold steady gaze.

"I don't want to be crass"—Jed, taking his cue from Deerman's words spoke solemnly—"but I know and you know—I'll never arrest you for anything. There isn't time."

At that Jed saw tears in Begay's eyes. "But it would be helpful; maybe in a small way it would even help square you with society, just to tell me what happened. Look, if it was payback for Morning Star; hell, I don't say it's right—but I sure understand."

Now there were tears on Begay's face.

"Is that what it was all about?" Jed knew he would have to press.

Begay shifted his gaze to stare at the ceiling.

"Communication, Buck." Jed pressed harder. "I need some answers here, friend."

For each centimeter his arm moved, it seemed to take the last ounce of energy Begay possessed. He managed to point to the top drawer of the small bedside chest. Jed assumed he was to open it and did so carefully. There was nothing—till he pulled it all the way out. At the back, something was wrapped neatly in a blue and white bandana.

"Don't mess it up," Buck whispered hoarsely.

Jed slowly unwound the bandana. Buck's dark eyes watched, waiting for Jed to reveal the treasure. The handkerchief contained a tobacco tin. Three Nuns was the brand name.

Jed looked at Buck, the question in his eyes, as to what the tin meant. The sick man motioned for Jed to bend close. "It was under her body," Begay whispered. "The police dispatcher told me. Course, they only suspect drunk 'injuns'—but you know 'bout that, doncha?"

"How did you get it?" Jed asked, choosing to ignore the insult.

"I have my ways. It wasn't a problem."

"But how do you tie this to Stickett?"

"No matter," came the whisper. Begay's eyes were full of disdain. "Just check the 'prints. White man knows how to do that, right?"

Jed gave a wan smile at the bitter sarcasm, re-wrapped the

tobacco tin, and slipped it in his pants pocket.

With great effort Buck Begay turned to the other side, his back to Jed. As he did so the top sheet pulled away, and there next to the frail body was a crumpled rosary. Deerman saw it too.

Jed wasn't sure whether to ask the next question or let Deerman handle it. He decided to do it himself. "Buck, it's none of my business but have you seen a priest?"

There was no sound in the room except Begay's labored breathing; then, "Been awhile." The hoarse whisper seemed all he could muster.

"Ya know, uh"—Jed was not good with these kinds of words—"man to man, it would make this whole ordeal go a little better." Jed paused, hoping Deerman would jump in. He didn't. "Couldn't hurt," Jed continued, "certainly in the next world."

No response.

"Shall I send up a priest?" Jed asked softly.

Silence.

"It's your decision, Buck." Deerman spoke for the first time since Jed started the interrogation.

Finally, an affirmative nod of the head—that was all Buck Begay could manage.

Jed, suitcase and Stetson retrieved, walked with Deerman to the street in front of the hospital. They shook hands. "Are you waiting to the end?" Jed asked.

"Of course," came the response. "And it won't be long."

"You need some rest, John. Ya goin' to your hotel?"

"No. I've already checked out. I'm going back to Buck's room. I want to be there, when"—Deerman turned quickly and walked away.

"Let me know when he, uh..," Jed called after him, "let me know."

Deerman did not turn around. He just waved and kept walking.

CHAPTER 39

Jed noticed it when he first arrived at the hospital: a small Catholic Church sat across the street, halfway down the block.

Now, he headed for the little chapel. *"Life is like a vapor..."* Jed couldn't remember where the scripture was found, but remembered some priest had used it in a sermon. He knew he'd just witnessed mortality about to kick in.

Church Of The Holy Spirit, proclaimed the modest wooden marquee. Jed lit a cigar on the front steps; then followed the narrow sidewalk to the rectory next door.

He tapped lightly on the front door and waited twenty seconds.

"May I help?" The priest was about fifty with thick eyeglasses and a ready smile.

"Yes, Father," Jed began, "across the street in the hospital—room 310. There's a young man, a Navajo. He'd very much like to see you."

"Does he have a name?"

"Begay—Buck Begay, Father."

"Begay, in room 310. Is this urgent?"

"Father, time is of the essence—very much so, I'd say."

"Thank you, sir, I'll take care of it," and the priest closed the door.

Jed walked back to the front steps of the church to finish his cigar. That's when he remembered the envelope John Little Deer had given him. *Mister Easton,* were the only words on its face and as he opened it Jed noticed the smell of perfume. He instantly knew whom it was from.

> "Dear Mister Easton—
> I hope this finds you well—and I trust you won't find this too forward, but I wanted to write.
> I think often of our wonderful night together at the Muehlebach (oooh, that sounds much more sexy than it actually was, doesn't it?), and I'll never forget it.
> But you were right. I have met a wonderful guy. His name is Eddie and we're to be married next month."

God help me—they're dropping like flies, Jed thought. The pain in his heart cut like a knife.

> "He's a very nice man and, rest assured, you'll never have to come cut his—well, you know the rest of that. Thank you for being so kind—and please forgive me if I always love you just a little.
> With fond memories forever,
> Blondie—"

Jed was a split second from ripping the note to bits but instead slipped it back in his jacket. He ground his cigar out with his boot heel and opened the door to the chapel.

It was a splendid study in how a small sanctuary should be. Jed had never seen such spiritual beauty. The highly varnished wood of the windowsills gleamed in the candlelight. Atop each sill, carved from the same wood, were the distinct faces (as imagined by the sculptor) of the twelve apostles. The realism of their expressions was remarkable for wood carvings. An engraved brass plaque was at the bottom of each window, telling which apostle was portrayed. There was also a single biographical phrase gleaned from scripture or tradition.

In church, Jed always sat or knelt at the back pew. But for

some reason he was drawn to the front of this chapel. He knelt at the prayer bench in the second row. He prayed for the soul of Buck Begay—and for his own soul. He couldn't bring himself to pray for the soul of Claude Stickett.

Behind the altar, the large ceramic Christ, on the cross, gazed back with sorrowful eyes. The red drops of blood beneath the crown of thorns glistened in the light. To Jed, at that moment, they appeared to be real.

Jed did not consider himself a man of deep faith, but from his earliest days he'd been a believer. Like everyone he had questions; but deep inside he also possessed a conviction: that the story told of those events in a faraway land two thousand years ago, was true. And he believed its truth sufficient to handle eternity for himself—and for Buck Begay. Again, he didn't have much faith for Claude Stickett.

Then he shifted his gaze to the smaller statue: Mary, Mother of God. A white shawl framed the Holy Virgin's face; a face so full of love, compassion, and understanding.

"Hail Mary, full of grace," Jed prayed. "Our Lord is with thee. Blessed art thou amongst women, and blessed is the fruit of thy womb, Jesus. Holy Mary, Mother of God, pray for us sinners, now and at the hour of our death. Amen."

Jed had heard of visions but like most people, had never experienced one. In days ahead, upon reflection, he still could not conclude whether "vision" was the proper description of what occurred; and if so, for what purpose? All that was beyond his range of spirituality; but it was something he'd never experienced before—and didn't expect to again.

He closed his eyes as tears streamed down his face. He put his forehead on the back of the pew in front, and in his mind, a face began to form. At first it was unrecognizable—but it was framed in abundant, luxurious red hair. He knew what was coming.

The face became clear. It was Erica's face; a portrait so

life-like she seemed to be breathing. It was as though an open frame hung suspended—and Erica stepped behind the open square to fill the void. But sadly, there was no consolation from her "appearance." If any message was communicated, Jed feared it was *not* in his favor.

The face faded away and Jed began to sob uncontrollably. He shook so violently he clinched each arm in the opposite hand, trying to stop the motion. For several moments this continued, as Jed began to accept with finality that Erica would be married this coming Saturday—*to someone else.* For the first time in his life he understood the poetic phrase, "a broken heart."

Jed believed the Christ of God could handle the hereafter. His faith was weaker that the Nazarene carpenter could solve this "Erica problem" in the here and now.

Time passed. Jed didn't really want to leave this place. Despite the disquieting "apparition," the chapel seemed truly a sanctuary from all the trouble in his life.

How long have I been here? He checked his father's pocket watch and was shocked to see it was almost six o'clock. He arose and walked from the chapel.

Jed paused on the front steps to light another cigar just as a Packard Clipper drove from the hospital driveway. As it reached the street it skidded to a sudden halt. The passenger door opened. A girl with long black hair *(the receptionist!)* alighted and slammed the door angrily behind her. The car roared away, the screech of tires leaving black marks on the pavement.

The girl walked slowly to a bus stop directly across from the church steps. Dusk was approaching but there was enough light for Jed to see tearstains on her face.

Jed knew this story without being told: the friggin' doctor would go home to his wife and kids. The pretty receptionist would go home alone—to heart-wrenching memories, and guilt.

Jed climbed aboard the eastbound *California Limited* at six-forty p.m. The train was ten minutes late. He headed immediately for the club car fully intent on arriving in Raton half crocked.

He quickly downed two Beefeater on the rocks—doubles—and ordered a third. But somehow it just wasn't working. Jed took two sips from the third glass but any "buzz" he was getting was far from sufficient. He put it down and touched it no more.

The train arrived in Raton just after midnight, right on time. But Jed didn't want to go home—he just didn't. And his war wound; it hurt like hell. Funny, he thought, the air is dry as a bone—but my leg still hurts.

He thought of the Nazi bastard who found his mark—or did he? Did he mean to kill Jed, or did he mean to miss? And Jed wondered if the German soldier was still alive. Did he too survive the battle? If they met today perhaps neither would think the other, a bastard. Somewhere across the Atlantic, perhaps—just perhaps—that man also mourned lost love.

Jed walked from the train to the depot parking lot and climbed behind the steering wheel of the old Chevy. However, he didn't start the engine. It was peaceful here too, just like the Albuquerque chapel. He slid down, resting his neck on the top of the padded seat, then pulled his Stetson over his eyes.

About one a.m., he finally dozed off. He was awakened by the sunrise—and the whistling winds of Raton.

CHAPTER 40

Thursday, July 7, 1949—

Jed hadn't been worth a damn all week. Since his return from Albuquerque, life went on around him—but without him. And it seemed to move in slow motion.

"What's wrong with you, boy?" Jody asked at breakfast. "You're dawdlin' over those eggs like you don't know whether to eat 'em or play wif 'em."

"Yeah, I know, Jody," Jed smiled at the cook. "Think I might as well've taken the westbound Santa Fe from Albuquerque—and jumped in the Grand Canyon."

"Fine wif me," Jody teased, "wouldn't haf to mess wif you 'round here."

Jed was glad TJ had taken Mrs. TJ to visit her mother in Roswell. Had the D.A. been in the office all week Jed was sure his boss would be convinced of suspicions already existent: that Jed was a hopeless case, unable to handle women, and probably going crazy.

Jed had somehow managed to start his final report on the Stickett case but was only half finished. He was waiting to hear from the FBI, as to their discovery or no, of Claude Stickett's fingerprints on the Three Nuns tobacco tin. If that was conclusive—if ol' Claude's 'prints were there, it would be <u>CASE CLOSED</u> so far as Jed was concerned.

"Good breakfast, Jody. Gotta get to the office," and Jed let the screen door slam behind him.

Jed wouldn't have admitted it to anyone at this moment—

but he knew he wasn't going to the office. He climbed in the '40 Chevy and headed south out of Raton.

The old car handled great with new tires purchased just yesterday, with his paycheck. Jed wondered if all county employees in New Mexico were paid on the sixth of the month—or if that was yet another idiosyncrasy of Miss Figger, the county auditor.

He arrived in Maxwell at mid-morning, too early for Jed to drink but he thought he needed one anyway. The old tavern was small and dark, but relatively cool for a July day. A large silver fan on a high stand whirred loudly at the back of the room. It was stationed to blow directly across the large galvanized washtub filled with ice and dark brown bottles of beer.

20 cents, said a crudely hand-lettered piece of cardboard taped to the tub. Jed, holding on to his Stetson so the fan wouldn't blow it off, pulled a longneck from the tub and laid thirty-five cents on the bar. The Mexican bartender nodded his thanks and opened the bottle with a "church key."

The place had the usual aroma of such places, half-pleasant, half-revolting: the smells of fried hamburger, fried 'tater' grease, and stale beer—the latter now dry on the floor. But the longneck was very cold, and the beer slid down easily.

"Anyone know where the Jenkins' spread is?" Jed directed his question at the two other customers in the tavern. They were middle-aged ranch hands in cowboy hats and Levi's, playing dominoes by the jukebox.

"You talkin' 'bout the rich guy from Texas—recently bought the Cameron place, right?"

"Yeah," Jed responded, hoping he was right.

"Never see him 'round here," said the second cowboy. "It's about fifteen miles east on the road to Farley. Then ya gotta turn back north a few miles. His place sets almost at the foot of Laughlin Peak."

"Ya here for his big weddin'?" asked the first cowboy.

"Yeah," Jed lied.

"Well, Jim, you're movin' up in the world," said the second cowboy, a sneer on his face. "How'd ya even know he's gettin' married? I didn't."

"Unlike a lotta people I know, I keep my eyes and ears open," came the jab back; then he warmed to the kill— *"instead* of *up* my butt!"

Everybody laughed, including the bartender; and he added a line of his own. "I also hear he redid the ol' house into a *purrrdy* li'l mansion out there."

As the cowboys talked, their game of dominoes slowed not at all.

"Who's he marryin'?" asked the second ranch hand.

"Don't know her name. Some fancy college teacher from Colorado, I hear."

"Oil money!" There was disgust in the cowhand's tone.

"Not against it—jest wish I had some of it!" said the first cowboy. He continued speaking while grinning suspiciously at Jed, as though wondering if *he* had oil money. "I'll say this: that Texan's got a mighty good eye. I saw his lady down at the gas station one day." The cowboy shook his head, like he couldn't believe what his mind's eye was remembering. "Least I think it were her, nobody else 'round here looks like that: *fiiine-lookin'* filly; *looong* red hair—and the cutest li'l ass you ever saw. *Wow-ee!* Make ya wanna stand up and slap yer mama!"

Jed had heard quite enough. "Thanks for the info'. Gotta go." He tipped his hat to the cowboys and the bartender as he left.

He checked his odometer and drove east on Highway 193. Exactly fifteen miles out of Maxwell a wide gravel road led off to the north. Jed assumed this was the one, had nothing to lose even if it weren't, and took it. Laughlin Peak loomed large in the distance. He drove several more miles then topped a low hill to look down on one of the most peaceful settings he'd ever beheld.

A long, low adobe ranch house sat in the middle of a lush green carpet of grass. Grass like that, particularly in these parts, could be kept that way only by irrigation. The house had an obviously new, red tile roof. Behind the house, to the left, was a large white barn. Two sleek chestnut horses grazed in front of the barn and a gleaming white board fence surrounded the entire complex. This was not the typical ranch in New Mexico—in fact, the white fence and green grass reminded Jed of a Kentucky Thoroughbred horse farm. He'd seen pictures of such in *Life* magazine at Derby time.

A quarter-mile behind the picturesque spread, Laughlin Peak began its sharp rise.

Jed let the Chevy coast slowly down the hill toward the ranch. At the driveway was a big black mailbox atop an old wagon wheel. The postal edifice, though rustic, looked new. "The Jenkins" were the words inscribed on the mailbox in fresh white letters.

Jed had no idea what to do next—or even why he was here. He drove on and the road began to rise away from the valley. A mile-and-a-quarter past the ranch it took an abrupt hairpin turn and snaked up and along the south face of Laughlin Peak. Jed soon found himself directly back of the ranch house at an overlook, sheltered by a small grove of mountain pine.

He felt foolish for what he was about to do—but did it anyway. He opened the Chevy's trunk lid and found the leather case he was looking for. Jed pulled his old Army binoculars from the pouch and rested his elbows on a low pine branch. He was about twenty-five hundred feet from the back of the house but as he fine-tuned the focus, it seemed he was in the Jenkins' back yard.

The highly polished flagstone, of what appeared to be a brand new patio, shone in the sunlight. A small concrete swimming pool, its tiny waves twinkling, flanked the patio. *Dear Lawd, ol' Bill's indeed fixin' up for the gal!*

Jed lowered the glasses and stood there taking in the magnificent view of the stunning countryside. The summer heat waves shimmered across the valley and a lone hawk circled lazily, its sharp eyes searching for prey. Some unsuspecting prairie dog pup was about to become lunch.

The thought came later to Jed: it might have been better had he left at this point—but he didn't.

Even with the natural eye Jed noticed a figure emerge from the back door. He brought the binoculars to his eyes—his quick gasp made him choke! It seemed he stopped breathing—he feared his heart had stopped beating.

The lady's hair was partially covered by a bright yellow kerchief, but the tiny piece of cloth couldn't begin to contain the mass. Frilly strands and curls billowed everywhere from under the kerchief. They were red, and gold, and bouncy—*it was Erica!*

She wore skimpy shorts that matched the kerchief, and a light green blouse, unbuttoned. The tails of the blouse were tied in a knot just under her bosom. From the ample display of cleavage, it was plain she wore nothing under the green top. Jed felt like a peeping tom—but refused to stop looking.

Erica adjusted the top half of a chaise-lounge backward, so she could better catch the rays. She sat down and lay back, facing Jed on the mountain; then, she donned dark glasses, settled in, and opened a book.

Jed stared at her through the binoculars. He watched, perfectly immobile; except for his hormones.

At one point Erica sat up, took off her glasses, and seemed to be looking directly at Jed. But he knew she couldn't see him. *I'm a half-mile away in a pine tree, for heaven's sake!*

Again, for the second time this week and for the briefest of moments, he fought an un-Jed-like impulse: this time it wasn't to run off to California with some would-be actress; but to drive to the ranch and beg—to *demand*—that Erica come away with him.

Yeah, right! She'd probably call the sheriff!

And Jed couldn't have blamed her. In fact, Jed knew if ol' Bill were around he'd likely not wait for the sheriff. Any rancher worth his salt could handle a gun—of which they all had plenty.

Jed tweaked the binoculars and his heart beat faster as Erica tucked her feet up next to her hips. The smooth rise of her hip line was clearly visible in the short shorts. Jed's hormone level raised another notch. Those thighs, like cream blended with ivory; but the blend had the slightest hint of cinnamon specks—they seemed so invitingly close; yet so far away.

Jed lowered the binoculars and prayed those lovely limbs wouldn't fall victim to sunburn. The thought of Erica experiencing pain brought pain to Jed.

But just as he'd known he must come here, even to see her from afar—he suddenly knew it was time to go.

"Goodbye, sweet Erica." Jed's lips actually formed the words. They came out in a whisper.

He put the army field glasses back in the trunk, climbed in the Chevy, and headed for Raton—but not back by the ranch. He didn't trust himself. Instead he headed for Sofia, Mt. Bora, and U.S. 64—the long, long way to Raton. He couldn't bear being any closer to Erica—not now. Now, he needed distance from her.

This time there were no tears. *Maybe I'm finally growing up.* Something had just transpired and Jed knew it. He'd said goodbye to Erica forever.

CHAPTER 41

Saturday, July 9, 1949—

Many July days were hot in Raton. This day was hotter than usual.

TJ listened intently to Jed's recounting of his visit with Buck Begay and John Little Deer. Every two minutes the heavy-set prosecutor wiped his wide round face with his handkerchief. The open windows in the office did no good today. At eleven a.m., long before Jed told his tale to TJ, the breeze had all but stopped—unusual for Raton. By two p.m., it was unbearable.

TJ said not a word until Jed finished. "So," he finally growled, "stop beatin' 'round the bush. Did he do it?" TJ held up his hand before Jed could respond. "Ah'm not askin' what he said or how he looked. Ah'm askin': do you—do you think he did it?"

"Hell, yes!" Jed responded. "You bet! Buck Begay knifed Claude Stickett as payback for Morning Star. I just hope for the sake of Buck's eternal soul, he killed the right man."

"D'ya think that'll square things up for Buck at the Vatican?" TJ asked the question in a dead serious manner—but Jed knew his boss was trying to get a rise out of him. TJ loved to needle Jed about his religion.

"Prob'ly not," Jed smiled, "not exactly—hadn't really thought about that. But I'm waitin' to hear anytime now, from the FBI on the Three Nuns tin; and I know damn good 'n' well it'll be conclusive."

Jed sure hoped he was right. The Arizona office of the FBI

had a mug shot and fingerprints of one Claude Stickett on file. They mailed a carbon copy to Jed, and even though the duplication was of poor quality, it was plainly Claude Stickett. He'd been arrested for a Tucson bank robbery a decade earlier; but they couldn't convince a jury.

Jed wondered if Buck Begay actually got the tobacco can dusted for prints. Maybe he was so convinced of Stickett's guilt he thought they just *had* to be there. The Colfax County D.A.'s office would like something more solid than mere dedicated family speculation, to make the circle complete.

"Well, it would all fit, wouldn't it?" TJ said. The prosecutor seemed resigned to (not to mention relieved *by*) the conclusion.

As though on cue from some archangel in heaven, the telephone rang and Jed reached for the stand-up model while still leaning back in his chair—which meant he knocked the receiver off the desk. It rattled and rolled on the wooden floor, almost pulling the entire apparatus off the desk. And another fraction of body weight applied to the chair's precarious position, and Jed would have been on the floor.

"D.A.'s office." Jed tried to sound collected. "Uh-huh…uh-*huh*…uh-huh. Well, thanks for callin'—'preciate it."

"Well," Jed gleamed, "that's that, seems to me! The FBI's *expert* experts; they say there were three clear prints matching Claude Stickett's on the Three Nuns tobacco tin."

"Damn! Great! It's 'bout time this office got some good news." TJ lumbered from his chair as he spoke. "There are more than enough loose ends in the course of a *normal* day." He paused and looked at Jed before continuing, "And this sure as hell ain't a normal day, is it?"

"Huh?"

"This is the day, isn't it, son?"

"What do you mean?" But Jed knew what he meant.

"You know, Jed—the little lady who turned you into Jell-o. She's gettin' married today, ain't she?"

A few days after seeing Erica's wedding announcement in the *Range* Jed had finally told TJ the full story, more or less. He had to tell someone or he felt his gut would burst.

"No big deal, TJ." Jed now feigned nonchalance, but carried it off in a less than spectacular manner. "Just life, TJ—just life."

"Well, upon occasion"—and TJ smiled more warmly than usual—"life goes better with a li'l pick-me-up—a li'l libation. Why don't ya go have a drink? By the way, Sarah's here, uh, when—Monday?"

Sarah Gillen was the District Attorney's secretary. She had been for years, long before TJ got the top job. She came in only three days a week unless they needed her more.

"I think so, TJ."

"Yeah—you head on over to El Portel. I'll dictate my wrap-up report to her then—that is, if Begay dies over the weekend. I ain't writin' nothin' down while he's alive."

"Why?"

"Son, you got a lot to learn 'bout politics." A look of disgust combined with appreciation was on TJ's face. He had a love-hate relationship with politics. "It's jest such stuff as that, that some prissy opponent will dig up and demand ya tell the people why ya didn't make an arrest."

"Oh, right." Jed wasn't sure he'd ever make a politician.

"'Course, such scalawag lame-brain politicians will never bother to mention that the guy could scarcely breathe and wouldn't even know he'd been arrested."

"And on that, TJ, I think I *do* need a drink." Jed pulled together all the clippings and reports of the Stickett case. "I'll get this stuff in some sort of order, just in case you need any particulars." He tossed the small stack of papers into a rust-colored accordion folder. "I believe I can do that at El Portel as well as anywhere."

Jed was about to walk out the main courthouse door on the ground floor when TJ bellowed his name from two stories up.

"Yeah?" Jed answered.

"John Little Deer just called," TJ yelled down the stairwell.

"And?"

"Mister Begay just 'bought the farm'—'bout an hour ago."

"Thanks, TJ."

Jed walked to El Portel. *"Life is like a vapor..."* and life goes on.

Jed took a stool at El Portel's polished wood and brass bar.

"The usual?" The bartender already had the fifth of Beefeater in his hand.

"You're a good man," Jed smiled.

He loved the ambience of a bar. Though it was a public place it was also a private place. In glad times you celebrated; in sad times you nursed the hurt. And Jed especially liked the El Portel bar on a hot day because it seemed the coolest spot in Raton.

The clock behind the bar said twenty minutes till three. An emotional tingle, not quite pain—but an unsettling twinge, went through Jed's solar plexus. He could see the words from the *Raton Range* like they were in front of him: *"...1 p.m., Saturday, July 9."* The deed was done. Erica was now married!

Jed hated hangovers. He promised himself that the trauma of this day would not become an excuse to over-imbibe. He wasn't usually a heavy drinker, but this "Erica experience" had made him all too often skirt the edge.

He sipped the English gin gingerly and buried himself in the clippings. The small stack of papers spread on the bar before him was a sad testimony to Claude Stickett's despicable life:

—the picture and newspaper story of his murder

—Sheriff Emwiler's description of the murder scene (this involved a total of three hard-to-read sentences, scrawled by pencil in the old lawman's longhand)

—the brief notes Jed had already written of the possible connection to Morning Star's murder in Gallup, and the clipping on that crime from the *Gallup Independent.*

Finally, there were a few notations of his Kansas City visit with John Little Deer. Jed had already destroyed anything suggesting that Deerman was ever a suspect.

A customer entered the bar and sat down at a table across the room. Jed did not look up as he pulled his yellow legal pad from the folder. He took his gold-topped Sheaffer fountain pen from his shirt, formulating in his mind a few remaining items to summarize: namely his conversations with Deerman and Buck Begay in Albuquerque.

Jed hated typewriters—at least he hated using one. He prided himself on penmanship and wrote all his notes in longhand. If two days passed with no writing required, Jed had to write something. It was therapeutic. On such occasions he performed an exercise originally assigned by one of his grade school teachers: he would write from memory, with his fountain pen, the Our Father and the First Amendment to the U.S. Constitution.

"Do it forever," Sister Anna had said, "it improves penmanship—and will focus the mind on things important!"

The bartender walked by Jed with the other customer's drink on a silver tray. "Here you are, ma'm, scotch and soda."

The words of the waiter stuck a dagger in Jed's soul. *How ironic!* At the very moment he needed most to forget Erica, someone had entered the barroom and ordered Erica's drink. *How long will it take to get over such nonsense?* Not long, he hoped. Scotch and soda, after all, was a very popular cocktail.

Jed concluded his notes on the Albuquerque visit. Only then did he glance across the room at the female customer. A newspaper hid the face—but what Jed could see was pleasant enough. Long, slender fingers gripped the newspaper, the nails covered in peach-colored polish; the same color as her lightweight summer dress. As Jed watched, the woman crossed her legs. Since she was holding the newspaper she didn't bother to tug at the hemline, and the upward slide of the fabric revealed a generous expanse of well-toned bare thigh.

Wow! But this gal needs some sunshine! However, the creamy paleness of the blemish-free skin was erotic in its own way. A couple of toenails—also polished in peach—peeked through her open-toe, slide pumps.

Jed again felt that twinge in the pit of his stomach. The lady's sunglasses, the rims matching the color of the dress, lay on the table. Something about the whole scene made his heart skip a beat. *Please, dear God, it can't be!* The lady lowered the newspaper and their eyes met. It was Erica!

Jed was too stunned to speak. He just stared at her. *Does God in heaven hate me?* That Erica and her new hubby would honeymoon at El Portel had never crossed Jed's mind. Why should it? <u>Nobody</u> honeymoons in Raton.

"Hello, Jed." Erica spoke first. The large brim of her fashionable hat, black straw like her pumps, was pulled low, almost hiding one eye.

Where in the devil does she find her wardrobe? It's a good thing I <u>didn't</u> get her—I can't afford her!

"Hello, Erica." Jed's heart was beating so loudly he was afraid it would drown out his voice—and for about the tenth time since he met her, he thought he would faint.

"I would ask you to join me at the bar," (Jed finally recovered enough to put together a sentence), "but I wouldn't want to upset the new hubby." He even managed a weak smile. "Congratulations, by the way. I wish you both the very best."

Erica got up from the table and picked up her sunglasses. She walked slowly toward the bar.

"I'd be happy to have a drink with you, Jed." Erica was dressed for the hot summer day. Daylight streamed through the window behind her and it was obvious she wore no slip. "You see,"—she hesitated—"there *is* no new hubby."

"What do you mean?" Jed was in no mood for a joke, cruel or otherwise.

"Just that, Jed." She now stood in front of him. "I couldn't do it. I—I just couldn't do it. I couldn't marry him."

"Then why the hell are you here?"

"I'm driving back to Colorado Springs. I left the Jenkins' ranch yesterday when I—when we decided—it...it just wasn't going to work."

Jed said nothing.

"I got to Raton last evening," Erica continued, "and I was just too tired—'distraught' is the proper word, I think—to go on. I just got out of bed an hour-and-a-half ago."

Jed was still wary. "So why aren't you back on the road to The Springs?" he asked.

"Okay—a little more honesty." Erica was still standing, unsure if she should sit down. "Jed, this is hard for me."

She looked at the floor and took a deep breath. Jed could tell she was very nervous.

"Look!" Erica said, taking another deep breath. "I just called your office. A Mister Johnson said you were here. I wanted to see *you,* Jed—I just wanted to see if—if you're the reason I couldn't marry Bill. Damn!" she whispered as she looked away, and a tear rolled down her cheek. "You're *not* making this easy, Jed!"

"Why do you want to see *me?*" Jed asked, "You told me not to bother you—*you* didn't even respond to a simple *Christmas card!*"

"Well, *here's* your damn Christmas card!" Erica, now angry, was fumbling in her purse. She took out an envelope and threw it at Jed. "Oh, this was a mistake!" she cried. She closed her purse with a vicious snap, slammed her sunglasses over her eyes, and headed for the door.

"No—no, Erica, please." Jed jumped up and grabbed her wrist. "I—I'm sorry," he continued, "I'm very confused—and, yeah, I'm a little angry. What am I supposed to say here?"

"Nothing, if you feel nothing." Erica was trying to free her wrist from Jed's grasp, "I shouldn't have come. You obviously don't want to see me."

"Oh, Erica!" Jed looked down at her sad face. "Erica, if you only knew."

Erica began to weep. "The Christmas card, Jed—that's how *I* knew. I tried to throw it away ten times a week but I just couldn't." Her voice trembled as she spoke. "Heaven help me, Jed, I even took it with me to Bill's ranch."

"Then why didn't you call, or write? Why this long silence?"

"I was engaged, Jed. Nice ladies don't write other men *when they're engaged.*" She paused and looked up at Jed as tears rolled from her eyes. "Yesterday morning at breakfast, I called Bill—*I called him Jed!*" The tears poured like a dam had broken and she threw her arms around Jed's neck.

Jed couldn't help himself. He began to laugh and buried his face in Erica's mass of red hair. In the process he knocked her hat and sunglasses to the floor. He put his hands on her tiny waist, his thumbs and fingers almost meeting around her.

Jed meant to kiss her gently but there was too much passion—pent-up passion—in each of them. They pressed their lips together, a gentle touch. Then Erica parted her lips. Their tongues touched, lightly at first, then eagerly.

Jed's reaction was automatic. He lifted her easily from the floor and set her on a barstool. With his left hand he gently stroked her thick hair and they kissed again, longer this time.

With a quick glance he made sure no one else was in the room, then found the hem of the summer frock..he slipped his hand beneath it. Upward, over her knees, caressing each inch of her smooth, creamy legs..slowly; first one then the other. Her soft thighs welcomed his touch..his fingertips edged under lace trim—

Erica suddenly shifted on the barstool. Their quick intake of breath was simultaneous—and audible—as his fingertips, for only a split second, brushed across soft curly down. Erica shivered.

Ten seconds more would have meant no turning back—and at the least, they'd have been subject to arrest. But as it turned out, Erica was the first to regain her sanity. The woman always is.

"No, Jed," and she gently pushed against his chest, "no, we can't. I'm not here for a one-night stand."

The words embarrassed Jed. "No! No, Erica. That's not my game." He took her face in his hands. "Sorry—I got carried away."

The bartender appeared abruptly from the kitchen and Erica blushed, as the hem of the peach-colored frock was still high, exposing her naked thighs.

"'Scuse me. Another drink?" the bartender asked uncomfortably.

"Of course," Jed responded with aplomb—then without missing a beat, he turned to Erica. "Will you marry me?"

"Seems like an appropriate thing," came the dry and barely audible rejoinder from the bartender—but then the impact of what he'd just heard, hit him. *"Whoopee!"* he shouted. "Congratulations, Jed—Miss! A real proposal right here in my bar." He grabbed two clean glasses from the back bar. "Drinks on the house!"

"Gosh, Jed! *Whoopee indeed!*" Erica exclaimed. Jed's abrupt proposal had taken her breath all over again. She fanned her face with her hand. "Let's—let's slow down a little. I'm really on a roller coaster here. I think we both are."

"Good idea," Jed laughed, and sat down beside her. They each took a deep breath, a small sip of El Portel's celebratory round, and great pleasure in looking silently, deeply, into each other's eyes.

If time is what she wants—time is what she'll get. If he had to, Jed knew he'd wait a hundred years for Erica. But he hoped it would be closer to a couple of days. For if they sat here much longer, just looking at each other, he also knew he'd *take her* atop the bar—the consequences be damned!

CHAPTER 42

Three months later—
Saturday, October 22, 1949—

> *"...a day in the country*
> *with someone you treasure—*
> *small conversations, caresses,*
> *and pleasure.*
>
> *...imagine this day,*
> *no clouds up above—*
> *then make it come true*
> *with someone you love."*

Good gosh! Jed thought. That he, Jed Easton, was walking around with poetry on the brain was more a surprise to him than anybody. He couldn't remember the entire poem, or who wrote it. He couldn't even remember where or when he read the verses—but he kept trying. Bits and pieces floated hauntingly through his mind:

> *"...in a quiet green meadow*
> *away from the rush—*
> *spread a soft silky blanket*
> *on grass, cool and lush.*
>
> *...then—the rustle of leaves,*
> *the song of the birds,*

*exchange of shy glances—
his hand touches hers."*

Jed washed the old black Chevy in preparation for the evening. He even swept out the inside and polished the dash. What a change in his life! There was joy in his countenance, boundless energy in his walk. Jed had been floating on "cloud nine" since the joyous call came, now seven weeks ago:

"It's fer you," TJ said to Jed. "Sounds like your li'l Colorado hotsy-totsy." The D.A. held his hand over the mouthpiece but his voice was so loud Jed knew Erica heard the remark anyway.

"Hello, Erica, I love you." Jed added the last three words in a whisper, hoping TJ wouldn't notice enough to rib him.

"Yes," she replied.

"Erica?"

"Yes—and yes."

"What do you mean?" Jed laughed, with more puzzlement than mirth.

"Yes, this is Erica—and *'Yes,'* to THE QUESTION you asked at El Portel."

Jed's war whoop could be heard throughout the entire courthouse. "TJ, she's going to marry me—she's *actually* going to marry me!"

"Any gal dumb enough to marry you—*deserves* you," was TJ's callous jab when Jed hung up the phone. Jed knew it was TJ's way of saying he was happy for him.

Jed was more than ready to consummate the deal. He was discovering that long distance courtship was unsatisfying, not to mention expensive. He dreaded the day each month when the telephone bill arrived, and vowed to call Erica every other day—instead of every day. It was a worthy goal; but one he usually failed to achieve.

The middle of October had come and gone, their wedding day was around the corner, but it had been five weeks since he'd seen her. The special events of the new school year had kept Erica chained to Colorado College.

It was just last evening, a Friday, when the phone rang again, this time at the house.

"Jed Easton." He picked it up on the first ring hoping it was Erica.

"You sound lonely, sweetheart." Her voice was always like music to Jed.

"I am, baby. Mom's cookin' dinner and I'm nursin' a gin and tonic. But I'd do a forty day fast and 'go on the wagon' if that's what it took to have you here."

"Speaking of which—I have great news!"

"What?"

"Doctor Gates—you know, Doctor Sherwood Gates, the college dean—he has the flu, and"—

"That's good news? He has the flu?"

"No, silly, but he was to speak tomorrow at the new library dedication in Trinidad. So, they're sending me instead."

"Great! What time?" Trinidad was about an hour's drive from Raton (the precarious mountain road notwithstanding), in even the old Chevy.

Erica explained there was a tea and reception at four p.m., it would last about an hour, she'd then say a few words and was free for the evening.

"Where are you staying?" Jed hoped she'd have a hotel room.

"Huh-uh, Jed, I know what you're thinking," Erica laughed, "but we must be circumspect. Remember, I'm a *highly respected* college professor." She made the tongue-in-cheek comment in a most persnickety accent.

She explained that the head librarian was offering a spare bedroom at her house, so she wouldn't have to drive back to Colorado Springs at night.

"You mean we gotta spend the evening with her?" Jed groused.

"No, no, Miss Seton has other plans; some function she was already invited to. I'm just sleeping there. "But," she quickly added, "don't get any ideas. She'll be home early."

"Well," Jed teased, "if you unlock the bedroom window, Miss Seton can write her own 'Lady Chatterly's Lover' when we're through."

"Naughty boy, Jed." Erica always scolded him for such remarks—but Jed knew she really loved it. "Find the new library and pick me up at quarter past five," she instructed. "I'd suggest you skip the tea and speech; don't want you asleep for the evening."

"Darlin', if I can just look at you, I don't care if you read me 'Winnie The Pooh.'" Jed hung up the phone and wasn't even embarrassed when he saw his mother shaking her head and smiling.

After the wedding Erica would arrange (for the second time), a four-day week at Colorado College and they'd swap off weekends in Raton and Colorado Springs.

"And we'll make up for the four days apart, on the weekend! Right?" Erica asked the question with a teasing, sensuous smile.

"Until," he promised in mock solemnity, "our strength gives out!" He delivered the sentence in an exaggerated stage whisper.

*"...the warmth of the sunshine,
the warmth of the wine—
arms reach out—
legs entwine!*

*...a day in the country
with someone you treasure...
small conversations—
caresses, and pleasure!"*

Following the European sabbatical, Erica would move to

Raton and seek a position in the public school system. Jed was thinking of running for sheriff. He could still practice law on the side so long as there was no conflict of interest. That meant he'd stay clear of criminal law, which was fine by him anyway.

There was one small hurdle to cross. Jed knew he'd eventually broach the subject, if for no other reason than to say he had. As expected, Jed's mother put the question on the table just one day after she and Erica met.

The three had enjoyed a lovely evening together, the same day as Jed and Erica's *torrid* reunion in the El Portel bar. Mrs. Easton fixed beefsteak, first browned atop the stove in a black iron skillet; then she covered it with mushroom soup and baked it slowly in the oven. The soup wound up as a thin succulent glaze over each piece of meat. The steak, so tender you could cut it with a spoon, was served with fried potatoes and lima beans. Not exactly the fare of the gourmet set but it was Jed's favorite "Mom Dish"; and apparently a big hit with Erica. Her plate scarcely needed washing when she finished.

Erica left in the Frazer Manhattan the next morning; the same stunning convertible she'd driven to Maxwell, New Mexico from Colorado Springs. The sky blue chariot was packed again with her belongings—belongings that Jed hoped would soon be in a home of their own.

Ten minutes after Erica's departure, Mrs. Easton spoke. "Will she do it?"

"Do what?" Jed was never good at "snowing" Mom. He knew what she was talking about.

"You know what I mean, Jed. You *have* to ask!"

"Mother, I love her. I am *going* to marry her—*if* she'll have me."

"Don't you love God, too?"

"Yes, Mother, I love God—and I love you," he added as he gave his mother a big bear hug. "Maybe—just maybe I'll ask if she'll convert. But you *must know,* Mom," (and he placed his big hands firmly but lovingly on his mother's shoulders), "Erica's answer on religion—one way or the other—will not change our plans one iota, so far as *I'm* concerned. *I* just pray she'll say, 'Yes,' to marriage."

Jed and Erica sat at a romantic table in the back of the Fabulous Martha-Lees Restaurant. It was the Trinidad café Miss Seton recommended and, erstwhile educator that she was, the librarian gave them much more information about the place than they really wanted or needed. She particularly liked certain Italian dishes served there and suggested they ask for the waiter, Luigi.

The native of Rome had managed, with his wife and two sons, to make it to America only two months before Mussolini—*Il Duce*—came to power.

"So happy they strunga sonuvabitcha upa!" Luigi's accent by now was seventy percent old-world Italian, thirty percent Colorado plains. At certain times he particularly enjoyed emphasizing the Italian part.

The flickering candle in the red vase, completely covered by wax drippings, highlighted the glow of Erica's cheeks.

"You had that glow the first day I saw you," Jed teased. "I thought you were embarrassed—hell, you *always* look that way."

Jed brought an even brighter flush to Erica's face with the mention of her wind-tossed skirt at Raton's depot.

"Had it not been for that li'l erotic pictorial," Jed teased, "we wouldn't be sittin' here tonight."

Erica stared him down, a wicked gleam in her eyes. "You ain't seen *nothin'* yet, cowboy!"

Jed chuckled—but his heart beat double-time at the promise.

There was one traumatic moment in the otherwise perfect evening: just after cocktails, before dinner arrived, Erica excused herself to freshen up. Jed pulled a cigar from the breast pocket of his jacket, fumbling in a side pocket for a box of Swan matches. He found the box, and pulled out with it a copy of the old *Raton Range* clipping on Claude Stickett's murder. It had been in the jacket since last fall—maybe the Kansas City trip. He laid it on the table, lit his cigar, and decided to see what else his pockets might yield. That's when he discovered the letter from Blondie, delivered by John Little Deer in Albuquerque. *Hell, is this the only travel jacket I ever wear? I need to buy another one!*

His next thought was of the Christmas card episode with Erica, in El Portel; how she'd confessed to holding on to Jed's card, even on the eve of her planned marriage to Bill Jenkins. Jed decided the wise thing was to get rid of Blondie's note—immediately. He went to the men's room, tore the letter to bits, and flushed it down the commode.

Upon his return, he could tell from across the room that something was dreadfully wrong. Erica was visibly shaking and white as a sheet.

"What's the matter?" Jed asked. He pulled his chair next to Erica, put his arms around her, and pulled her close.

"Oh, Jed!" Erica whispered, "that *man!* How did this get here?" She pointed to the Stickett clipping—the one with the snapshot of Stickett and his shotgun. Jed could feel her body shiver. "He—he tried to kidnap me a long time ago!" Erica sounded like she'd seen a ghost!

In a matter of moments she spilled out the whole story of Stickett's unsuccessful abduction attempt, many years ago, when she was a student in 1936. "I *know* that's him—I could *never* forget those eyes—*or* that face!"

Jed soothed her, rubbing her back, patting her hair, and reminding her it was over; that Stickett could never harm anyone again.

"The 'what-ifs' of life," Jed said soberly as their dinner arrived. "Dear God, I don't even wanna think about it. Stickett could've deprived the world of *you!*"

His fingertips touched her face, love and fondness in his eyes. "I can't imagine *never* knowing you," he whispered.

"But isn't it eerie?" Erica replied. "It was his *own* murder that caused *us* to meet."

"Yeah, eerie; or maybe destiny." Jed took another sip of the light Italian grigio. "I'm sure we don't know *half* the misery that ol' geezer caused."

He filled her in on details of the case: John Little Deer and Buck Begay; how the fingerprints on the knife matched Begay's, and those on the Three Nuns tin matched the prints on Stickett's shotgun, as well as those from his old arrest in the Arizona bank robbery.

"But hell, enough of this cop talk!" Jed exclaimed. "A toast: to a brighter tomorrow!" They linked arms before bringing their glasses to their lips.

"Besides, Stickett got what he deserved," Jed concluded, "the ol' bastard is dead!"

For the first time in moments Erica laughed out loud. "*The ol' bastard!* That's what I called him. I think it saved my life. He'd never heard a lady talk that way."

As they were ready to leave, Jed decided, for his mom's sake, to bring up that other small matter. "Erica, I want you to know, it makes no difference to *me,* uh—as to your answer"—

"You want me to convert." Erica said matter-of-factly, her eyes unblinking.

"Do you read *minds?*" Jed was astounded.

"No," Erica chuckled. "I met your mother, remember?"

"Oh, right." Jed joined Erica in wry laughter.

"I knew instantly," Erica continued, "if our relationship got this far, *this* conversation would occur." Erica reached over to caress his cheek.

"Yeah. I guess you would," Jed said. "But *again* it makes no difference to me."

"Don't you want to know my answer?"

"Not really," Jed said with a shrug.

"Men!" Erica exploded in feigned disgust.

"Well, I thought you might wanna *think* about it," Jed explained.

"I have," she replied.

Jed hoped her explanation would be short because, frankly, his mind was on things most would consider less spiritual. But he could tell Erica was determined to lay it out.

"Here's the way I see it," she began.

As Jed listened, he stared adoringly at her cover girl face, and was overcome by the poise with which she explained her reasoning. He wondered if any young man in her class ever learned anything. The girls, sure—because Erica was obviously a great teacher.

But Jed knew *he'd* spend each hour in her classroom just waiting—waiting to watch her walk across the room, or turn to the blackboard. Then, he would ogle those curvaceous hips; or he would hope she'd look out the window so her pin-up girl breasts would rise and fall in profile.

Maybe someday—just maybe—he'd tell her of the day he watched her through binoculars at Bill Jenkins' ranch. And how sad he'd been at saying goodbye; or so he thought.

But now she was here, and he was here with her—*and* she'd soon be his wife.

As she talked, she pointed out the window, up into the sky. "Are you listening, Jed?"

"Yeah. Uh, yes—of course." He was happy he managed any response from such a deep reverie.

"So. It's all very simple," Erica continued, "child-like even. That's why I love that star."

Again she pointed out the window. Jed's eyes followed to a bright evening star in the Colorado sky.

"Wait—wait a minute. Okay, I guess I wasn't listening

very well. You—you believe in *Venus?*"

"You *jerk!*" Erica laughed. "You've heard nothing I said." She began to tickle him in the ribs—which sent Jed into convulsive laughter.

"I'm sorry," he laughed, "don't do that. *Please!* I'm very ticklish, I can't stand that."

"Thanks for telling me," she said menacingly.

"Please, I'm sorry," Jed pleaded. "I want to understand what you're talking about. Uh, start over. I'll try to keep my mind off your—off..your..body," he concluded with resignation. Maybe God would at least give him brownie points for honesty.

"I was merely trying to explain why conversion is not difficult for me," Erica said. "I believe in the Star of Bethlehem; the Babe in the manger; The Man He became." Her eyes gleamed with conviction. "It's not just a fable, Jed, not to me."

She gripped his hand firmly. "That's why Catholic or Episcopalian; Rome or Canterbury; that's not my debate," Erica said. "I'll leave that for others. It's simple faith that counts."

Jed thought no lawyer had ever made a more convincing summation; to the point. Basic.

Erica was saying precisely what Jed believed; but had trouble verbalizing. *Skip through the high-toned words—get to the bottom line!*

"So!" Erica concluded her thesis with a smile that was almost beatific to Jed. "Not only am I happy to convert—I've already started!"

"*What?*" Jed was flabbergasted.

"Jed, I started instructions the day I decided to accept your proposal."

"You are some grand dame, Erica. What will your parents say?"

"Heather and Doctor Harlan?" Erica again laughed loudly. "Are you kidding? They're just delighted to have a kid who actually attends church. Besides, you know the 'old saw' on

Episcopalians, don't you?"

"What's that?"

"They're Catholics," Erica responded—"Catholics who vote Republican."

"Right!" Jed laughed at the clever joke—and wondered why he'd never heard it.

He reached across the table, tenderly touching both his hands to her cheeks. His necktie was dangerously close to the spaghetti. But still he kissed her—and he kissed her.

Luigi approached quietly and unscrewed the light bulb nearest their table. Neither noticed the softer glow. They noticed nothing at all—except each other.

When they arrived at Miss Seton's the house was dark, but she'd given Erica a key. Jed carried Erica's suitcase—the one just like his—to the small guest room.

"How long before she's home?" he asked mischievously, his eyes on the bed.

"Oh, no you don't," Erica laughed. She turned him around to push him back through the open bedroom door. "I'm escorting you to the front porch before things get out of hand."

"Gettin' some things *in* hand was what I had in mind!" He scooped her off the floor, pressing her body to his.

She had to grip his hips with her legs to stay there. They kissed again and again, their passion about to boil over.

"Down, boy, *down! And go home!*" But as she slid to the floor, she hunched her pelvis so firmly against Jed he had to steady himself against the wall.

"Not sure I can wait, babe!" Jed pleaded.

"Not only *can* you wait"—she turned him again toward the door to the front porch—"you *will* wait! *Heavens,* Jed. The wedding is a mere ten days away!"

They heard the creak of the hinges as the front door opened. How much Miss Seton had witnessed through the window they weren't sure; but Erica calmly introduced her fiancé.

Jed said a gracious goodnight to both ladies, gave Erica a peck on the cheek, and walked onto the porch.

"See ya in a week," he said as he turned to gaze at Erica.

"Oh, Jed," she whispered. "I can't wait!"

"But—I thought you said we'd *have* to."

Miss Seton raised her eyebrows in a mixture of shock and amusement, and Erica whispered one final scolding. *"Get out of here, you ass!"*

Jed saw a completely new tinge of color in Erica's blush. He thought it resembled a blend of her hair color—and the New Mexico sunset!

Jed walked slowly to the Chevy, a little angry that such an opportune moment had been interrupted. *The nerve! Someone coming* home *to her own house!* The idiocy of his disgust made him laugh.

A twenty-four hour diner was just outside the Trinidad city limits. It was approaching midnight and Jed thought he'd better have a cup of strong coffee for the drive back. The waitress looked like a high school homecoming queen; red hair, and freckles across her nose, under sparkling blue eyes. Jed wondered if Erica looked like that in high school. He realized he'd never seen snapshots of a teenage Erica. He must remember to ask if she had any.

The waitress poured his coffee in a white Pyrex cup and gave him a teasing smile. She reminded Jed of Lucille Ball, the actress; but with short hair.

"You headin' home to the wife?" she asked.

"Why?" Jed wondered exactly *where* this conversation was going.

"'Cause if you are," said Miss Teen Queen, leaning close to his face, "I'd suggest you wipe that lipstick off your mouth."

"Oh," Jed laughed and reached for a napkin. "Thanks. No problem, 'cause that's where I got it—well, she ain't my wife yet; but will be in a few days."

"Great! Congratulations!" As she spoke the waitress proudly held her left hand aloft, showing off a gold band. "I've been married six months."

"You're *married?*" Jed thought it incredulous. "How old are you?"

"Sixteen," she teased, "and *trust* me"—the waitress again gave Jed that knowing smile—"that's old enough."

"Yeah—yeah, I reckon." Jed knew he was blushing. *She's young and fresh!* "How old is your husband?"

"Thirty-five."

"*Thirty-five?*" Jed was flabbergasted. "*Hell!* That cradle-robber oughta be horse-whipped!"

"Well, if you think you're up to it," (and as the waitress spoke she looked over Jed's shoulder), "here he comes. We both get off at midnight and he's here to pick me up."

Jed looked out the diner window to see a brand new '50 Ford sedan slowing to a stop. The fact that it was shiny, and new—that didn't impress Jed; that it was a Colorado Highway Patrol cruiser; that impressed him.

"Oh, help!" Jed cackled, spilling some coffee. "You're married to a 'highway cowboy?'"

Good Lawd! Jed was suddenly as nervous as a cat. "Don't tell him I called him a cradle-robber—hell, I don't care if he kidnapped you at age ten!"

The patrolman filled the doorway. He was six-foot six, if he were an inch.

"Hi, Sweet Pea." The cop smiled at the waitress; then, as a man with more important things on his mind, nodded toward Jed.

"Mornin', officer. See you got a new wagon." Jed tried to smile his brightest.

"Yeah. She's a honey." And that was all the time the

patrolman had for Jed—or the new patrol car. He moved behind the counter to kiss his teenage wife.

Jed envied the couple. They were locked in an unashamed, passionate embrace, oblivious to anyone or anything around them. They kissed like it was a hobby. Jed had no doubt it was. And there was no mystery at all, as to their plans for the remainder of the night, and wee hours of the morning.

Jed felt warm desire well up, as he remembered the moments he'd just spent with Erica. It hit him like a lightning bolt! He knew what he was going to do, and chuckled at the devilish thought.

Jed laid fifty cents on the counter and walked out the door. The newlyweds didn't even notice he left.

All the houses on Miss Seton's street were dark; but bright moonlight bathed the night. Jed parked a few doors down and across the street. The chill of the October mountain air was invigorating and it heightened Jed's anticipation as he walked stealthily to the back of the librarian's manicured white bungalow.

He rounded the corner and thought for a moment he must be dreaming. Erica was sitting in a low, open window, a sheer negligee wrapped loosely around her otherwise naked body. The moonlight made her appear as a mythological Greek siren, bathed in silver; like a picture he'd seen in a college textbook, the one he didn't read—which meant he almost flunked the course.

"You *scamp!*" Erica whispered. "I knew you'd come."

"Aren't you freezing?" he asked. With one hand he touched her shoulder—with the other her bare tummy.

"No," came the response, "feel." She took his hand and placed it next to her hips. She was seated, not on the window ledge itself, but on a long narrow cushion just inside. It was warm to the touch. The cushion was atop a strong metal shelf, and under the shelf was a piping hot steam radiator.

"Isn't this neat? I'm warm as toast!" Erica whispered excitedly, like a little girl with a new doll. "I hope we get a house with one of these." She put her arms around Jed and kissed him before he could reply.

As she pulled him close the negligee fell away, and Jed felt her bare breasts against his shirt. He wanted to rip the shirt off his back—but couldn't bear to let go of Erica.

"What the hell!" Erica suddenly breathed in his ear, "come on in here. If we scandalize Trinidad—we *scandalize* Trinidad!"

And it would have happened—save for the German shepherd next door. Why the dog had been quiet thus far, Jed could not imagine, but the sudden uproarious barking made the hair stand up on the back of his neck. The dog was only ten yards away and Jed prayed the yard fence was strong enough; *and high enough,* to keep the animal contained. Lights began to blaze one by one, in houses up and down the street.

"Get out of here!" Erica giggled as she rolled from the window cushion; out of the moonlight, away from any prying eyes that might peer from a nearby window. *"Run, Jed, run!"*

And he did! Across the lawn he streaked, and down the street, making a combination broad jump and headlong dive into the old Chevy. He was grateful he'd left the keys in the ignition.

Jed didn't turn on his headlights till he was five blocks away. And he kept checking his rearview mirror to make sure no one had called the cops. No flashing lights appeared. He finally breathed a huge sigh of relief, and threw back his head in boisterous laughter. Jed headed out of Trinidad for Raton.

Thirty minutes later the old Chevy rounded a curve, one of many in Raton Pass. He was a mile short of the zenith on the New Mexico state line. The moon, which had been hidden behind a mountain, suddenly burst over the landscape like a giant, yet soft, spotlight.

Jed pulled into a fenced overlook, got out of the car, and walked to the edge of the precipice. He couldn't begin to calculate how far he could actually see in the clear nighttime glow—but it was miles.

He stood there for several minutes and was overcome by a sense of amazement. He, Jedidiah D Easton, was about to marry the girl of his dreams. It occurred to him now, that Erica was the girl he'd *always* dreamed of; long before he knew her, or even knew *how* to dream of her.

Why was he so lucky? But in the next second he knew it wasn't luck.

Jed didn't believe God's home was on the moon; at least no nun ever taught him that. But on a night like this, the moon was the focal point of the universe. It was easy to *believe* God lived on the moon.

"Thank you, God," Jed said, as he looked up. "Thank you, for bringing Erica to me." His voice broke; he was embarrassed at the loss of control though no one else was there to see it.

He wished he were more comfortable expressing this sort of thing; like Erica. He looked at the ground, drawing circles in the gravel with the toe of his boot. "I know"—Jed looked at the sky again, his voice and soul still choked with emotion—"I know it was no accident."

Jed opened the Chevy door; but before sliding under the steering wheel, he looked back at the moon once more. As silly as it seemed, he tipped his Stetson.

Jed drove down the New Mexico side of Raton Pass. En route home, he passed by Claude Stickett's old house. He breathed another prayer, thanking God for sparing Erica from this terrible man. And for only a moment, he again wondered: how much misery had that wretch of a person caused?

He drove on home, slipped stealthily up the stairs so as not to awaken his mother, and lay down across his bed without removing his clothes.

Jedidiah D Easton slept like a baby.

CHAPTER 43

One final look back—

Claude Stickett had seldom if ever thought of marriage. It was nothing he ever thought he needed. He definitely didn't want it.

Until!

Perhaps it was because he was getting older. To have someone cook a hot meal for him; maybe a woman would even wash the sheets on his bed from time to time; to have someone wait on him at his beck and call—now *that* was an attractive idea.

He had none of these thoughts until he bought the house in Raton in 1944; the first home he'd ever owned. He paid cash. The owner didn't ask where it came from. He didn't care. It was cash.

As it happened, this was about the time the woman came to town—at least Claude had never seen before. She became the fry cook at the dingy little diner where he occasionally got black coffee and a hamburger after playing pool. Chico's was just across the street.

From the stool at the café counter where he sat, he could see her through the tiny window where she set the freshly cooked food. She was not pretty; her hair was too gray—her face too lined. But she didn't move like an old woman. Stickett thought she was likely younger than she looked. But frankly, he cared about none of those things. Her cooking was tolerable and he surmised she was capable of keeping house. That's all that mattered to him.

Today, Stickett was at the counter at closing time. A waitress was wiping down the tables and stacking chairs, when the lady fry cook came out front to pour herself a cup of coffee and smoke a cigarette. She sat down at the counter, five stools away.

"You're lookin' especially pretty today, ma'm." Stickett used charm so rarely it was surprising he possessed any competence at all in the craft.

At first the woman looked almost frightened. Then—"Thank you," she said quietly, knowing he was a regular customer.

A couple of minutes later Stickett spoke again: "Uh—be glad to buy you a beer, and walk you home."

Again, the frightened look; then she smiled. "I am home," she said. "The owner let's me sleep in the little room upstairs."

"Do tell!" But Stickett would not give up so easily. "Well, Chico's has a back room with a jukebox. And" he added, "the beer is real cold. Guess I wouldn't have far to walk you home, would I?"

She even laughed at his attempt at humor. "Uh—fine. But let me put on some lipstick. I'll be right back."

It became something of a routine for the couple once or twice weekly. Stickett, knowing what he was after, was on his best behavior.

Then, the unexpected happened and Stickett had his opening.

The diner burned one night, an accidental electrical fire. Fortunately, the lady fry cook in residence smelled the smoke and got out safely. But the owner had no money to refurbish or open in a new location, and the cook was jobless—and homeless.

"You're welcome to sleep at my house—until you get on your feet," Claude said in his kindest manner. "I travel a lot—and usually sleep on the couch, anyway."

The woman was taken aback—but desperate; and too proud to ask for un-offered help. She moved into Stickett's bedroom and he continued on his best behavior. Just as he promised, when home, he slept on the couch.

"What *is* your business, Claude?" She dared ask the question after she'd lived in his house for three weeks—and he'd been gone half the time.

"Oh, I guess you could say I'm a trader, ma'm. I buy and sell," he lied. "Sometimes horses; sometimes machinery—even furniture."

The answer seemed to satisfy the woman. She concluded that was the reason the furnishings in his house, though simple and sparse, were of decent quality. She even bought his explanation for strapping on the holstered derringer every time he left the house.

"People know me," he told her. "And they know in my business, you carry a lotta cash. You gotta protect yourself."

She had been in his house a full month and was still unsuccessful in finding work. She had tried, almost daily. They would not tell her, but most potential employers thought something unsettling about her reticence. She displayed a pronounced lack of confidence, and seemed uncomfortable asking for even the most menial jobs. She appeared to be a person, who had been knocked down too many times. And rightly or wrongly, most suspected she was mentally unstable. Also—it didn't help at all (word had begun to spread), that she was living with Claude Stickett.

Stickett had been around Raton for years, living in one crummy little hole in the wall after another. Even though he'd finally bought a home, to most of Raton he was still "the drifter."

The day arrived when Stickett made his move. He hopped off the freight on the outskirts of Raton and walked home. His pockets were stuffed with cash from three overnight break-ins; businesses, all in a four-block area of Albuquerque. He'd been especially good at staking them out this time.

"Ma'm," he said quietly over the ham and eggs she had cooked, "I'd be mighty glad—uh—if you'd agree to—to be my woman," he smiled.

Again, she gave him that brief frightened look. But she was desperate.

"We'd have to go before a preacher, Claude. That's—that's the only way I could do that."

"Ain't much for church-goin', ma'am. But a judge can marry us just fine."

And so they were married. It did not take long for the woman to regret her decision. Sex, on the wedding night, was terribly rough; even painful. She tried to tell herself, that was just the way with some men; and she'd have to live with her commitment.

But the telltale moment came ten days later. Stickett had just returned from a three-day trip and seemed to be relishing (or so she thought), the pot roast she had prepared.

"More mashed potatoes?" *she asked.*

"Naw," *he grumped*, "too much salt."

"My, my, Claude"—*she teased him with a smile*—"now you're soundin' just like my first husband."

The noise was startling as Stickett slammed his fork against his plate. The look in his eyes made the woman's blood run cold.

"Ya never told me ya been married before!" *he growled.*

"Well, Claude"—*she tried to speak as calmly and sweetly as possible*—"you didn't ask."

They finished the meal in silence.

He rose from the table and she got up to clear the plates. As he walked by, he suddenly doubled his fist and punched her in the stomach as hard as he could. The blow slammed her into the corner where she collapsed, gasping for breath. She could not get up. Stickett walked from the room.

But he returned immediately. "You listen to me, you miserable bitch! If you got anything else to confess, ya best do it now—or keep it to your damn self."

The woman still lay on the floor, struggling to get her breath.

"And if you got any frickin' ideas," *he continued,* "'bout runnin' away, or tellin' anybody what goes on behind these four walls—you need to know I got people—powerful people, indebted to me. They watch this house every time I'm away. They know every move you make—and they'll never let you outa this town alive!"

That was all a total lie; but the woman had no way to know that—as he knew she wouldn't. She believed him—as he knew she would. So. In essence, from that day, she was a prisoner in her own house.

What had so embittered him? Why such hate? In the years ahead, those were questions the fearful woman often asked in her mind—but would not dare ask him.

She did not know his story. No one in Raton knew his story; because, it was a story he told no one at any time in his life: The story of a young boy in west Texas, whose mother died at his birth; of a father who drank too much because of it. Then, in his drunken state, the father would usually respond to the boy with a harsh slap to the face, or an even more painful kick to the rump or back, with his sharp-toed boot. The boy would pick himself up stone-faced; but at night he would cry himself to sleep.

However, one night, at age eleven, he did not cry himself to sleep. He cried—but suddenly he was through crying. He felt dry, emotionless, uncaring.

He vowed never to cry again—and he didn't. Not even when his father died in a mysterious hunting accident. The boy, by now fourteen, was the only witness.

Stickett arrived home, if possible, in a worse mood than usual.

"Don't want no supper, woman. I'm tired of your cookin'. Got me a steak at the truck stop."

"All right, Claude," she said softly.

"Goin' to the porch—to smoke," he growled. "Don't bother me." He un-strapped the holstered derringer from his leg, tossed it on the table, and walked out the door. But something from the holster had bounced on the floor. She picked it up and put it by the holster.

Then, she picked it up again for a closer look. She took the item to the bedroom, got a magnifying glass from the dresser, and turned on the bedside lamp.

She froze as she heard him come in from the porch.

"Colder than hell out there," he muttered. Without seeing her in the bedroom, he got his sheepskin jacket and shotgun and returned to the porch.

Now, as she returned to the magnifying glass, she sensed a spine-tingling horror at what she saw. There were undoubtedly countless antique coins throughout the world, engraved with the Coliseum of Rome on one side, and the image of Julius Caesar on the other. But the magnifying glass told her all she needed to know.

"It would be worth a lot of money, were it flawless. But then"—her coin-collector father had laughed—"then, I couldn't afford it. See the imperfection?" He pointed to the wreath around Caesar's head. "A couple of the leaves," he continued, "see—they're almost worn away. Anyway—a nice little keepsake for you. Happy eighteenth birthday!"

Proof? Proof enough for the courtroom? Not really—but it was enough for Mrs. Stickett. Tears rolled down her face; tears of sorrow and fear. In her mind she was again in that little clapboard house near Dalies, New Mexico. She relived those moments of terror from years ago; she was again huddled beneath the huge trunk. The gunshot was as loud in her memory as it had been that rainy night. She heard the crash of the broken chair, and the jangle of coins from his pocket, as her dead husband fell to the floor. She cried even more as she recalled crawling to the kitchen, to wipe blood from her dear Charlie's face; and she had scoured the floor in vain, for that precious coin she had given him on their wedding night. And to think! She was now <u>married</u>—to the murderer of her first husband.

Now, she slipped the coin into the pocket of her dress, hoping Claude would not miss it, and moved in the darkness to her rocking chair. She smelled the aroma of his pipe tobacco on the back porch.

She had made up her mind. His threats notwithstanding, she would go to the authorities—as soon as possible, hopefully tomorrow. They might not believe her but she had to try. She would tell them what she knew. Surely they would, at the least, provide sanctuary.

Little did she know, Claude Stickett would not be able to harm her much longer—not directly. Moments later, Dora Webb Sarles Stickett, heard the pain-wracked death scream of her second husband, as the blade of a bone-handled knife pierced his heart.

It was October 14, 1948.

CHAPTER 44

Jed and Erica were married November 1, 1949, in St. Patrick's Church on Second Street, in Raton. They went three days earlier for a consultation with the priest.

"We'd like the ceremony short, Father." Erica spoke with all the confidence of a young lady used to getting her way.

Father Pedro Kennedy (yes, his mother was Mexican, his father Irish) was now approaching ninety. He looked at her with a twinkle in his eyes. "Young lady, you are indeed beautiful. Makes me wonder if I chose the right vocation!" he added dryly. Then his voice became authoritative, even stern. "This is a Catholic wedding. It will be over, when it's *over!*"

"Yes, Father," was all Erica managed and Jed suppressed a laugh. It was always the new Catholics who tried to tell a priest what to do.

"Excuse me a moment." Father Kennedy arose spryly from his chair. "My sister in Amarillo sent me an exquisite bottle of brandy for my upcoming birthday. Methinks we'll open it early."

As the priest left the room, Jed for some reason remembered something he'd wanted to tell Erica for a year. "By the way, Miss Erica Elaine Harlan Swanson soon-to-be Easton! You'll never guess who I saw in ol' Kansas City." And Jed proceeded to tell of his night at the Muehlebach Hotel (he did not mention Blondie) and his first-hand look at The President of the United States.

There was a sly look in Erica's eyes as he finished.

"*What?* You don't believe me?" Jed asked.

Then Erica told her story: of her and sister Jean's evening at The Elms in Excelsior Springs, and their own experience with Ol' Harry. She especially savored the part about her and The President "scaring him up" a sandwich.

Jed shook his head. "I just can't top you, can I, Erica?"

"*Well!* I certainly *hope so!*" was her comeback. They were still giggling in the naughty, conspiratorial manner of little kids when Father Kennedy returned. He brought three sparkling crystal glasses and a small bottle of cognac on a silver tray. At the end of the consultation the newly opened bottle had a mere two fingers to return to the priest's liquor cabinet.

The wedding was at eleven a.m., and the reception (complete with lunch, margaritas, and marachi band), got underway at twelve forty-five at El Portel. At one-thirty Doctor Harlan, Heather, and Jean approached.

"TJ and Arthur just brought the car around," the doctor said. TJ, Professor Aldridge, and Erica's father had all become fast friends in the last three days. "And, a little something to look at later this evening." As Doctor Harlan spoke he stuffed a large envelope in Erica's tiny purse. There were hugs and kisses all around and the happy couple left with the party still going full blast.

At one fifty-five p.m., one year to the moment when Jed Easton first laid eyes on those titillating green garters, he and Erica stood on the passenger platform at Raton's Santa Fe depot. *The Chief*, No. 20, was running ten minutes late today.

"That's okay," said Jed, "means she'll really be highballin'. I love to ride 'em when they're makin' up time."

Erica's going away outfit did not disappoint. She wore an eye-catching silk dress; a two-piece suit, really. It was rust-colored, and of course, had a matching hat. Jed was carrying the luggage and was sad that Erica's hands were free to guard her skirt from the Sangre de Cristo winds. But he consoled himself that on this trip there'd be ample opportunity to discover whether the undies matched the outfit.

They were off to Philadelphia. Neither had ever seen Independence Hall and the Liberty Bell. An unusual honeymoon spot, most would say, but for Erica and Jed it was just right.

As they waited for *The Chief,* Erica opened the envelope from Doctor Harlan. "Oh, Jed!" she exclaimed.

The envelope held the biggest wad of cash Jed had ever seen and a small piece of greenish-blue paper. "What's that?" he asked.

"Your ticket, Jed—on the boat to Europe next summer. Daddy's sending you with me on sabbatical. I told him it was the only wedding present I wanted. I know you'll have to return early; but at least we'll experience Europe together."

Just as forecast, No. 20 rolled in exactly ten minutes late.

This time as the porter took their luggage, they went not in opposite directions, but to the same drawing room. "The largest ya got!" Jed had told the reservations agent.

Again, just as one year ago, they had cocktails in the club car and dinner in the diner. Jed even dug deep to order the same vintage of Chateau Lafite Rothschild presented to them by the over-served gentleman that fated evening. But this time they didn't linger over dinner.

"We'll take the rest of the bottle with us," Jed told the steward. And he made Erica an offer at the bedroom door. "If you want a little privacy I'll grab a drink in the club car."

Erica grabbed him by the necktie. "How *crazy* do you think I am?" Her question was rife with mock suspicion. "I remember! That's where you picked *me* up!" She opened the door and pointed to the edge of the turned-down bed. "Here. Sit down." But her command was gentle…and tantalizing.

She took from her makeup case a tiny plug-in nightlight; then switched off the overhead bulb. The room was filled with a dim, amber glow. Erica turned to face Jed and slowly unbuttoned the silk top of her rust-colored suit.

She slipped it from her shoulders. It slid to the floor. She reached behind to unhook her lacey bra. *It* slid to the floor—and so did Jed, almost. She was more beautiful than he'd ever imagined.

It was a sensual floorshow—but a very short floorshow. For when Erica's rust, silk skirt dropped to the floor, Jed could take no more.

She stood before him in rust high heels, sheer silk stockings, a frilly, rust-colored garter belt, and—but there was no 'and'! This time, the short silk tap panty was missing!

Jed's reaction was akin to a football tackle—a very tender, very loving football tackle.

Between the crisp cool sheets Jed and Erica again rocked with—*and against*—the train. But this time it was no dream. This time, the stars: rust, green—all colors of the spectrum—were real. As was his sensual and loving release inside her!

They slept in each other's arms, the clickety-clack of *The Chief's* journey lulling them peacefully.

Somewhere in Kansas around midnight, Erica's soft laughter awakened Jed.

"What is it?" he mumbled groggily.

Erica put her lips to Jed's ear and whispered, "So, *that's* what you mean by *highballing!*"

The *Santa Fe Chief* roared eastward.

AUTHOR'S NOTE

Santa Fe Cocktail is a work of fiction, but certain historical facts are contained therein: President Harry S Truman actually spent Election Night, 1948, at The Elms in Excelsior Springs, Missouri. And he visited the Muehlebach Hotel in Kansas City, early the next morning. Many of the particulars I gleaned from David McCullough's wonderful biography, "Truman," (Simon & Schuster, 1992), and the archives of the *Kansas City Star & Times*. Of course, the insertion of *this* story's characters into history occurred only in the author's mind.

It is also doubtful that The President's private railroad car, the *Ferdinand Magellan*, would have been parked at Kansas City's Union Station—but it helped the story to have it there. In fact, The President usually disembarked at the Missouri Pacific station in Independence.

My thanks to the public librarians and newspaper archivists, in Missouri, New Mexico, and Colorado—also to the archivists at the Truman Library in Independence, Missouri. All were most helpful and kind, as were other fine citizens who are interested in the history of their communities, and this great land.

—JLM, Nashville, 2005

Printed in the United States
73541LV00002B/64-69